The Chase Is On

A Novel of Suspense

Marc E. Overlock

Printed in the United States of America
First Printing: December 2015
Published by Sojourn Publishing, LLC

ISBN: 978-1-62747-184-8
Ebook ISBN: 978-1-62747-185-5

For Wendy

33 years and counting.

*Behold, I know your thoughts
and your schemes to wrong me.*
Job 21:27

NOVEL CHARACTERS

Name	Age	Comment / Characteristics
John Adams, Ed.D.	49	President—Fitchburg State Teachers College.
Chuck Ames	39	Mark's former drill sergeant. Former farm boy. Taught troops value of rebel yell. Told Mark about the Hawaiian coffee. Sends him Kona beans.
Al Angelotti	42	Pit Boss—Antonio's Club; Boston.
Mrs. Lacey Anttonen	68	Witness to kidnapping in progress.
Mr. Collin Anttonen	68	Witness to kidnapping in progress.
Paul Bowen	6	Medic Alert student whom Helen Murphy helped at Farnsworth Elementary.
Dan Brodie	39	Ship Welder; General Dynamics; gambling addict.
Butch Brodie	58	Dan Brodie's father. Tattooed.
Uncle Howie Brodie	56	Dan's Uncle—the garbage man
Velma (Koskinen) Brodie	38	Dr. Rebovitz's receptionist / transcriptionist. Drives a Dodge Coronet Lancer. Weighs 96 pounds.

Ronnie Bryant	42	Barber Shop owner.
Phil Cochran	22	Rollstone youth—still in Vietnam.
Dr. Copoulos	48	Jeremy Hergenroeder's family doctor.
Kelsey Cotter	24	Alex's middle sister.
Nathan Cotter	58	Alexandria Hergenroeder's father; road crew boss for Massachusetts Dept. of Public Works.
Patience Cotter	22	Alex's youngest sister.
Kurt Crider	42	Rollstone UCC Moderator.
Cordero Díaz	16	Fitchburg High School Mechanics Student.
Linda Dunn	35	Rollstone UCC Office Secretary.
Andrea Faust	24	Pinehurst nurse's aide; helps bathe Eva R.
Joey Fenn	45	Antonio's Bar Keep
Bill Fontaine	40	Rollstone Organist.
Mark Gallagher	29	Karate / Judo instructor. Studio next to Rollstone Church; Vietnam Vet; former MP.
Dr. Alfred Gonyer	49	Fitchburg High School principal. A small mouse of a man.
Sgt. Finch Hudson	43	Fitchburg Police Desk Sergeant.
Daniella Gutierrez	62	José's grandmother.
José Gutierrez	35	Rican Ranger Leader / El Jefe.
Pilar Gutierrez	29	José's cousin; Rican Ranger #3.
Ricardo Gutierrez	36	José's cousin; Rican Ranger #2. Huge guy; no neck. Likes to do anti-grav work on low lifes.
Matthew Hannah	13	Advanced karate student.

Jeremy Nathan Hergenroeder	5	Main character; reads people's minds.
Alexandria Hergenroeder	29	Jeremy's mother; minister's wife.
Rev. David Hergenroeder	31	Minister Rollstone Congregational Church. Jeremy's Dad. Trained at VU Divinity School.
Daniel Hergenroeder	Deceased	Phillip's father—Union Maine
Edith (Thompson) Hergenroeder	54	Nanna—Jeremy's paternal grandmother.
Luke Hergenroeder	36	David's older brother by five years.
Phillip Hergenroeder	55	David Hergenroeder's father.
Mattie Hergenroeder	Deceased	David's grandmother. "Everyone's got to shit."
Christopher Johnson	30	Fitchburg Assistant District Attorney General.
Harvey Jones	Deceased	Grandpa Phillip's first construction boss.
Mitch Jones	Deceased	Harvey Jones' uncle who gave him his writing tablet box.
Jimmy Kendall	5	Jeremy's neighbor; Friend; also in accelerated kindergarten class.
Lori Kendall	9	Jimmy's sister; Jeremy has a crush on her.
Sean Kirkpatrick	51	Fitchburg Mayor.
Marian Koshgarian	33	Fitchburg librarian— children's section.
Joy Koskinen	65	Velma's mother. Finnish immigrant.
Leonard Koskinen	65	Velma's father. Finnish immigrant.

Landis	32	Church member who drove Mattie and Phillip to Worcester. Betty is Landis' wife.
Walter Liston	59	David's pastoral care professor in divinity school.
Paula Lovejoy	37	Edgerly 5th Grade Teacher whom Velma met in grocery store; chided "scripting". Platinum blond; searching eyes.
Clancy Marshall	10	Rollstone Congregational Kid [dials 888].
Trixie McLoughlin	44	Bar Maid; crime tipster re Rican Rangers.
Det. Rodney McNamara	40	Fitchburg Police Detective. Third generation police officer. Irish émigré. Wiley student of game theory before it became part of the public lexicon. Been married 15 years.
Agnes McNamara	38	Det. McNamara's wife.
Rod McNamara, Jr.	17	Twin son of Det. McNamara; takes Ray Peterson's auto mechanics class.
Conor McNamara	17	Twin son of Det. McNamara.
Col. Edward McPherson	55	Retired Army Colonel; Korean War Veteran; Rollstone member; Son Truman died in Vietnam.
Mrs. Lily McPherson	53	Wife of Col. McPherson.
Truman McPherson	20	Col. McPherson's son killed in Vietnam War.
Julio Mendez	17	Fitchburg High School Mechanics Student.
Bishop Horace Montgomery	53	Local Episcopalian Bishop.

Ms. Helen Murphy, Prof.	38	Fitchburg State Professor; advanced kindergarten teacher of Jeremy's.
Arthur O'Callaghan	23	Karate student.
Robert Peeler	11	Rollstone Congregational Kid Ring Leader [dials 888].
Jeff Pelletier	32	General Dynamics' co-worker.
Ray Peterson	51	Fitchburg High School Shop Teacher—Auto Mechanics.
Ted Pluchinsky	24	Karate student.
Amy Quinn	29	Pinehurst Nursing Home receptionist.
Dr. Azriel Rebovitz	42	Jeremy's treating psychiatrist; 6'5" tall; German émigré; Jewish.
Eva Rebovitz	67	Dr. Rebovitz's mother; German émigré; Jewish. Room 109 at Pinehurst.
Lance Rice	21	Rollstone youth—still in Vietnam.
Dominick Sangria	37	Shipyard welder and colleague of Dan Brodie. Hooked up Dan with José for a loan. José is Dominick's Uncle.

PROLOGUE

Monday July 22, 1968—10:42 a.m.

Fitchburg, Massachusetts Courthouse
Grand Jury Room—4th floor

"**B**efore we move on, ladies and gentleman, I want to direct your attention to one final exhibit," said Assistant District Attorney Christopher Johnson. "I'm handing you what's been marked as Exhibit 12. It's a letter from *Dr.* John Adams of Fitchburg State Teachers College to The Rev. and Mrs. David Hergenroeder concerning their son." Johnson stressed the "doctor" portion of Adams' title for effect, not that he needed to since he could tell that several grand-jury members had already made up their minds about probable cause in the case.

The 30-year-old Johnson stood five-foot-eight inches tall, but resembled a linebacker and stalked the grand jury room as if he needed the exercise. This created the effect he intended—of a sporting event where lots of action happened and happened quickly. The 18 members of the grand jury, mostly white, of Finnish heritage, and male, came from a cross section of Fitchburg neighborhoods. They'd taken an immediate liking to "General" Johnson, as DA's were called by everyone who knew any better.

1

They'd been poring over the evidence in this case since 9:00 a.m. and were shocked at the three defendants' behavior in the prior months.

"Take a minute and read the Exhibit please," Johnson asked. The 18 took their time just as they had in studying the prior eleven exhibits.

Worcester County Grand Jury
State v. Gutierrez, et. al.
Docket No. 68-2-138 22

Exhibit 12

Fitchburg State Teachers College
Office of the President
160 Pearl Street
Fitchburg, MA 01420

14 March 1968

The Rev. and Mrs. David Hergenroeder
123 Pearl Hill Road
Fitchburg, MA 01422

Re: Accelerated Kindergarten Class

Dear Rev. and Mrs. Hergenroeder:

It gives me great pleasure to announce to you that we have accepted your son Jeremy into our first ever accelerated kindergarten class. Based both on his IQ test and the battery of aptitude tests our researchers conducted, Jeremy is by any measure a remarkable youngster. He far outpaced most of his peers, scoring quite high even in logic and reasoning skills. We estimate that he is already reading at a fourth-grade level. His math scores indicate a similar level of aptitude. Therefore, we would be honored to have your family participate in this special program. We are limiting the class size to 15 students.

Our Director of Education, Professor Helen Murphy, Ed.D, is leading the class instruction and mentoring both the students as well as the specialized additional instructors we will be providing. Joining Dr. Murphy will be three Fitchburg State College student teachers, all rising seniors and all at the top decile of their class. This exceptional team will offer each student individualized instruction, coaching and support throughout the 12-month program. Yes, the program lasts an entire year, which is why we will commence classes Thursday May 30th. I emphasize that this accelerated learning environment will be far different than anything our U.S. educational system has ever before offered.

We are deploying the latest pedagogical research so that each student, at his or her own pace and comfort level, will advance in reading, writing, math and reasoning aptitudes. What's more, we've structured the program to ensure that each participant will capture a foundational understanding of civics and history. I suspect this program may sound remarkable. I assure you it is. To succeed, we must have your active support, in covenant, to join our teaching team to help Jeremy explore this world and universe.

3

Most compelling of all, based on our pilot studies with control groups made up of Jeremy's peers, when he completes his studies in June, 1969, he should have achieved a two-year jump in aptitude equivalency. In other words, we reasonably expect that Jeremy would be prepared to start 6th grade. So as not to worry you that we would then place him outside his age group, our design team plans to keep this exceptional class of youngsters together through elementary school.

I hope you are as excited about my message in this letter as I was in conveying it to you both. My staff will be in touch in the coming days to outline the program logistics and provide a date for a formal orientation. If you both agree to have Jeremy participate, please sign, date and return the participation form in the enclosed reply envelope. This will establish our covenantal relationship with your family.

Please do call me with any questions or suggestions you may have. Thank you and welcome to our accelerated program.

Sincerely,
John Adams, Ed.D
President

"Everyone finished?" Johnson asked. Most jurors nodded their heads. "Good. Now, remember your job is to find probable cause here—is it more likely than not that the Gutierrez defendants committed the crimes for which the police arrested them? I want to reinforce in your minds that the child here was no doubt quite gifted at the time the letter was written. Your role is not to see if there are any reasonable doubts as to guilt or innocence—that's for a *petit* jury to find. I'm only asking that, in light of what I've presented, would you all hand down the indictments...?" Johnson let the thought sink in as he moved back to his table, which was stacked high with documents and case law books. Part of the show.

Johnson, brown-eyed with matching hair, had graduated five years earlier from Suffolk University Law School, having taken evening classes while he worked days at his father Rudy's print shop, Kaleidographics in Malden, Massachusetts. He'd worked his way up to a printer after apprenticing next to his Uncle Ned, Rudy's half-brother. Apprentice was a loose concept that meant silk-screen cleaner, gofer, and gossip vessel. He also cleaned the bathrooms. It was hard work and he made enough money to pay his way through Suffolk. He moved to Fitchburg right after the bar exam in July, 1963. Always industrious, he'd sent letters to 25 different district attorneys' offices offering his post-exam services. Only Fitchburg's D.A. took the time to call him for an interview.

Now, he leaned back in his grand-jury room chair listening to the jurors debate the indictment for all of 68 seconds. He chuckled to himself in gratitude for his trusted friend, Detective Rod McNamara. McNamara had called him right after the arrests to get his advice on processing the case to make it bulletproof.

Northboro, Massachusetts—The Back Woods
Spring, 1967

"Shhh," Nanna warned, "the frogs can *feel* you coming up to the pond's edge, Jeremy. Gotta be real quiet—like you're holding a big secret inside! The froggie hears our footfalls in the grass. We've gotta tread lightly. Like the Indians used to. No animal could hear an Indian hunter approaching!"

Four-year-old Jeremy Hergenroeder took his Nanna's warning to heart. "I'm tip-toeing! How'd the Indians do it, Nanna?"

Edith Hergenroeder thought for a minute, taking in the scenery. Her husband Phillip, Jeremy's grandfather, had bought this land and the accompanying forested acreage a few years back—an investment on which he hoped someday to build a subdivision. A carpenter by trade, Phillip could craft a home in his head and then draw it out with a sharp pencil. Edith breathed in the pine-tree scent and loved hearing the wind slide through the branches above her head. The high breeze made her feel like she was flying to faraway places, her imagination in high gear.

"The Indians practiced right from the moment they started walking. You weren't invited along on a hunt if you'd give away your hunting party by breaking sticks under foot. So let's us start practicing, too."

Jeremy got down on all fours and crept up to the edge of Grandpa's pond. The bright sun reflected off the reeds and grasses that held fast at the water's edge. Jeremy reached up and broke off a stalk of grass with seeds on top. He stuck it in his mouth like he'd seen his Grandpa do. Sort of like smoking a pipe the way his father David did.

David was Edith's second son who at age three had contracted polio. David's older brother by five years, Luke, had cried all day when the family got the diagnosis. David hadn't understood his brother's problem that day, but he soon enough found out. The polio started in his right leg but mysteriously moved up to attack his left arm instead. Eventually the disease withered his arm, rendering his fingers and hand virtually useless. Edith persevered, however, and took it as a personal challenge to help David do everything from tying his shoes and a necktie one-handed (using the left palm to hold things in place), to playing catch—alternating with catching the ball with his right-handed glove, slipping off the glove, tucking it under his arm, and then throwing the ball back. It proved a neat choreography after hours of practice. Edith taught David how to type one handed, too, using Phillip's construction-office typewriter. Years later, Jeremy would marvel at his Dad's ability to do anything one-handed, even driving a car with a stick shift! Jeremy also thought his Dad's right arm surely was the size that Superman had for both his arms. And David never complained or mentioned what the polio did to his arm. Neither did Jeremy's mother, Alexandria. His Dad liked to say he passed along the gift of immunity to Jeremy, even though Jeremy had gotten the vaccine when he was three. Jeremy understood this to mean that since his Dad had beaten the disease and didn't die from it, he had a double shot of protection and couldn't catch polio.

As Jeremy crept to the muddy edge, he saw a bullfrog's head just above the water's shiny surface. Three skate bugs whisked by the frog, but he ignored them, perhaps sensing Jeremy's presence. Under the surface Jeremy marveled at the tadpoles swimming along the bottom. They came in all sizes and some had both a tail like a fish and hind legs on either side of their tails. He'd ask Nanna later how that could happen to a frog.

Quick as you like Jeremy grabbed for the frog—from beneath the water where he'd slipped his hand down, all before the frog knew what predator had captured him. Jeremy held up his prize for Nanna to see.

"You'd have made a good Indian, Jeremy. Let's take a look at him. Don't worry Mr. Froggie, we're not going to let Grandpa Phillip fry your legs. We just need to finish our zoology experiment here."

"What's zoo...aw...lagee, Nanna?"

"Oh, it's the science where they study animals of all kinds. I suppose that's where they got the word "zoo" from. Anytime you come up with a science—they add 'ology' onto the end of it and it's a big deal. Didn't you tell me you wanted to be a scientist?"

"Yes ma'am."

"Well, I'm studying you and so is Mr. Froggie. That makes the two of us "Jeremologists!" Nanna let out a shriek—her way of starting a belly laugh. Jeremy thought she had surely scared away all the tigers they'd come to hunt beyond the pond. But he giggled too. Jeremologist indeed!

"OK, Jeremy, ease Mr. Froggie back in the water and let's see him scoot away from us as fast as he can."

Jeremy gave the frog a kiss on its head and slowly put his hand beneath the surface. As soon as he let go, the frog dashed forward, reveling in its new-found freedom.

The sun arched up in the sky toward its apex just as the town's noon whistle blew. Jeremy saw a fish jump in the middle of the pond, startling two ducks nearby.

"How'd fish get in the pond after Grandpa dug it out, Nanna?"

"Remember how much your grandfather loves to fish? Lots of times when he goes to other lakes he'll bring home live fish in a bucket of water and toss them in the pond. Nature helps out, too. Duckologists tell me that those birds carry fish eggs on their feet as they move from pond to pond. Fish eggs are sticky and they fall off when the ducks land here. Grab your "rifle" and let's continue our tiger hunt."

Edith had grown up outside Worcester, Massachusetts and had one sister, Cora. She and Cora were inseparable during their childhood and had to sleep in the same bed almost until they graduated from high school. Cora would howl loudly in the winter, complaining that Edith's toes were "so cold you could freeze the sun in July!" Edith would just say, "Shush sister, quit your beefin' and roll over so I can sleep." After high school, Cora's childless marriage to a local man of suspect character didn't last long and she spent the rest of her adult years in the leadership ranks of the Girl Scouts. The girls loved her stories and she mentored them lovingly, supervising trips to the big cities of Boston and New York. Her goal was to open the girls' eyes to a bigger world—explore now so when you get bogged down with a family you'll have stories of your own to tell, or maybe you'll find a career of your own. Her mantra became "college first, marriage later...those boys can wait!"

Phillip had carved a circuitous route to Edith. As a 10-year-old living in Union, Maine, he had come home from school one day only to find his mother, Mattie, outside the house in a pick-up truck with a man from their church. Phillip was startled to see his mother's every possession tied down in the truck bed. As the engine idled, Mattie leaned her head out the passenger window and gave Phillip a choice. "I'm leaving your Pa. You can come with me to Massachusetts or stay with your Dad here. I'm tired of his carousing and shenanigans."

Phillip didn't know what carousing meant, but it didn't sound good. He knew his father, a mail carrier named Daniel, would disappear for days at a time, but he'd always figured it was mail-call duty. Phillip looked up the cement steps toward the screen door. Through the prism of his tears he saw his father staring back at him. He made a snap judgment and hopped in the truck. As it lumbered off down the hill toward Route 1, Phillip wondered about his clothes and school books. Would he ever see his Dad again? He wept quietly and Mattie put her arm around him, whispering that this was for the best. "I'm sorry honey. You just have yourself a good cry. We'll make it. I've found us a new home in Worcester, Massachusetts, Phillip. I've got a few dollars saved and I'll figure something out."

Phillip barely heard what she said. The farther down the hill they got the worse his stomach felt. As he turned three shades of green, Mattie asked the truck driver, Landis, a sinewy fellow church member with a heart of gold, to pull over to the side of the road. Mattie had cornered Landis after church one day asking him if she could "mosey along" the next time he headed to Boston on a work assignment so she could attend to "some family legal business."

"Of course, Mattie. Do you want to bring a lunch or should I have Betty make some extra sandwiches? I'm headed there on Tuesday." Mattie's tears told Landis everything he needed to know. He didn't ask any more questions. He'd never seen Daniel in church and knew the stories. He and Betty often wondered why Mattie put up with the abuse—more emotional than physical, which just meant it hurt all the more and all the longer.

Phillip jumped out of the front seat just in time, hurling his lunch *and* breakfast. Funny, with a newly emptied stomach he didn't feel hungry when he hopped back in the truck.

A few years later, after the two of them settled down on Dawson Road in Worcester, Phillip finished high school. He got a job with a construction crew that built townhouses outside Boston. He'd always been handy and loved tools. His boss, Harvey Jones, saw the gleam in Phillip's eye and knew how he'd helped Mattie scratch a living out of nothing more than will power. One day on the job, Harvey asked Phillip to come into the construction trailer where Harvey kept the books and crew schedules all laid out on a card table. "Listen, Phillip, I need help with getting out payroll and the payables. You wanna' lend a hand?"

"Sure boss. Just point me in the direction you need me to go!" Phillip responded.

"OK, let's see how well you write. I need clear penmanship. Copy down this bill of lading and then hand write a second copy of this letter I wrote a few minutes ago. Let's see how you do."

Phillip sat down in earnest and did his best to copy the words precisely. When he finished he held up the work product to Harvey, who just shook his head.

"All right, that's what I figured. Good with tools and good at helping your Ma, but you write like a damned doctor. Here, take this cursive book home and practice your handwriting at night. Get your mother Mattie to watch over your chicken scratch. *Take her advice because she knows how to write.* My uncle Mitch gave me this handy writing desk—portable, fits right on top of any table. Look, the top opens to a compartment where you can keep your pencils and erasers, not to mention a ruler. Have at it, and come back to me in three weeks when you've gotten the hang of it."

Phillip couldn't believe his luck. Not only was he learning construction, Harvey had invited him into the secret world of business—where the clarion call was "inside job, no heavy lifting!" Best of all, someday he could pursue his dream of building houses on his own, be his own boss and make some real money. Three weeks later, Phillip had practiced so much he could match the best calligrapher. Not only was it readable; in Harvey's estimation, Phillip had style!

"Back to the hunt!" Nanna whispered to Jeremy. They left the pond behind and continued down the service road Phillip had carved out of the pine forest. Jeremy carried the poplar rifle Phillip had carved for him. It had a trigger and a sight down the end of the barrel, perfect for spotting tigers before they spotted you. Jeremy marveled at how Grandpa had sanded down the rough edges—no chance of getting a sliver from this gun! He knew Grandpa had shellacked the gun, but he wasn't sure what shellac was. Just that it made the gun the color of a real rifle. It was good enough for him and, by gum, good enough for those tigers lurking about.

Jeremy loved the service road—with the grass growing down the middle of the two tire ruts. He could play for hours on the private road near the house all day with his Tonka dump truck, grader, and steam shovel. Being an only child did have its benefits—he long ago had learned to occupy himself and take full advantage of his imagination. He created whole worlds and outer spacescapes with his Tinker Toys and the Erector Set Grandpa had given him for Christmas when he was three. Lincoln Logs didn't really fit in with outer space, so Jeremy only used those after watching the Lone Ranger. Jeremy most loved to watch *The Twilight Zone*, but was only allowed to watch the first 30 minutes of the show, thanks to a 7:00 p.m. bedtime. It really did drive him crazy, particularly a rerun episode he saw called, *A Penny For Your Thoughts,* which starred actor Dick York as a bank loan officer. York's character, Hector Poole, purchases a newspaper from a street vendor on his way to work and tosses a coin into the metal payment box. The coin lands on its edge and just sits there, a million-to-one shot. At that moment he suddenly gains the ability to hear other people's thoughts. Jeremy was perplexed because Mr. Poole didn't seem to make use of his power. What happened at the end, he wondered? Could

Poole tell the difference between people's fantasy thoughts and their actual intentions, as he usually could? Hopefully something good had come out of it.

No worries about traffic on Grandpa's service road. Phillip had long ago installed at the entrance a log chain between two fence posts. He even painted and hung a no-trespassing/no hunting sign ("We happily will and have prosecuted!"). Thus, no ne'er-do-wells dared sneak down the road for some drinking, make-out sessions or adult tiger hunts. Ants and beetles often ignored the signage and would parade through and around Jeremy's road projects, never paying him any mind or he them. He did worry about bumblebees though because he got stung at the age of two when the Hergenroeders lived in New Bedford. That was the location of his Dad's first congregational church—right after he graduated from Vanderbilt Divinity School in Nashville. A bumblebee had latched on to a Macintosh apple Jeremy was learning how to eat. His parents had shouted at him to drop the apple or throw it away. Try as Jeremy might, he could only get the throw motion, not the letting-go part. Pretty soon he'd angered the bee who gladly stung him. Jeremy never would forget the waves of pain from the stinger as his mother put mud on the wound. She had managed to get out some of the venom but it still hurt like nothing he'd ever felt before.

Edith and Jeremy heard something moving about in the brush just beyond their sight. "Look, quick Jeremy! A tiger's coming straight for us! Oh my!"

Jeremy took careful aim and yelled "pow" and "boom" as the tiger fell just inches from where they stood. "That was a close call. We better watch out for its brother—don't they hunt in pairs?"

"I don't know, Nanna!"

"Look out behind you—here comes his sister and she's angry!"

Jeremy barely got the gun up in time. The tiger's head blew off and, as he looked down, saw the tiger's body still twitching. He couldn't believe his luck. Two tigers in the span of one minute. Any big-game hunter should be so lucky.

"I've got to catch my breath, Jeremy. What say you and I head in for a tiger sandwich? You gather up that one and I'll grab her brother. We'll have us a tiger barbeque. I think I just heard Grandpa pull in the driveway for his lunch. Let's skedaddle and get him fed or he may start roaring!"

"Yes, ma'am." Jeremy replied. He *felt* Nanna's head and Grandpa's too and sensed that they both were hungry. Grandpa seemed a bit antsy for some reason that Jeremy couldn't fathom. He'd have to ask him at lunch or maybe he'd figure it out as they ate.

CHAPTER 1

Friday May 31, 1968
Fitchburg, Massachusetts
Skipping the second day of the accelerated kindergarten class—and for good reason.

"**M**om, why do you think I have stickso-frame-ee-ya?" Jeremy asked.

"Oh Lord, honey. Please let the doctor worry about that, OK?" Alex answered, shaking her head in hopes that Jeremy would remain calm.

"Look, son, your Mom and I have been worried the last few weeks about what you've been telling us...you know, those voices in your head," David said, trying to assuage his son's fears. "You're barely five years old so it's probably nothing, but Mom and I just want to see if there's any medicine that the doctor might have that will help you."

David and Alex knew Jeremy was a gifted child. After reading about a special accelerated kindergarten class touted in the *Fitchburg Sentinel*, they completed the application and hand delivered it to Fitchburg State Teacher's College. The school was right along David's morning trek to Rollstone Congregational Church, where he was the pastor. Everything proceeded swimmingly after they got Jeremy's acceptance letter in April from none other than college president John Adams, Ed.D. The Hergenroeders celebrated with a Friendly's ice cream cake complete with five candles. The program meant that Jeremy would be truly challenged and not shunted into a peer group who had yet to learn their ABCs. Jeremy had figured out the alphabet at age two, and could read with the skill of an older child, even tackling complicated Old Testament passages ("what is the jaw bone of someone's ass, Dad?"). Then the first day of school hit and their world seemed to collapse. Jeremy had cried inconsolably, much more so than David thought possible for first-day jitters. He even intimated to his teacher, Mrs. Murphy (Dr. Murphy, thank you very much) that he could read books *and people*. David took him out of class on the excuse that he just needed some time to get used to the idea of school. Now David understood how the owner of Mr. Ed the talking horse on that TV show must have felt every time the neighbors heard "him" talking to himself.

"What do you think the doctor will say?" Jeremy asked from the back seat of their 1964 VW Beetle.

"I'm not sure, Jeremy. Let's just all breathe and give him a chance," David said as they pulled into the parking lot of the psychiatrist's office.

Jeremy sounded out the name on the brown and gold sign affixed to the doctor's front door: "Dr. Israel Reeb..."

David piped up, "Yeah, that's a tough one Jeremy. Good job, though. I think he pronounces his name Azriel Rebovitz. We'll just call him Dr. Rebovitz, OK?"

One of the benefits of being a big time minister in a small town like Fitchburg was that you got to know most of the star players who were part of the helping professions. David had heard about Dr. Rebovitz's work with Korean War veterans and came away impressed. He also knew that Dr. Rebovitz had for some reason switched to treating children instead.

Brooding for a moment, Jeremy nodded and hopped out of the back seat as Alex held it open for him. He'd felt his parents' fears for months, even as far back as age three. He couldn't help it if he knew what other people were thinking! As the family entered the office, Jeremy heard a little bell attached to the door jamb announce their presence.

The Hergenroeders felt the whoosh of refrigerated air escape the office as they entered. It was the rare office indeed that had air conditioning. Jeremy eyeballed the receptionist who smiled and said, "Hello, young man and welcome to our office. My name is Velma Brodie. You must be the Hergenroeders, and you must be Jeremy. How are you today?"

Jeremy could sense Velma's thoughts and felt worry and fear in her heart. He could tell that her marriage was in a shambles, but kept it to himself. "I'm fine, Mrs. Brodie," Jeremy answered.

Velma wondered how Jeremy knew she was married, but ignored the thought. "Well, good. Please have a seat and I'll let Dr. Rebovitz know you're here early. He may be able to sneak you in."

The family took a seat and Jeremy pushed aside the lame "Highlights" magazines, grabbing instead a Superman comic in the middle of the pile. He couldn't believe a doctor's office had comic books! As he lifted the comic he saw a Batman comic and another with Captain America on the cover. *This might just turn out all right*, Jeremy thought.

The family took in the smells and bells of the outer office. Pictures of Dr. Rebovitz with Army and Air Force brass looked back at them, as did several commendations for meritorious service to Korean veterans all over the country. Jeremy zeroed in on a picture of a big black Lab sitting on the front steps of a mansion with its tongue hanging out. He read the inscription underneath—Phil-a-da. Sounded like Philadelphia to him. *Why wouldn't you just call your dog Philadelphia—why leave off the rest of the name?*

Just then a huge man walked out through the passageway door. Jeremy craned his neck to see the man's face. At six foot five inches tall the gentleman's head nearly touched the ceiling.

"Greetings, I'm Dr. Azriel Rebovitz. I'm glad that we had a cancellation. You all must be the Hergenroeder family and you, young man, must be Mr. Jeremy. I saw you admiring my dog Philada. Spoiled rotten she is."

David and Alex stood up to greet Dr. Rebovitz. "Yes, this is Jeremy, I'm David and this is my wife Alexandria." David reached to shake Dr. Rebovitz's hand.

Dr. R. welcomed everyone and bent over to shake Jeremy's hand before turning to Velma. "I'm expecting a call from Boston Children's Hospital, a Dr. Pick. Do put him through if he calls while I visit with the Hergenroeders."

"Yes, sir," Velma said pleasantly.

Jeremy felt Dr. R's head and knew that the call from Dr. Pick involved a teenager who had been arrested for trying to kill himself. He also realized that Dr. R used to treat adults, mostly war veterans, but gave it up because the mounting sadness overwhelmed him. Dr. R had heard so many awful war stories that his cup runneth over.

Before everyone headed into the inner sanctum, Dr. R. turned to David and Alex and said, "I think things'll work better if I meet with Jeremy one-on-one. I know you said you needed an emergency appointment and I'm glad we could fit you in on short notice. Your phone call the other day helped me a good deal in terms of background information, David. Would it be OK with you two if I brought you in toward the end of my interview with Jeremy—after I've gotten to know him a bit?"

Alex stammered, "Sure, I just thought we might be part of your initial intake."

Alex didn't trust psychiatry and hated revealing family secrets to anyone, especially someone who might *write down* those secrets in some sort of *permanent record*. Now this doctor wanted to meet with her son in private. She wondered if she was somehow shirking her parental duties. Her family was big on secrets, at least her mother had been, and her father had just given up fighting. Alex was the oldest of three sisters, with the second sister, Kelsey, five years her junior and the youngest, Patience, named after one of the first babies born after the Pilgrims landed at Plymouth Rock in 1620, coming two years after Kelsey. Alex's father, Nathan Cotter, worked as a Massachusetts State road crew boss. Every day he worked outside and went to work in his bright orange Department of Public

Works pick-up truck. Nathan was a by-the-book kind of guy, which meant even in a blinding snowstorm he would drive by his daughters as they trudged home from school. No one was allowed in that truck, period. State regulations, don't you know. Or at least his understanding of them. Sort of like what the Israelites did to protect and expand on the 10 Commandments—they created the Book of Leviticus, every regulation imaginable. Granny Cotter never really wanted children to begin with and motherhood proved a struggle. As often as she could she'd get Kelsey and Patience to play outside, and then no sooner had they exited, she'd lock the door and ignore their pleas later to let them in so they could go potty.

Alex had long suffered similar treatment, which convinced her to get a summer job after her 14th birthday teaching swimming at Camp Putnam in New Braintree. For her trouble over the nine-week season, the Camp paid her and the other junior workers $25, barely $3.00 per week. She'd have worked for free just to be away from her mother. A strong swimmer, she found teaching swimming a breeze, except for the leeches that feasted on her students. Camp policy involved asking the children to come out of the water every 15 minutes to check for "water worms", the corporate euphemism for leeches. The kids didn't know any better and of course the leeches didn't hurt since they injected an anesthetic into their victims when they chomped down on the skin. Counselors advised the kids to put the leeches into a bucket of kerosene that the Camp kept to the side of the beach.

Alex first met David, a senior counselor, at the camp. It wasn't until she reached the age of 17 that she even noticed him. For the prior three years she thought of David and the other veteran counselors as Camp bigwigs. Then one day she and her fellow counselor Patty stood in line for watermelon slices. Sure enough, David served them. He greeted Alex with a becoming smile and raised his eyebrow to ask if she was ready for a slice. Alex nodded and David held his own slice between his teeth to free up his cutting hand. Later Patty scolded Alex for making David cut her a piece—*how could you not have noticed his withered left hand?* Alex felt a deep shame, but at that moment David saw in her an innocence about his affliction. Alex always focused on people's hearts and their non-verbal communication, not their outer beauty or disabilities. Later in life she would finally come to understand her gift when she heard The Rev. Dr. Martin Luther King, Jr., advise everyone to pay attention to the content of their neighbors' character, not the color of their skin. She'd made that a habit since childhood. A few weeks later, David asked Alex to go to the Worcester County Fair with him. She readily agreed and their love blossomed over the next few months.

Alex pined at night in her camp cot for her homebound younger sisters as her sense of helplessness paralyzed her spirit. Child abuse had not yet entered the popular lexicon. There didn't yet exist an abuse investigative division within the Massachusetts Department of Children's Services. Back then, DCS focused on orphan placements or when no one volunteered to take in the orphans, DCS housed the children in big orphanages. Alex knew her father had long ago decided a strained peace was far better than confronting the issues of a shared parenthood. Through her lens, unless he proved to be a miracle-worker, Dr. Rebovitz fell into her father's cadre of non-committals. The closed door behind which her son ventured only reinforced the angst she felt over her own mother's locked-door policy.

Snapping back to the present, Alex heard Dr. Rebovitz say, "Yes, Mrs. Hergenroeder, you are correct. That's sometimes helpful, to have the parents in right at the start. And I'm not trying to exclude anyone. I'd just like to visit with Jeremy first. Let him tell me what he thinks is going on."

Dr. Rebovitz got caught up in Alex's beauty. She stood five feet four inches tall, had fetching azure blue eyes and flaming strawberry blonde hair. She presented a marked contrast to David's six-foot-one-inch frame and jet black hair that he always slicked back with a dab of pomade.

"You're the doctor," David responded without any hint of sarcasm. "We're both just grateful for your time. My colleagues have nothing but praise for your insights and healing powers. They said you're something of a miracle worker."

"Oh, I don't know about that. All my patients are miracles, some just waiting to happen. C'mon Jeremy, and do bring that Superman comic you've got in your hands. He's my favorite superhero!"

Jeremy followed, clutching the comic book. Velma eyeballed the two person parade, and thought to herself that the Hergenroeders better just trust Dr. Rebovitz. Imagine questioning his judgment and advice! They were lucky to get some of his time. She watched out of the corner of her eye as the Hergenroeders took a seat. As she typed correspondence, she chuckled to herself at the Hergenroeders' muted displeasure. Velma ran a tight ship and would not cotton to any criticism of her boss. She'd let them have it if they so much as mouthed a "what for."

As Dr. Rebovitz sat down and invited Jeremy to do the same, Jeremy said, "My other doctor that Mom takes me to, Dr. Copoulos, he doesn't have comic books in his waiting room. Just that 'Highlights' magazine."

"I know Dr. C. He's a good doctor, Jeremy. I bet he gives you shots, doesn't he?"

"Yes! And they hurt. He tries to fool me into thinking I won't need a shot, but I can always tell I'm going to get one. It's easy—he has the needle lying out. Keeps it on a towel up by the sink!"

"Thank you for coming today, Jeremy. I always like to get to know my patients a bit before we jump into any kind of therapy. Or, before I offer any medicine. Please, tell me what's going on. Why do you think you're here? And do call me Dr. R."

"My parents are worried. I guess they think I hear voices. In my head. I see things about people I meet at church that nobody else sees. Sometimes I tell them. That's when they get scared of what I say. Scared of me."

Jeremy looked around the cozy office. He admired the odd looking couch that seemed to have some sort of hinge thingy, like a chaise lounge. The comics in the waiting room were one thing, but Dr. R had a huge assortment of toys in two big boxes on the floor. He also had a Rube Goldberg device with all sorts of twists and turns for a steel marble to follow. He also saw a GI Joe and a Barbie Doll, sitting in a pink Corvette. Ken rode shotgun. Jeremy so wanted to jump out of his chair and play!

"My, my Jeremy," Dr. R responded as he admired Jeremy's emerald green eyes. "Sounds like you bear quite a burden. I'm trying to understand. By the way, you seem pretty smart for a five year old. Have you ever heard anyone use the word 'precocious' when they talk about you?

"No," said Jeremy, "but my Grannie Cotter calls me 'Sweetie Pie.'"

"Do you like your Grannie? Is she nice to you?"

"Oh, yes. She never makes me eat anything on my plate that I don't like. My Mom makes me sit there until it's gone, even parsnips. Boy, do I hate parsnips. I don't think my aunts like Grannie."

"Why do you say that?"

"Well I can feel in their heads that Grannie might not have been very nice to them. When they were growing up. My Mom, too."

"Really? Have they ever said anything to you about your Grannie?"

"No. But I know! Guess what! Grannie told me a secret last week when we visited her and Grandpa in Winchendon."

"Winchendon? I know that town. It's called the 'Original Toy Town.' They used to make lots of toys there and shipped them all over the country—to boys and girls just like you."

"Yup. I've read the sign. When we drive into town. Grandpa said the same thing about how important Winchendon was to Santa Claus. He kept elves there to help make the toys. But I know there's no Santa. It's a good story, though. My friends still believe in him. I don't tell them they're wrong."

As Dr. R started establishing rapport with his new patient, he knew he had to revisit Grannie's secret and find out how Jeremy managed to say things that scared church folk. That last one could be a real career killer for Rev. David, thought Dr. R.

"So Jeremy, you mentioned that Grannie told you a secret last week. What did she tell you?"

"I'm not supposed to tell my Mom and Dad. I don't want to upset Grannie. She knows I can feel other people's heads. She told me that she had a cousin named Grace who read people's heads too. Grace and Grannie lived near each other. They played together a lot. Grace called it 'going to other people's libraries.'"

"Really? And your parents never heard this story?"

"Grannie said she'd never told. Grace died of measles when she was 10. Plus, I can tell they don't know when I feel their heads. Grannie was right."

Stunned, Dr. R caught his breath for a moment and then focused in on the head-feeling statement. "What do you mean when you say you and Grace could feel people's heads? Do you touch their heads?"

Jeremy was nonplussed. Recovering quickly, he said, "No, that's just what I call it when I can tell what someone's thinking. I can feel when they're worried about me. Like if I feel the head of one of the ladies at church."

"Yes, you mentioned church folk getting scared of you. Please tell me when that's happened before. Does it happen a lot?"

"All the time," Jeremy said with a worried look. "My parents said you might have a medicine that you'd give me to make this go away. But, when I feel your head, I know that's not true."

"You're feeling my head now, Jeremy?"

"Yes," Jeremy said sheepishly.

"What do you feel in my head?"

"I can tell you think I'm smart and not stick-o-phrenic. But you've never seen a kid like me before."

"That's an understatement, Jeremy. You are one of a kind. And that's what we're here to explore. Sort of like a journey. Have you ever been down a country road, Jeremy?"

"Oh yes. My Grandpa Hergenroeder has his very own country road. It leads to two ponds he's made. I love to catch frogs in the main pond—the one we're allowed to go swimming in. The other one is sort of a feeder pond. It's gross. Dark and muddy."

"Good example. So think about our conversation as if you and I are hiking down your Grandpa's road, way out in the woods. We may see crickets, tree frogs, a crow, a dove, all sorts of song birds, you name it. Let's explore your imagination and please think of this office as a safe place, Jeremy. Do you feel safe?"

Pondering the idea of safety, Jeremy said, "Last week our family went for breakfast at the diner. When we sat down at our booth, I saw a big policeman at the counter. He was eating an egg sandwich. He had a big gun on his belt. I said 'wow' too loud and my Dad told me to hush. He said I might embarrass the policeman. Dad said he needed privacy. He asked me the Golden Rule thing—how'd I like it if someone saw me and said wow too loud? But that gun! I guess it keeps the policeman safe. Maybe us, too. You know I felt the policeman's head. He was glad I said 'Wow!' Yup, I feel safe. When I feel your head I can tell you're a good person. You're not like that bully I ran into at nursery school last year. A boy named Mike punched me in the belly. I didn't think I'd ever breathe again. My teacher said he was from the trailer park and I should stay clear of him. I could have taken him though. I'm pretty strong, ya know."

"OK, but I'm glad you didn't punch him back. Not a good move for the minister's kid. So you're in kindergarten now?"

"Sort of. My Dad took me yesterday for the first day, but we only stayed fifteen minutes."

"OK, fifteen minutes. Tell me what happened? Why didn't you stay?"

Jeremy thought about the day before and told Dr. R the story. "I woke up early since I was nervous. The sunshine made it a nice day. I did my push-ups, pull-ups and sit-ups. I'm trying to get stronger. Wanna see my muscle?" Jeremy pulled back his short-sleeved shirt and imitated Charles Atlas.

"Wow—you have been working out. I'm impressed." Dr. R. thought about his pediatric training in the fourth year of medical school. Jeremy did seem to have unusually well-developed biceps for a five year old. He recalled reading some research about a muscle anomaly in one of his medical journals. He only subscribed to the New England Journal of Medicine and an obscure family practice journal that rejected pharmaceutical company-funded research. He found the psychiatric journals too focused on Freudian research. He racked his brain for the name of the genetic condition. *Some German kid had it. Perfect—another Aryan. Yes, I remember! The researchers called it...myostatin-related muscle hypertrophy. Sort of the opposite of muscular dystrophy. The six-year-old patient weighed 63 pounds and could carry his 155-pound mother around the house! Focus,* he thought, *focus—let's stick with the problem at hand, not on other problems Jeremy might face as he develops physically.*

"Yup. I don't want to be a weakling. I've read those ads in the magazines. I saw one that said 'Strength in 77 seconds.' I couldn't figure out what they were selling though, so I started exercising. I can do 45 pull-ups in a row, and 100 push-ups! Sit-ups are just too easy. I could do those all day."

"I'm letting us get off track. Please tell me what happened at school."

"OK. Dad and I left the house about 7:30. Mom said I had butterflies in my tummy. I told her butterflies don't live in my belly. She just laughed as we left the house. We got to school and when we walked into the classroom I could feel all the other kids' heads. It scared me at first. You know, some of them were crying. I felt like a big beach pail. Everyone dumped their crying into my bucket. I started crying, too. My Dad moved me toward the back of the class. He rubbed my back after I sat down."

"Did that help you, Jeremy? Calm you down some?"

"Yeah. For a minute. I wasn't scared myself. I just couldn't handle feeling everyone's heads all at once."

"OK, go on. I didn't mean to interrupt you."

"My teacher, Mrs. Murphy, came over to us. She wanted to know my name. I couldn't get the words out. I couldn't breathe very good because I was crying. Sort of like when Mike punched me. I did say my name finally. She said, 'Welcome to my class.'"

"Well, that's good. You could speak to your teacher. Lots of kids on the first day can't even do that. Go on."

"I said thank you and Dad said, "Ma'am, I'm David Hergenroeder, and I guess my son's just a little nervous." Mrs. Murphy said, 'Aw, that's OK. School's such a new experience. It takes some getting used to—even I cried on my first day.' But I knew she was lying. I felt her head and saw her first day of school. She lived in Peabody, where we used to live. I saw the name Farnsworth Elementary on her school building. Big cement letters above the front door. Her classroom was on the second floor. I saw her in a new dress. She wore keen red shoes like Dorothy. In the Wizard of Oz. I counted 43 students. She and maybe six students weren't crying. I saw her holding another student's hand, I guess to calm him down. His name was Paul Bowen. He was a tiny kid and had a real red face. I think he had some sort of disease or something. He wore a necklace that said *Medic Alert*."

"Whoa, Jeremy! You seem to be able to tell me exactly what everyone said word for word. Plus you saw so clearly into and *through* Mrs. Murphy's mind. You must have a good memory."

"Yeah. Other people's words float around in my head. I can put them back together like a puzzle."

"OK, a puzzle. I understand, I think. Tell me what happened next."

"When Mrs. Murphy lied to me I got upset. My Dad worried about me disturbing the class. So he said he'd take me home. Maybe we could try again tomorrow. He asked Mrs. Murphy if that was OK. She looked at me and said, 'Certainly. Let's let Jeremy sleep on the idea overnight and he might get a better feeling.' She told me the class was a safe place and I'd make lots of new friends. Get to know new kids, play games and learn how to read. I told her I already knew how to read books and people."

"You told her you could read *people*?"

"Yeah. I shouldn'ta said that. She looked at me real funny. Asked my Dad what I meant. Dad said I was just precious."

"Precious or precocious Jeremy?" I bet he said precocious like we talked about earlier. It's a big word that just means you're advanced for your age—ahead of your time, so to speak. It's why Fitchburg State chose you for the accelerated class."

"OK. Mrs. Murphy asked Dad if I really meant I could read people. 'Why would he say that?' she asked. Dad said he was the minister at Rollstone and he had told me that being a good minister meant being good at reading people. He lied to her. She said she remembered that I was a minister's kid. She seemed OK with Dad's answer. That's what I could see when I felt her head again. The rest of the class just stared at me and Dad. The other moms had left and everyone else had stopped crying."

"So are you going to go back, Jeremy?"

"Yes, maybe Monday. I was too upset and just wanted to play at home."

"I see. You say you heard what everyone was thinking including your teacher, Mrs. Murphy?"

"No, I felt their heads and hers too!" Jeremy responded.

"I'm sorry, yes you 'felt their heads.' But you also said you knew Mrs. Murphy lied when she said she cried on her first day of school. Did you feel that or see it?"

"Both, I guess."

"You're a preacher's kid. A'PK.' Has anyone ever called you that?"

"Yes. I've heard adults at Rollstone say that. They usually say it and then tell me I'm cute—like Rudolph the Red Nosed Reindeer. Rudolph's girlfriend Clarice said he looked cute. After she said that, he jumped higher than all of the other young bucks!"

"Yes, he sure did. I like that Christmas special. It has a good message for all of us. Keep trying even when all the odds are against you."

"Yup. Even if you're the Abominable Snow Monster!"

Dr. R. found Jeremy's powers of concentration highly advanced for his age. The doctor would fill in more details as they got to know each other better. Jeremy wouldn't know ADHD if it occupied a whole edition of one of his cherished Little Golden Books. Focusing never had been Jeremy's problem—but daydreaming had been, at least once in a while at nursery school when his teacher, Mrs. Tesser, would ask everyone to close their eyes and nap. Why shut off my daydreams, Jeremy wondered? So, he'd learned to squint his eyes to make it *look* like they were shut. He didn't fool Mrs. Tesser. She chose to say nothing as long as Jeremy kept quiet and didn't disturb his classmates, some of whom actually snored. His daydreams took him into the minds of his classmates—he just didn't realize it at the tender age of four. He thought he was visiting other worlds—still on earth, but with his friends along for the ride, except *they* always seemed to be driving.

"Jeremy, look, I don't think you need any medicine. You're just fine. Usually I'd want you back for several visits so we could find a medicine that might help. We doctors think we can spot a disease or illness in a patient's body or mind. Then we try some drugs to see if they will help. A pill here or there. But I'll admit—if you'll keep this a secret, sometimes we psychiatrists just guess. We miss the mark and people get worse! That's not the case here Jeremy. You are a healthy and wise-beyond-your-years PK! I have a good picture of what is going on with your special gift, Jeremy. I'm going to invite your parents in so we all can discuss this further. Is that OK with you?"

"Yes, sir," Jeremy said.

As Dr. R. stood to poke his head out of the office door and invite in the Hergenroeders, he thought back to his own childhood in Germany. He and his parents lived through the Nazi's rise to power. They hid in a false walled room that their gentile friends had constructed up in the eve of their home. They got caught eventually and the soldiers sent *both* families to Dachau, just weeks before the Allies broke through and won the war. Thank God Jeremy won't have to live through a hell like that, Dr. R. mused.

As he opened the door he breathed a sigh of relief, both that Dachau was long behind him and that Jeremy didn't have a mental illness. He informed Alex and David that he was ready to discuss their PK with them. David Hergenroeder, sensing a lighter moment after fearing his son really was schizophrenic, said, "'PK' is old school Dr. Rebovitz. We prefer 'Theologian's Offspring' or 'T.O.' for short."

Dr. R gave vent to a long hearty belly laugh. Jeremy could feel in Dr. R's head a warm feeling and he, too, relaxed.

"OK," said Dr. R. "What's going on here? And, before I offer my professional opinion after visiting with Jeremy for twenty-five minutes, I want to get your take, David and Alexandria. What do you think is going on with your son?"

Alex spoke up. "First, please call me Alex. Second, Jeremy has always been special to us. We know he's smart. It's why he got invited to attend this twelve month accelerated kindergarten program that Fitchburg Teachers College has launched. This is going to sound crazy, and I know that's not a word I should use around a psychiatrist, but I'm a fan of the Star Trek TV series on CBS. Have you ever watched it, Dr. Rebovitz?"

"Why, yes, I'm quite a fan of space exploration."

"Perfect. There's a recent episode where Captain Kirk and Spock are transported against their will to some planet. They encounter these beings wearing long silver robes that grab Dr. McCoy and put him in some sort of near-death state—with wounds all over his body. Next to McCoy is this beautiful kind-hearted woman who is completely mute. You can see the graciousness in her face. And she's also got a deeply pained look as she considers McCoy. She goes and touches him and soon where she touched McCoy's wounds they transfer to her body and then disappear. Meanwhile, Spock and Kirk watch in horror from their light beam jail cell. Every time this woman, Spock calls her an 'empath,' heals Dr. McCoy, the pumpkin headed jailers add more injuries. It's like a test—will she give up her life to save Dr. McCoy? The ultimate sacrifice, I suppose. Anyway, she ends up saving the doctor and it all ends happily when the pumpkin guys save the woman, the empath, from final death."

"Yes, I've seen the episode."

"That show was a revelation for me. I finally realized Jeremy may have that skill or something like it."

"Good. I agree, which is part of the reason I wanted all of us to talk. David, what are your thoughts?"

"OK, I get the empathy idea—although I don't think Jeremy is 'with healing powers' as my peers in the ministry trade might say. But he clearly has a special gift. I took enough pastoral care classes and have made plenty of hospital visits to ailing parishioners to know medical science is imprecise. But that's why we are here. We need answers. I'm just worried sick."

"I understand," replied Dr. R. "I'd be worried too. There's a new type of brain scan that Mass General is using—it's quite experimental. They inject a radio pharmaceutical into a patient's blood stream and the researchers tell me they see which parts of a patient's brain light up as they ask him questions or pose problems to him. It requires this special marker chemical that lights up the active portions of the brain. I'm sure you all are wondering how this mind gift works. The new experimental imaging procedure might give us some insights. But before I even advise such a test, I have a deeper concern.

David spoke up. "I don't care much for Star Trek. And I don't like the sound of 'radio pharmaceutical.' It sounds radioactive. And I'm concerned about having chemicals racing around Jeremy's brain—is it dangerous? What are its long-term effects, and…."

Alex interrupted, "Look, if you say he's OK, no mental illness and he's not schizoid, why do this?"

Dr. R saw where this was headed. "Hearing your objections, I think you may be right, but for a completely different reason. First, I don't trust that we could keep Jeremy's gift or talent under wraps. Yes, medical care is confidential. But rumors will fly and manipulative people would want to take advantage of Jeremy. Second, I don't know if he's told you this story, but yesterday at kindergarten when he was crying, his teacher, Mrs. Helen Murphy, told him a little white lie. She said she cried on her first day of school. Not only did she not cry, according to Jeremy, she comforted a classmate of hers who was quite short for his age, underdeveloped. Jeremy—you even remembered or 'saw,' felt as you would say, that the boy had a medic alert necklace on!"

David responded, "No, we hadn't heard that story. But it matches what Jeremy's told us about some of my parishioners. Sometimes he'll tell them things about themselves that they had long forgotten, especially at funerals that he's attended with me, even at the graveside. To say he spooks some of my flock would be a 'grave' understatement." David's attempt at humor fell flat. "I've been afraid, frankly, for my pastorate. Our denomination, the UCC, United Church of Christ, is quite progressive, liberal even. But not that liberal!"

"I get it," said Dr. R. "Since we all like comics, there's an older Superman comic I read as a boy that reminds me of you, Jeremy, and your gift. The story takes place right after Superman starts working at the Daily Planet. He's just left his boyhood home in Smallville to come to Metropolis. Big city, big lights, right? At one point, after putting away a few bad guys, he rockets his way to the stratosphere. He closes his eyes and hears millions of conversations around the globe. Billions, I suppose. No matter. My point is he has a choice. Help where he can, then prioritize and tune out the rest. He filters the white noise down to a manageable level. This is what we need to teach Jeremy. And I suggest...."

Alex interrupted again, "We can't afford your fees. We just wanted a quick read on whether our son was psychotic. Now you're trying to sign us up for long-term therapy. David only makes $180 per week. And that's his gross. You charge over $100 per hour!"

Alex didn't have a stingy bone in her body. She kept a tight ship at home, clipped coupons and planned family meals at least one week in advance, making her shopping all the more efficient. She learned the *waste not want not* motto from her own grandmother, and even went so far as to make her own laundry soap in the parsonage basement with lye poured out to cure in several baking pans laid out across the floor. She'd grind the soap into flakes with a cheese grinder, and then bag it for later use. She didn't consider the cost of her time, or that getting a job as a secretary would have brought in far more resources than she ever could couponing or making soap. After all her father was raised on a poor farm after *his* dad died at age 35 of a massive heart attack. Alex's grandfather had been the superintendent of the poor farm and his family got free room and board. When he died, the family members suddenly found themselves as farm clients. They had always worked hard at the farm, but now were like sharecroppers. At the time, the Worcester town fathers ordained that "It shall be the duty of the superintendent and matron to see that *inmates* labor in such a way...that no one may be permitted to lead an idle life... No person shall be allowed to converse or have intercourse with any person...without permission... no pauper shall leave..." and on and on the directive went.

Alex never had read that mean-spirited statement, but still took to heart saving money. She knitted gloves and hats for David and Jeremy to wear during the cold Fitchburg winters. She taught herself how to sew her own skirts and blouses, getting template designs from patterns she borrowed from friends. Alex even started a sewing club at Rollstone and the women members happily traded patterns, all with an eye to saving precious nickels and dimes.

Dr. R. struggled to respond to Alex's monetary concerns. "You are correct, Alex. A hundred dollars per hour is my *normal* charge. I suggest we use the barter system, a trade, if you will."

"Trade with my son? I don't like the sound of this. Nor do I like you going all radioactive on Jeremy's brain. My son is not a lab rat," Alex exclaimed.

"Of course, Alex. I didn't mean to suggest anything inappropriate. I am suggesting we work as a team—the four of us. Perhaps there's something you all can do for me. David, let's say I could help you all professionally, not only to get to the bottom of Jeremy's gift, but also to help him develop a filter for it. Could you help me with your pastoral care skills?"

"Me? Counsel you, a psychiatrist? Sure, I'd like to avoid bankruptcy from your incurred charges. What did you have in mind? If it's you personally, I'd first suggest you talk with your rabbi. In my professional opinion."

Dr. R laughed. Watching the adults, Jeremy thought Dr. R looked a lot like the fattened Santa who laughs during the Rudolph cartoon, when Santa figures out Rudolph's red nose can guide his sleigh through the blizzard of the century. He also chuckled a lot just like Nanna. He took in a big breath and then out the laugh came, unbridled.

"No, I've tried the rabbi and I've had some concerns about chemical impairment. You know we professionals are ripe for addictions of all kinds. Med school and residency work involve shame based training, rife with hazing rituals. I suspect the ministerial course of study has its own hazing—whether Jewish or Christian. No, no, what I need is a kind minister to look in on my mother each week at Pinehurst Nursing Home. She's a holocaust survivor. Would you do that for me, David?"

"I could, but won't your Mom want a rabbi?"

"Yes, of course, but she has the beginning stages of senility—we are now calling it dementia. Sometimes she recognizes me, sometimes not. Anyway it's handy that your name is David—like the King. Just tell her you are a friend of mine and you heard about what a great mother she is and was in raising me. Befriend her. She's asked me more than once why only her roommate gets wine and bread from her chaplain. Bring her wine and bread, can you do that?

"Certainly. Even though I'm not Methodist, I can take a page out of John Wesley's book and give her a love feast. That's what the Methodists used to do when they didn't have an ordained elder handy. Since I won't have a rabbi with me, I'll get her the spiritual sustenance she has been asking for. Good old Mr. Wesley, a physician and minister to boot, used to recommend the love feast for his first support groups at their camp meetings. They could get a quasi-communion without running afoul of the ordination rules. So, yes, I can help you and your mother."

"Fine, fine. My next appointment is waiting outside; I see my line blinking. Please get my mother's contact info from my secretary Velma, and let's see you all for a two hour session early next week. Will that suit? See, there is an alternative economy. Completely untaxed. Fair trade. I scratch your backs and you scratch mine and my mother's. I love it. Jeremy, I know we've been ignoring you for a few minutes of adult talk, but I think we are all about to help you unwrap that 'feeling heads' gift of yours. And it is a gift, perhaps from God. Bye now."

CHAPTER 2

Friday May 31, 1968
Off for home at 123 Pearl Hill Road

As the family paraded to the door, Velma gave them their next appointment and the info for Dr. R's mother. She said, "I'm glad we could squeeze you in on such short notice. We don't get many last-minute cancellations like that."

Obsessively curious, Velma wondered why David needed Dr. Rebovitz's mother's contact information. She dared not ask and figured later she'd ask her boss.

The Hergenroeders hopped into their Bahama blue VW Beetle and headed back to their Pearl Hill Road parsonage. It was an aptly named street with a lumber company three miles past their house near the summit. Jeremy loved to ogle the big lumber trucks as they struggled to carry their massive logs up that hill every day. The street flared right off Route 2 and coursed across a bridge over a small waterfall that flowed from Putts Pond. A pristine river fed the pond and had an ample stock of rainbow trout and bass. Lots of kids and adults loved to fish that river. Just another reason why the Hergenroeders adored Fitchburg. After their move from Peabody, the Hergenroeders discovered that Fitchburg had the highest concentration of Finnish immigrants and their descendants in the U.S. Fitchburg's bragging rights included lots of paper mills and chair manufacturers, which made it the chair capital of America. The city proved convenient to Boston, thanks to a mere 90-minute drive. So many hills everywhere that the locals dubbed the city the second hilliest in the country. Pittsburgh was first, or so they said.

As they pulled into the driveway, David's thoughts turned to his Friday sermon preparation. *I need to get to work!* Gone were the divinity-school days when sermon writing seemed so exciting.

Alex overheard him. "Something wrong, honey?"

As they sat in the car, David responded, "Yeah. I can't reconcile how I'm going to preach a Gospel of peace. This week's lectionary aims squarely at the Vietnam War. The passages call the anti-war movement just. The New Testament *command*s all the protests we see on the nightly news. The young people are spot on as they march in so many cities across the U.S. So how do I relay *that* Word of God to my flock when there are so many high-profile military families in the congregation? You know their church attendance is as regular as Old Faithful in Yellowstone. They'd storm out if I bad-mouthed the War."

"I don't know, David," Alex whispered.

"I've done more historical research on the War. President Johnson's former arguments for continuing the War, hell, even escalating the War, really were moving us in the wrong direction. So many folks still hold to that philosophy. Those arguments go against all of Christ's teachings. How do I reconcile the two? Lots of martyred prophets made the same choice. Even contemporary ones who are still alive like Robert Kennedy. Imagine him as President—if he could just win the upcoming California primary!"

"Dad, who's Robert Kennedy?" asked Jeremy.

Jeremy caught his father by surprise. "Why, son, his brother John was President until some nut job killed him with a rifle shot from a book storage building in Dallas. Robert was President Kennedy's Attorney General—the top cop in the whole wide US of A."

"OK," said Jeremy. "Then what's a primary?"

"It's the process we use to start electing our nation's President. Every state has a say-so in an election. There are two steps. First, each party, the Democrats and the Republicans, figures out who their man will be to run for President. That guy is their candidate. They hold contests in every state called primaries. You have to get lots of voters to back your man—in all 50 states. They have 50 mini elections. Then, whichever guys win the Democrat and Republican primaries, they have a second race to see who should be President. You don't really 'run' like you and I do around the yard or when a mean ole dog chases us, but you make phone calls and send letters to voters asking them to vote for you on election day. Why do you ask, Jeremy?"

"I don't know, but I felt someone's head in that state you were talking about for Mr. Kennedy."

"You mean California? What about it?"

"I think there's a guy out there who doesn't like Mr. Kennedy."

David laughed for a half minute. "I love your insights Jeremy. I never know what's going to come out of your mouth next! Lots of folks hate the Kennedys!"

Alex interceded thanks to her mother's intuition, "Honey, why do you care about California or some guy who doesn't like Mr. Kennedy?"

"Mom, it's just a question."

"I know, baby, but I want us to pay careful attention any time you mention feeling someone else's head. You heard what Dr. Rebovitz said. You have to learn, no, *we* have to learn, how to help you filter your thoughts and these *head feelings,* OK?"

"Sure, Mom. Will I learn to filter next week with Dr. R? Just like Superman did? How about Mighty Mouse? Does he filter?"

"Oh Jeremy, you always ask great questions. Let's not worry any more about it. As your Nanna likes to say, there's just no sense in frettin' about things you can't control."

"All right, Mom."

The Hergenroeders hopped out of the car. Jeremy tried to go first, but the two-door Beetle wouldn't accommodate his effort. His buddy Jimmy Kendall wouldn't be home from the accelerated kindergarten class until 2:15 p.m. That was play time—especially when he could talk his Mom out of the day's forced nap. Napping seemed such a waste of time, especially when all the other kids played kickball or the game Red Light/Green Light, while he was locked tight under his covers.

Jimmy lived right next door in a big purple house with lots of nooks and crannies for playing hide and seek, not to mention a screened in, wrap-around porch. His parents had wealth, inherited, don't you know, but their blue-blooded upbringing had taught them how to keep that wealth and not squander it on frivolities. They didn't hold back, though, when it came to fostering Jimmy's development. That meant they got him out on the ski slopes at the age of two. They even bought him the nicest junior pair of Head skis available and of course Look bindings and Scott poles. Middle and Western Massachusetts had so many great little ski areas around that every weekend the family ventured to the slopes. Jimmy learned to run at the same time he learned how to slalom and hit the moguls. He loved adventure and took to Jeremy as soon as they met, right after the Hergenroeders moved in. Jimmy sensed something special in Jeremy, but he couldn't put his finger on what it was. Jeremy just seemed nice, and he seemed to listen so well that Jimmy hardly had to say a word or make a playtime suggestion before Jeremy was saying "Let's go and do that—great idea, Jimmy."

As Alex busied herself in the kitchen whipping up egg salad, she realized she was going to have to go against her family pedigree and start trusting people like Dr. R. Her parents had few friends and felt like the bottom could drop out of their lives at any moment, just like grandpa's heart attack had changed everything a generation before. It had taken her quite some time to trust David when he first started courting her. She figured he was like all the other young men she encountered, all charm and bull, hoping to bed her as their next conquest. David never made a move on her and she was the one that blurted out she loved him at the end of one of their dates. David was speechless at first and then uttered those same magical words, *I love you too.* At that moment, Alex felt like she could trust David—he'd earned it.

Back in his study, David wondered how he could "feel the heads" of his flock? How silly would it be to ask Jeremy what to say to his parishioners? It wasn't an issue of avoiding vulnerability in front of Jeremy—he liked to teach by example and Jeremy had seen him plenty of times discussing his fears about the pastorate with Alex. Those military families were both humble and proud of the sacrifices their sons were making and had made. Just trying to take out Ho Chi Minh.

The Interpreters Bible series often offered David some solace and he hoped that maybe he could find a notation with sound advice. Alone in his thoughts amidst many of his divinity school books including several that friends and family had gifted him over the years, he started to drift off when Alex's "C'mon boys, lunch is served" rang down the hallway. David almost fell out of his lawyer's style high-back chair. Thankfully the solid oak underpinnings and the spring-loaded back support caught his fall. He loved to lean back in the chair and contemplate the cosmos. David had long ago mastered the tipping point where he pinioned his body just right so he felt like he was levitating. Pure pleasure. *No such cantilever in the pulpit,* David thought to himself. *Can't have the Reverend relaxing prior to the show.*

As the family lunched on egg salad and Campbell's tomato bisque soup, the clock struck 1:30 p.m. Ever the news junkie, Alex tuned in the radio. A reporter came on announcing, "Today Robert Kennedy, former U.S. Attorney General of the United States, landed with his campaign staff in California to a cheering crowd that greeted him on the tarmac. The Kennedy campaign finds itself in a pitched battle against Vice President Hubert Humphrey and Minnesota Senator Eugene McCarthy. In typical fashion, Kennedy proclaimed his optimism for American's future—free of war and filled with prosperity for all." The reporter finished off the segment with a few more sound bites.

Jeremy asked, "That's who we're voting for right Mom?" As he posed the question, he pictured himself alternately standing in the voting booth, driving a car, giving blood, and heading off to college. Everything that he couldn't do now because he was just too dang young.

"Yes, Jeremy, that's who. He's a good man and helped get the Civil Rights movement on the right track—to give everyone the same rights no matter their skin color." Alex cherished the franchise right, having studied the suffragette movement in high school. Nothing said liberation as much as the right to vote. She often shuddered at how her forebears viewed women as a form of chattel, or at least unable to own property. Talk about helpless! It's the one thing she never wanted to be. She made that clear to David during their courtship. Yes, he was saving her from continued heartache at the hands of her abusive mother, but she was going to be independent and saved every penny she scraped together so their family would never be beholden to anyone.

"I'm worried about Mr. Kennedy, Mom."

"We are too, Honey. He's got a lot of campaigning ahead of him, lots of travel, and lots of speeches. It's hard work. Plus everyone's worried that someone might try to assassinate him like they did his brother, John."

"What's 'assinate' Mom?"

"I'm sorry. It means to be killed. Shot."

"Then, that's what I mean, Mom. There's some guy out there. I can feel his head and I'm scared."

Stupefied, Alex retorted, "Jeremy, enough now. You can't feel people's heads across 3,000 miles. That doesn't make any sense." As if the 'gift' had some sort of logic from even three feet away.

Just then the doorbell rang. David got up and answered the door. In walked Jimmy Kendall. "They let us out early so the teachers could plan," Jimmy said with a smirk. He caught a glimpse of Rev. Hergenroeder's left arm. He just couldn't imagine not having two hands that worked. *How did the guy get along, let alone tie his shoes? Jimmy thought. But at least I never heard him complain.*

"You've got to be kidding me—a half day already," laughed Alex. "On your second day of school? Boy this *is* an experimental classroom experience."

"C'mon Jeremy let's go play, or do you have to help with the dishes?"

"Nope, I've got the dishes. You all go play—no nap today, Jeremy," Alex offered.

As the boys ran outside, Jimmy said, "Look what I have—it's brand new!" Jimmy held up a blue rectangular object with a mirror on one end and a spy hole on the other. "It's military! They call it a Long Tom Combat Scope! You can see your enemy around corners and they don't even know you're looking! Jeremy, go stand on the side of the house where I can't see you and hold up your fingers. Just not all of them and I'll tell you how many you're holding up—when I look through the scope!"

Jeremy watched as Jimmy expanded the scope to its full length. "Ready, Jeremy!"

Jeremy ran to the side of the house and held up a clenched fist. Jimmy hollered, "Hey, no fair. You ain't holding up any fingers!"

"That means you got it right. I tried to trick you. Let me give it a try."

The boys traded off using the scope, and then later ran down Pearl Hill to look through the neighbors' windows. Some mothers were hanging out laundry (boring), others were sweeping up their homes (even more boring), while others were in their kitchens reading magazines (gimme a break!). Alex let Jeremy skip his nap since he'd been so cooperative with Dr. Rebovitz. Plus, thank goodness, he wasn't mentally ill.

The way-cool combat scope tapped right into Jeremy's love of games. All kinds. His favorites? Red Light/Green Light, and kickball. Jimmy's sister Lori, who was four years older, often led the games for the neighborhood kids. Jeremy had a hopeless crush on Lori and thought about her at odd hours. Her deep-brown eyes bewitched him as did her pearly smile. She often let Jeremy win at Red Light, Green Light, especially when older boys twice his size played. The object of the game was to run as fast as you could up the sidewalk after Lori yelled 'green light.' and before she hollered 'red light' and turned around after counting to five. Anyone still moving got sent back to the starting line. The first one to tag Lori won. Lori always heaped praise on the winner, which made victory for Jeremy all the sweeter.

Lori had taken the time to show Jeremy how to tie his shoes, a real feat for a three-year-old. Trouble was he just stared at her in abject wonder and later had to sneak peeks at his parents tying theirs before he really got the hang of it. Lori had said something about bringing the "bunny ear" loops together, but he couldn't quite get the hang of it the first try because his heart pounded so hard in his chest, the force of his young crush getting the best of him. He hoped against hope that she liked him too, but no matter, his heart also aimed its cupid arrow at Helen Clause, who sat beside him in nursery school *and* Sunday school class. Helen had blonde hair and a smattering of freckles on her nose that pointed the way to deep-blue eyes. She was quiet and liked hanging around Jeremy, just for the fun of it and could sense in him goodness, tenderness and mercy. Jeremy thought Helen smelled good, almost like one of his Dad's shirts his Mom had ironed with all that extra starch, all ready for a good sermon. Jeremy couldn't fathom why his older peers hated girls. *What's to hate? Girls were just the best.*

Back in the kitchen, Alex mechanically did the dishes. She thought to herself about a story a TV reporter offered following his interview with a mother participating in a new pregnancy support group. "Yes, when we all joined, we couldn't contain our excitement. A first birth for each of us. We shared wisdom and stories from our own mothers and how to plan for our as yet unborn children's lives," the mother had said. "We even discussed paint choices for the baby's rooms, what the best bassinet brand was to buy. Everyone's future all bright, shiny and gold-plated. Like those sugar-plum visions from the poem, *Twas The Night*

Before Christmas. We were all headed to Hawaii or Tahiti—somewhere idyllic. Then, as I birthed my baby, I saw the shocked look on the doctor's face. The little tyke had cerebral palsy. All my friends disappeared, headed for Hawaii and I got stuck in Bakersfield or worse, Truth or Consequences, New Mexico. No one knew what to say to me. I rarely saw any of those friends ever again."

Alex realized that none of those so-called friends had David's pastoral care training. Had they gone to divinity school or maybe lived in the 1800s, where community was more interconnected, interdependent even, they would have known it was enough just to be present. *Silence speaks volumes,* Alex thought. *Even a simple hug would have made all the difference instead of abject abandonment. I'll never let that happen to Jeremy or our family. Sort of like when my friends abandoned me just because I was dating a ministry student. I still can't believe they shunned me—as if David was a cult leader aiming to woo them into a religious trance, forever his slave.*

David glanced out the study window and saw Jeremy and Jimmy playing with the scope. "Alex, come watch these two. They're hilarious!"

Alex came running and, for just a moment, enjoyed the boys' frivolity. Their spy game took her mind off the coming storm clouds of doubt she clung to about her family's safety. And those doubts, like her mother's intuition, were well founded.

CHAPTER 3

Friday May 31, 1968—Afternoon
Dictating the Chart

*T*his may be the most unusual chart I've ever dictated!
Dr. R thought to himself. *And that's saying a lot after
all my Korean War vets and that trauma work.*

Azriel leaned back in his chair to contemplate precisely
what to say. He said aloud, "Maybe I don't need a chart.
The last thing this kid needs is a psychiatric record on file. I
wonder if Jeremy's 'feeling my head' as I ponder this
question. Let's just grab the old oracle here," he said aloud
as he palmed the small granite sign that sat on the front of
his desk. It read, *Just remember Doc, most patients get
better without your help!*

Azriel Rebovitz, MD, long ago had discarded his
"MDeity" ego. Doing so took real effort and discipline. He
mused to himself. *Med school really did it to me. All that
hazing, and for what? My medical education could have
been so much smoother without the professors foisting on
us a myth of invulnerability! It set me up for failure—
especially when I couldn't fathom shedding tears when I
heard my Korean vet patients tell me of their battlefield
horrors. Their traumas became my traumas; their shell*

shock infused my psyche. So much for professional detachment!

He'd finally found a non-MD therapist who helped him work through the pain with a final recommendation that he give up his vets' practice altogether.

One day, four years earlier, Azriel woke up with the rising sun and decided right then and there to focus his practice on children. Ever since, he'd travelled the wards of Boston Children's Hospital and "juvie" halls, helping younger trauma victims. His practice found him commuting from Fitchburg to Boston and the surrounding bedroom communities. He had gained a reputation for unlocking trauma. He used a form of hypnosis that would later be termed "EMDR," short for eye movement desensitization and reprocessing. By semi-hypnotizing Korean War vets, Dr. R had gotten them to move their eyes side to side or tap their hands on their laps in alternating staccato and, boom, he could get them to engage both brain hemispheres. In this way, he'd take them back to the original traumatizing events that had paralyzed them in the first place. Dr. R helped his patients unlock their demons. "Dang Doc, I feel liberated finally," more than one veteran had told him at discharge.

One vet named Peter started off his first session right in the heat of battle. "Man, I'm the one that called in the napalm drop, Doc. Next thing I know the Chair Force guys missed the target and nailed a bunch of women and children. Their bodies all smoldering and unrecognizable. Hell, they bombed a school! Their relatives clawed and screamed at me!" Another vet, a platoon leader named Job, had a theory. "We got it in training. You know, we had to learn to think of the enemy as non-human. Me and my guys utterly objectified them because you can't kill as easily if you think they're someone's mother, father, aunt or uncle. Oh yeah, drill sergeant taught us to call them gooks. Made killing easier, or so we thought." And yet another vet poured out his soul for having fallen asleep on watch. "Yessirree, there I was Doc at oh-four hundred (that's in the a.m., Doc) snoozing to the sound of those Korean crickets. Thank God my buddy heard the enemy patrol snap a twig. Got me and the other guys up pronto. Saved all of us. Worse thing, Doc, he never said a word about me sleeping! That killed me!"

As he took notes while that vet relayed his war tales on the therapy couch, Azriel flashed back to Germany. A different war, a different kind of attrition. The German soldiers and city officials insisted they wear special patches signifying their Jewish faith. Not Aryan by a long shot. Scapegoats through and through. Hard to hide with that declaration affixed to his tunic. Somehow his father had made arrangements with a neighbor family to hide them. They lasted in that claustrophobic attic for a couple of years, completely useless to anyone or the society to which they used to belong. Someone somewhere ratted them out and the SS showed up at 2:00 a.m. one morning near the end of the war to haul them off to the train to Dachau.

"Enough dwelling in the past! Gotta finish this dictation," Azriel exclaimed to himself as he stood his six-foot-five-inch frame all the way up for a good stretch. Sitting back down, he began to speak into his Dictaphone:

"Patient Jeremy Nathan Hergenroeder, five-year-old male seen for initial visit. Patient's primary care physician is Hercules Copoulos, MD. Visit attended by patient and parents; history obtained from both. Parents report patient has been accepted into an accelerated kindergarten class, apparently experimental. Tested out at the fourth grade reading level. Parents concerned about early onset schizophrenia. No suicide or other psychiatric disorders in immediate family members.

"On initial intake call, Father posited patient experiencing hallucinations. Following intake and thorough interview, patient appears quite articulate. Patient does not appear distracted. Parents and patient deny depression or sleep problems. No signs of sadness or irritability. Appetite appears to be excellent. Patient doing well until 5/30/68 when, during first day of accelerated kindergarten class, he had an episode of crying and appeared to his teacher and his father to be nearly inconsolable. Some concern, however, about patient hearing voices.

Following general workup, patient appears to have substantial capacity to read minds of other individuals, including this clinician. Parents believed patient to be delusional. Further inquiry revealed the patient has substantial capacity to recite, word for word, conversations from several days ago. Patient likely has eidetic memory. Following general examination, parents invited into session and advised of mind reading gift. Offered to enroll patient in experimental PET scan program, but mother adamantly refused.

Warned family that further therapy of some sort advisable to provide patient with a filter since his articulations cause concern in others around him. Must maintain absolute confidentiality on this case—gift could be abused in the wrong hands. Will set weekly appointments to aid patient in establishing filter. No charges—case to be handled pro bono.

Azriel put the finishing touches on the dictation including the idea of the Mass General brain scan. As he hung up the recorder in its cradle, he recalled trying to calm down Rev. Hergenroeder when he called for his son's appointment. The Reverend seemed panic stricken. "Sir, we just have to get in to see you. It's an emergency." David had pleaded. "Please understand. We fear Jeremy has developed schizophrenia. He's certainly delusional sometimes. Scares the bejesus out of us *and* my parishioners. Even today Jeremy started hearing voices from the minute we walked into his kindergarten classroom. He started crying and held his ears with both hands, as if trying to shut out all the sound. I ended up taking him home."

"Let's slow down a minute, Rev. Hergenroeder. First things first. Yes, I can get you in tomorrow. I had a last minute cancellation. And no, Reverend, it's probably not schizophrenia. In fact, I've never heard of a single case of that organic brain disease in anyone so young. It manifests in the late teens for most victims. So let's leave the diagnosing to me and I'll leave the parenting to you. Make sense?"

"I guess so," said David, not completely ungrateful.

"Good. Then we'll see you tomorrow at 10:00 a.m."

As Azriel left his office, he dropped off the file folder on Velma's desk with a note stating the dictation was ready. Finally he felt the solace of the weekend upon him— time to play in his flower beds, mow his lawn using his handy dandy Craftsman tractor and dare Philada to chase him. His house sat high up on a ridge overlooking the city below. Perfect for keeping a watchful eye out for any German Panzer divisions coming his way.

you'll spend these two bits either!" Every quarter helped Jeremy get another Matchbox car added to his collection. He'd just started dabbling in the world of Hot Wheels, which came with a special slide track, and a housing motor that fit neatly over the track. Its foam wheels captured the cars and shot them out the other end making sure the cars could make it around the oval. The darned Matchboxes couldn't even roll one quarter of the way around the track. Worse, they only got down the slide part way, which meant the Hot Wheels would kick their butts off the track like the little leaguers they were.

Jeremy, of course, couldn't afford all the Hot Wheels' accessories, but his friend Jimmy could. Jimmy's dad worked at one of the paper mills along the shores of the Nashua River that ran through town. Jeremy remembered driving with his father to an adjoining hamlet called Cleghorn, passing the Digital Equipment Corporation and seeing the river full of green or pink dye, the color that the mills spewed that day. "Dad, how can fish live in that river?" Ever the budding scientist, Jeremy figured that Jacques Cousteau could fix the problem.

Jeremy invested a lot of his time in scientific exploration, usually via his imagination. He devoured books the way big African crocodiles devour wildebeests. He often accompanied David to the library and headed straight for the science fiction shelves, sometimes with the books a bit too high for his reach. Marian Koshgarian, the head children's librarian, often helped him get the titles he wanted. She'd give him a boost up on a special stool on wheels that would "plant" itself the minute Jeremy climbed aboard. She often held back newer editions from the crowds just so she could ensure Jeremy got a first read. Marian marveled at how well Jeremy could read and thought him a sure-fire prodigy. She told no one about his exploits because she figured he was having a hard enough time avoiding the lime light as the son of a local minister from one of the biggest churches in town. She had hand sewn a special book bag for Jeremy with his name on it. The cotton proved quite sturdy and Jeremy could cram three books at a time into his new bag. David encouraged Jeremy by paying him 25 cents for every book he read as long as he wrote a one page report. Alex had taught him his ABCs, all the colors of the rainbow, and how to count to 100 by the time he reached the age of two. He started cursive writing when he was three years old. His effusive love of books really took off on his fourth birthday when he unwrapped a special science book David had stumbled on called, *Tell Me Why*. The book explained almost every question Jeremy had about the earth, space and animal life. His next favorite book was a big Time Life edition that outlined earth's history starting with the primordial soup and ending with the fall of the dinosaurs. He loved the triceratops with its three horns, and thought that beast must have been the grandfather of today's rhinoceros.

Volcanoes also captivated Jeremy's budding imagination. He read a short story about a Mexican farmer who went out to his fields one day to find a small mound that he thought was another ant hill. But instead of ants scurrying about, out spouted a bit of molten lava. Within hours the ant hill had become quite large and the earth shook around the farm. The farmer and his family ran for their lives to avoid getting burned alive. They carried all their possessions on a small cart that their donkey pulled. Jeremy felt sure the tragedy could have been avoided had the farmer merely covered up the hill with dirt from the field. He figured the dirt would have cooled down the lava and perhaps encouraged it to "move on."

One night at the dinner table, a huge crack of thunder shook the Hergenroeder's home. It scared Jeremy out of his wits, not because of the danger it represented but because of how loud it was. Jeremy had hyper-sensitive hearing and loud noises hurt his ears. David explained that thunder came from clouds banging into each other. Jeremy thought that was silly, especially since he often lay in the grass on summer days admiring the big cumulonimbus clouds bumping into each other. The collisions never made a sound. After dinner he ran to his *Tell Me Why* book and learned that lightning causes thunder. You could count the seconds between seeing lighting and hearing the thunder and know how far off it was. Jeremy didn't tell his Dad, though.

Just then Jeremy felt the head of Mr. Edward McPherson. He drank in the utter grief the man clung to over the tragic death of Truman. "Even he's wondering about the War!" Jeremy spouted.

"What's that son? Who is questioning the War?" David asked.

"Mr. McPherson. I can feel his head. He had been so proud when Truman joined the Army."

David realized that when Jeremy used his gift he might be invading people's privacy. Ignoring the thought, he said, "Yes, I know Col. McPherson is proud of his son. He couldn't wait to follow in his father's footsteps.

Enlisted on his 18th birthday. Just like his father had a generation earlier. But Truman was on point one day leading his platoon on a patrol through the Me Kong Delta. Then, out of nowhere, some 12-year-old sniper shot him. We held a closed-casket funeral. Had to," David offered, shaking his head.

Jeremy looked up and said, "Dad, just tell them *we* all love them. Just like Jesus. Remember they're doing the best they can. They need to know we're thankful."

David and Alex both nodded. David's eyes filled with tears as he responded, "Of course, Jeremy. Tibetan monks spend much of their lives contemplating gratitude. That's a great offering. I'll invite the congregation to meditate on gratitude. Thank you for your advice, young man. I think you've given me what I need to craft a decent sermon. Let's let Sunday take care of itself."

CHAPTER 5

Saturday June 1, 1968—Morning
Transcribing Trouble

"**I**'ve gotta get to the office today," Velma Brodie said to no one, as she woke up to an empty bed. "I'll kill two birds with one stone—get Dr. Rebovitz's dictation done and pull some overtime."

As she drove across town in her Dodge Coronet Lancer, she admired its glorious tail fins. *This car cuts through the air like a shark through water!* Her thoughts turned to the odd boy who turned up yesterday. *What about that Hergenroeder family? So sad to have a five year old with psychiatric problems. That's way too early! Hergenroeder. What the heck kinda name is that anyway? Gotta be German. Wonder if they have any Nazi relatives hidden in their closet? If they did, why come to a Jewish psychiatrist? Boy, that would be one helluva legacy for any five year old to carry around: 'I'm sorry, son, your granddad served as a guard at Auschwitz. Your great uncle captained a U-Boat.' What would Jeremy say to his friends on the school yard? 'Oh yeah, never met my grandfather, but I heard he was a nice guy.' Kids could be so cruel to each other.* Velma shuddered at the thought.

As she parked her car she thought to herself, *Thank God for work. Gives me respite from Dan. I know he's a gambling addict, but does he carouse around behind my back, too? How could things have gone so wrong? How do you go from high school sweetheart to wage slave and mother of none? Those baby blues caught me so off guard. Then, the junior prom and me a senior hoping for a college run. I coulda been a nurse for cryin' out loud instead of....*

****

Like lots of North Shore high schools, Peabody High where Velma and Dan attended, held their prom event in Saugus at the Italian American Club, right off Route 1. "That old highway runs the entire east coast," Velma reflected. "From Fort Kent, Maine near the Canadian border all the way to Florida. I should have bolted after graduation to Florida State like I dreamed and gone to nursing school. But, no, I took the road more traveled. Dan's football prowess and dancing skills ain't done me a bit a good since. He'd never a followed me to Florida State. Too late now. All those shop classes molded him in the image of his dad, Butch. Straight to the shipyard, matey!" Velma chuckled, as she envisioned Butch, all full of military tattoos, including the name "Jill" on his upper bicep. "Couldn't remember her," he'd say, "must have been a whirlwind romance in some Filipino dive. Always looked forward to them ports a call during the Big War," he'd muse. Now, Butch and Dan welded the big ships at General Dynamics in the Quincy shipyards. Dan promised himself only idiots signed up to volunteer for the Vietnam War. In his heart of hearts, though, he knew he'd been damned lucky to get that high draft number. It was the one lottery he actually won, without even having to fork over any hard earned cash.

Shortly after Velma graduated from Peabody High, Dan quit school and they got married. Velma's parents Joy and Leonard Koskinen didn't object. Dan's lock on the General Dynamics' welding job gave the Koskinens great comfort in the knowledge that their daughter would live like they did in middle class comfort, all thanks to Butch's union connections. Great bucks for steady work. Shippers the world over knew the big boats' payload capacity beat the higher costs of moving their freight by rail or semi-trailers. Pennies per load instead of greenbacks. Plus, the Vietnam War meant constant construction work, not to mention the Cold War submarine contracts. Most subs came out of Groton, Connecticut, right on the coast. General Dynamics had lots of feeder contracts and sub work right there in the Bay State. Dan should have been set for life.

As Velma sat at her desk she wondered how Dan had caught the gambling bug. *I can't remember the last time he actually won. That moron cashes his damn paycheck at those gambling dives! No wonder we never have enough cash on hand to pay the mortgage. 'Sure, step right up Danny boy, just put down your John Hancock right here on the signature line. Don't forget, we run a lottery every weekend on the check numbers. Your number might hit tonight!' Come to think of it, Dan's never mentioned if any* *of his compadres ever scored on that $10,000 lottery...bet it's rigged.* Bile rose in Velma's throat.

Velma started to realize that the little lottery tease just juiced up Dan for his game. Craps. His specialty. "No, that loser is the game's specialty. The harder I work the more he gambles!" Velma shouted to the empty office. "Maybe it's time I started my own slush fund. Thank the Lordy Dr. Rebovitz is so generous with overtime. I could squirrel away the $15 an hour I make for O.T. on Saturdays. Someday I might just bolt town and get that nursing degree!"

Dr. Rebovitz had the latest Dictaphone technology, making typing a snap. On a good day, Velma could type 100 words a minute with hardly any mistakes. Usually. She popped the machine into the go position and listened to Jeremy's story, utterly transfixed at this young seer. "Just five years old!" Velma said out loud. And, Dr. Rebovitz sounding like Dr. Frankenstein—"We can't let anyone learn of Jeremy's gift. Gift indeed!" thought Velma. Just then her co-dependency kicked in. "I wonder if, nah, well maybe, could this little PK pull off a gambling trick or two? Maybe turn the house's odds in Dan's favor just once? We could pretend Jeremy was Dan's nephew or something," Velma schemed. "I'm away, tending my sick aunt in Freeport, Maine. Last minute thing. Called away—an emergency, don't you know. Dan gets stuck babysitting." She could hear the Pit Boss, Al Angelotti, right now with a chewed up stogie clenched in his brown teeth saying, "All right, kid, just this once. But if you start belly aching or whining, you and your uncle here can take the Red Line all the way to Mattapan Station. I'll even cover your fare, ha ha!"

As she proofed her transcription, Dr. Rebovitz's tone started to scare her. If word got out, the mob would love to get their hands on this kid. What a pay-day bonanza. *Step right up folks, get your front row seat, we got a PK here with the green eyes of God and the Devil. Pick a problem, any problem. Think your wife's cheatin' on you? Is that politician trying to squeeze you out of some graft? Did your bribe stick? Is the Mayor going to stay bought? Is your stoolie rattin' you out to the feds? We can test anyone's loyalty boys!*

Velma rarely listened to transcription content—just wanting to get through the trunk line recordings and get the filing done. She became a conduit from the Dictaphone to the chart. But Jeremy's story riveted her. *Who is this kid? An experimental brain scan? Hell, that's Mass General, and a trip to Beantown. Ye olde Fitchburg ain't got that technology. Suppose word got out—and it would with those radiation techs—right there in the lunch room. This kid would go to the highest bidder or some real muscle. This was way above Dan's station. He might could sell the information. But how? Once the word was out, they'd kill Dan the messenger. Yeah, he was a village tough, but they don't come at you so you see them. They out flank and blind side most victims! Boston Harbor is filled with visionaries who forgot to look in the rear view.*

As she kept editing, she started to hatch a plan. *All's I need is to, what's that fancy word, oh yeah, "ingratiate" myself with the young lad. I'll make him look forward to Dr. Rebovitz's counseling sessions. Jeremy calls my boss*

Dr. R, so I'll suggest he call me Mrs. V. Nice and pretty.
'Hershey bar for you today? No, how about a Tootsie Pop?
Bet you can't not bite it to get to the chocolate center!
Velma pondered the possibilities.

CHAPTER 6

Saturday June 1, 1968
Pinehurst Nursing Home—First Visit

David awoke from a catnap, appreciating Dr. Rebovitz's offer to trade pastoral visits to his mother for therapy for Jeremy. *This is like manna from heaven!* David thought. *With my salary and Alex a homemaker, every penny counts. Too bad most parishioners assume my colleagues and I work for Jesus Christ like those disciples did—no salary or benefits for them.*

This theme always percolated to the top of the agenda when the church voted on whether or not to give David a raise. Congregants voiced diatribes like, "I always was taught that the minister ought to think of the church finances first—ensure the flock gets fed before expecting the flock to cough up more salary dollars!" Or, "I didn't get a raise this year, why should our minister?" David's moderator, Kurt Crider, who headed up the church administrative board, always handled the objections with aplomb and disarming humor: "I got to say Reverend, some of these folks may have a point. I think you and your family ought to work eight days a week if we're going to raise your salary one percent, don't you? All right folks, it's just one percent. How many of you have called David in the middle of the night asking his counsel or prayers on all manner of things? How about if we cut back his hours to just 40, say, and have him work 8:00 to 5:00 Monday through Thursday, and then Sunday? No? I didn't think so. Would someone please call the question?" And so the mob would move on to another concern and David would get his subsistence raise. Enough to keep the VW Beetle in running condition.

On his way to Pinehurst Nursing Home, David reflected on the odd course of recent events and this barter deal he'd made with Dr. Rebovitz. Then it occurred to him. *How ironic that Dr. Rebovitz's mother's first name is Eva. Almost like the first woman in the world. Everyone blamed her for getting humanity kicked out of paradise. What a crock. Sure made Adam look the fool. Three-thousand years of scapegoating!*

As his VW chugged up the Pinehurst driveway, David thought about all the times he'd made pastoral visits here. He remembered his first visit to the locked unit where Rollstone had three parishioners. "Man, it was like the bum's rush as soon as I walked through the door," David chuckled to himself. "All points bulletin! Step right up, ladies. Handsome man in a suit!" No sooner had he made it to the nurse's station, when five elderly women crowded around him. "Hey, you're handsome!" the first yodeled. The second asked, "Are you married?" When David answered yes, she said, "That don't matter!"

David downshifted and looked at the lush spread of pine trees he was passing. His window down, David breathed in the holiday-like scent. Squirrels dashed hither and yon, gathering and burying nuts for the winter. "Hey squirrel!" David shouted to one. "You and your buddies are just like some of my parishioners with your memory issues. Now, just where *did* I bury that mother lode of acorns last year? Why am I doing this again?"

David reminisced about his first history survey course where the students read the Lewis and Clark expedition journal. As the explorers left on their rafts from Pennsylvania and entered the Ohio River, they feasted one night on scores of squirrels. Turns out that a herd of 10,000 of the varmints made the mistake of fording the river just as the explorers rafted by. Ten-thousand, not 50, not 60, or the 15 he could spot on the Pinehurst property today. Then he thought of the billions of now extinct passenger pigeons that could alternatively block out the sunlight or destroy a stand of trees with their droppings as they roosted for the night. As David's grandmother, Mattie, remarked one time as they drove through a high-end neighborhood in Cambridge where some rich family's septic system had failed, "Well, everyone's gotta shit!" The family had to stop the car since his father Phillip couldn't see the road through the tears of laughter. Yessirree. Ten million birds could paint any town white; so don't look up!

Before the advent of streptomycin, the Pinehurst facility served as a tuberculosis hospital. New owners swooped into town and bought the facility from the county. They infused buckets of cash to refurbish all the rooms and common areas. They even broke up the long hospital-style hallways and took out the central nurses' stations, where the nurses used to congregate to visit, instead of attending their patients. Wisely, they placed the stations off to the side in favor of wide living rooms for residents. The patients then could gather to visit, play games, nap and socialize. Every resident now had a private room that had a nice front-door entrance, just like home.

David tromped in through the big columned entrance and greeted Amy Quinn, the diminutive 29-year-old receptionist, sitting at the front desk. "I need to visit Eva Rebovitz today."

"Good afternoon Rev. Hergenroeder," Amy smiled. "Yes, Mrs. Eva is in Room 109."

David thanked Amy and ambled down the hall to 109. He rang the doorbell and heard a faint "Come in." As he opened the door, he saw Eva sitting in an easy chair with an IV in her arm. Saline—David read the label. He had great eyesight, 20:10 in both eyes. David figured the drip meant that Eva likely was a bit dehydrated which, if left untreated, could lead to kidney problems and "UTIs," urinary tract infections. David remembered his pastoral care professor warning the class that UTIs also affected brain function—making nursing home residents like Eva seem psychotic at times. "Kidneys," Professor Walter Liston said, "are ideal filters, but they need water to push the poisons and detritus out of the bloodstream!"

"Hello, Mrs. Rebovitz, I'm David Hergenroeder," David greeted Eva with a smile.

"Nice to meet you, Mr. Hergenroeder. That's German isn't it? H-e-r-g-e-n-r-**Ö**-d-e-r. I bet you dropped the umlaut on the O didn't you!" Eva suggested with a sly smile.

"Yes, my father did that since it was a pain to print. He added in the E for integrity purposes, I guess.

"I'm making my pastoral care rounds today and thought I'd stop in to meet you. Say hello, visit if you've got time."

As Eva raised her free hand to shake David's, her sleeve fell back and David saw a Nazi tattoo designating her as a former resident of another facility altogether. "I'm a local minister and I like to bring to my friends here at Pinehurst a love meal. Slices of bread and grape juice. Are you by any chance hungry today, Mrs. Rebovitz?"

"Not really no, Reverend. But I am not impolite. Please serve us both. You know I'm Jewish and we Jews don't really take communion."

"Yes, Ma'am, I do know. I'm not here to convert you," David said sheepishly. He felt comfortable with the mild humor because Mrs. Eva had a smile and kind eyes behind her statement.

As he served the bread and the cup, Eva said, "I saw you noticed my tattoo from Dachau. I entered the camp as a 38 year old right before the Allied Liberation. I saw enough, of course, to begin to appreciate the horror, but I was not there long enough for them to gas me. Right there on the entrance gate the Nazi's had posted their slogan *Arbeit macht frei*. Do you know what that phrase means?"

"No, Mrs. Rebovitz, I'm ashamed to say I do not."

"Oh, please call me Eva. No need to feel shame. It means 'Work will make you free.' We all knew better, of course. What I do remember most was the looks on the guards' faces as the English and U.S. soldiers hauled them off to their own prison camps, their worlds turned upside down. Never will forget that. You have any Nazis in your lineage, David?"

Before David answered, he realized Mrs. Eva was far smarter and on point than most rest home residents. Her room appeared clean as a whistle with family pictures set out for all to see, black and white, color, even a few fading Polaroids. "No, no Nazis that I'm aware of."

"I see your admiring my photo legacy. My late husband made a living as a photographer here in town. You know, after the War. That meant *I* had to take all the family photos!" Eva said, giggling. "He was too, I don't know, unwilling—since that was his vocation, but not his avocation. So, do you know my son? He's a psychiatrist. He says I have 'lucid intervals' and he's quite concerned, always hounding the staff when he visits. Likes to rifle through my chart, double check my meds, and Lord knows what else. What's a mother to do?"

"I do know your son, Ma'am. He's got a fine reputation in town. I actually took my son, Jeremy, to see him yesterday. He's got some developmental issues, or so I had thought."

"Well, does he or doesn't he?"

Eva's answer/question shocked David. He realized he had underestimated her again. She was astute. "You have an incisive mind, Ma'am. No, no issues. Your son gave him a clean bill of mental health. I figured a psychiatrist would take weeks of therapy before making such a firm decision."

"I didn't raise no bull shitter, David. He'll get right to the nub of the matter. 'Say it, don't spray it,' my classmates and I used to say on the school yard."

Eva's doorbell rang just as David finished a belly laugh. Eva bade the caller to enter. Her nurse's aide, Andrea Faust, came in and announced that it was time for Eva's bath. Eva turned to David and said, "As beautiful as this place looks by our bucolic driveway, they do have rules and a schedule to which I must adapt. Or is it adhere? It was a pleasure meeting you and you can tell my son you stopped by. Please don't visit again out of obligation. But I'd love to meet Jeremy the next time you bring by a Methodist love feast. Yes, I know what it's called. That's such a nice name for it, too. And I don't even need the food, just the grace of good company, especially with my suite mate Marie out for two weeks visiting her family in New Hampshire."

As David departed and drove past the scavenging squirrels, he wondered about Eva. *What was she like when she was not lucid? What brain processes affected lucidity? Surely the moon's phases had an effect? Even our cells have a tide, thanks to the moon, he thought.*

CHAPTER 7

Sunday June 2, 1968
Rollstone Congregational Church—Sunday Service

T he never-shy Rollstone Congregation gave organist, Bill Fontaine, whom they had recruited, err, stolen for more money from a bigger church in Poughkeepsie, NY, a standing ovation. Bill really could pull out all of the stops—make everyone sizzle down through their bones. Hand of God, they said.

David jumped to the pulpit, nodding his head, "Whew! I'm usually as humble as the next guy, Bill, but wow. You should know it's every preacher's dream to get a standing O after a sermon. We are all thankful for your artistry. You are a blessing to us." David said as he glanced at the younger congregants half off of their pews, "Time for the children to head to Sunday school!"

The kids knew it was almost time and many sat on the edge of their pews just chompin' at the bit to get out of adult church. They took their cue and dashed for the exits. Only time their parents allowed them to run in church! As Nick Sulkinen, Clancy Marshall and Robert Peeler ran, they made sure to touch the metal heat shields above the banks of radiators. The shield delivered a walloping and, yes, visible electric shock. Their bodies electrified, the boys chased down some of the girls to deliver the jolt just by touch. A wonderful feature of Rollstone—it probably had something to do with a lack of grounding in the heating element. No matter.

Robert caught Clancy and Nick as they exited. "Hey, time to call the operator!" He pointed at the hall phone, laughing. Nick and Clancy nodded their assent. Robert picked up the receiver, dialed 888, and hung up. This novel feature delivered a message to Ma Bell to ring-test the hall phone. At least once every Sunday the ringing phone called forth the custodian, Roger Tomlinson, to come running, lest the service or prayers be disturbed.

Sitting in his office watching through the crack in his office door, Roger heard the phone ring as the boys tiptoed by. Dutifully, he came out of the office and answered the call. "Hello, Rollstone Church." Immediately he heard the dial tone, but was ready with a play of his own. He heard the muffled giggles of the boys down the hall. This time he used some of that fancy sy-call-o-gee, and said, "Why yes, Ma'am, I do believe the three boys you are looking for are right this very minute in their church-school classes. What's that? You need them or their parents? You want *both* them and their parents! Please, if you'll give me a minute I'll see about pulling them out of class and roust their parents from the sanctuary. I'll do it forthwith. No delay. Oh, yes, this does sound serious. And you say the police are involved? Oh my. Let me grab a pen. OK, Nick Sulkinen, Clancy Marshall, Robert Peeler. Yes, Nick and Clancy are 10 years old, and Robert is 11, I believe. Got it. Now, give me your number so their parents can call you right back."

Down the hall the giggling ceased. Nick, Clancy and, yes, their spiritual, wise-cracking leader, Robert, were peeing their pants. They ducked into the rest room to hide. Roger meanwhile ambled down the hall in the opposite direction with a new spring in his step. He'd dreamed up that little counter ploy when he heard David's wife, Alexandria, at a recent staff potluck supper at the parsonage offer the perfect solution to the phone pranks kids were playing on her.

"I never would have thought of it, but a Ma Bell staffer told me how to hoist those hooligans on their own petard," Alex said, beaming. "Get this. She says, 'Ma'am, the next time those boys call or are listening in on your party line, say the following, word for word, and you'll probably want to write this down and tape it next to the phone: Hello? Hello, Operator? Yes, I've got these prank callers on the line right now. Yes, what? Oh yes, please trace their number. Oh, bless you. Thank you so much!' I asked her where she came up with that idea and she tells me her colleague thought of it. She said, 'It's worked for some folks, hopefully it will for you.' I tell you I tried it the very next time and those clowns have never called back or sat there breathing in to the phone!" Roger knew he had the solution to the 888 conspiracy—only he'd dress it up a bit with the threat of the police.

David took a deep cleansing breath and launched into his sermon. He used a "move" system for his homiletical style. Tie together five or six logical sentences, and then add a story or two under each sentence heading. Never use "I" because the sermon ain't about the preacher. That was ego-building idolatry. No, a good sermon had an interior logic to it. The problem was anytime you were speaking to more than eight people you were confronted with a "group mind." That meant that unless you added stories and imagery, you'd lose the audience in 90 seconds. It's why congregants hardly ever could recall what scripture passages their peers had read. And, don't cite chapter and verse numbers. No one remembers that stuff either. This is to say nothing about the danger of infusing humor into the sermon. One man's joke is another's tragedy. Jokes are for the back-slapping coffee hour after church.

David longed for a good joke now and again. But he was a preacher—this meant that when he and Jeremy or he alone walked into Ronnie Bryant's barber shop down the street all the belly laughs stopped. "Oh, hi Preacher. Didn't notice you come in," Ron would bellow to his customers, putting them on notice. Instantly, all the light banter ceased, every time. Felt like a mortuary sometimes to David. Maybe if he was lucky they'd discuss the Red Sox game or the Bruins or Celts. But no one would cuss or drop the F bomb in front of him. He often mused and so wanted to tell the barbershop patrons the F bomb was the most versatile word in the English language, citing the old joke about it being a verb, noun, adverb, adjective, preposition, a definite article and even a gerund in front of itself, "f-ing, f____!" But he knew they'd only laugh *after* he left and mock him for trying to be one of the guys. Then, word would get out to his parishioners that the "preacher's got one hell of an effin mouth. And he's in charge of our children's vacation Bible school!"

This may be the shortest homily ever, Dave thought. He began: "The news report the other night announced that last month another 612 U.S. soldiers were killed in action in Vietnam. Are we giving up our treasure, our progeny, in a noble cause? What do you all think? Gandhi's been dead for 20 years. He talked about what would happen if we followed the eye for an eye rule of the ancient Israelites. Pretty soon, he said, the whole world would be blind. Who would lead us then? The history of this War doesn't just go back thirty or forty years with French colonialism. It goes back 1,000 years or more. The people of Vietnam, and they are people just like us, have fought all manner of feudal conquerors from various Chinese dynasties to the Dutch and the Japanese, just to name a few. These people have fought for millennia just to keep their homeland.

"Apparently, while fighting the French, Ho Chi Minh asked President Truman to aid him in stopping the needless bloodshed. Truman refused of course, not wanting, I suppose, to insult a NATO ally. Now here we are years later, and how many French, Vietnamese, Chinese, Japanese and Dutch soldiers have been killed over this plot of land—about the size of New Mexico. I'm offering not a solution or a diatribe against President Johnson or General Westmoreland. No, instead, I ask that we join in a prayer, not for peace, but for the hope and promise of peace. Let us bow our heads and close our eyes to avoid looking into the heart of the burning bush. Dear and precious God, abide in us and all world leaders to help us all find a better way of transforming our conflicts, large and small, local and international. Call us to be better stewards of this Earth and the life that came from your primordial soup."

David paused and then said, "I invite us to consider what the Tibetan monks do with much of their lives. They spend hour upon hour each day contemplating gratitude. How often do we give thanks for what we have? Most of us worry about the future, always asking what if? What if I could make $10,000 more a year in salary? Why didn't I stay in school or study more when I had the chance? Or, we ruminate on mistakes we've made—errors that haunt us every day, keep us up at night. I urge us to consider living in the present. Let tomorrow take care of itself. But while we live for today, we must give thanks for our spiritual bounty. God loves us just like God loves all the soldiers who are serving in Vietnam and who have lost their lives there. For their lives we also should give thanks.

"Please, let us pray to honor the memory of Truman McPherson, who was killed while on patrol protecting his comrades and us. Yes, us. We pray for Corporal Lance Rice and Phil Cochran, who are still in Vietnam with the 3rd Battalion, 3rd Marines, or *America's Battalion,* as they are known across the military. Envelop them and their families—our church family, with your love and encouragement. Come quick God, make haste, for we feel lost in a wilderness of despair, no manna from heaven in sight to feed or sustain us. Please, in the name of your Son, in the names of all our sons, pull us out of the abyss. Amen."

David sat down as a hushed silence fell over the gathering. He spied only a few dry eyes in the congregation. Most everyone shed tears for the fallen and for those who might fall soon, any day now. After the benediction, Colonel Edward McPherson came through the receiving line and reached out and shook David's hand in an iron grip, where he'd usually just nod politely and say hello. "Preacher, I hope this War isn't a waste. I didn't consider that one-thousand year thing you mentioned and didn't know the story about Ho's contacting President Truman. But I was primed to storm out of this church for good—if you took my son Truman's name in vain. Instead, you reconnected me and Mom here with our son in the cosmic scheme of things. I'm grateful for your taking my thinking in a new direction—away from that God-be-damned shame spiral our family's been in since Truman died. Bless you. If I can ever return the favor just holler. The War I fought back in the day is nothin' like this one."

David's spine tingled as he eyed Col. McPherson and quietly thanked God for Jeremy's insight. He felt his sermon sparked a new day even though the War would drag on for seven more years. And little did David realize, Col. McPherson would soon be a huge help to the Hergenroeder family.

CHAPTER 8

Tuesday June 4, 1968—Afternoon
The Gambler

"**I** can't wait to get off shift!" Dan Brodie chortled to himself as he welded another seam on the ship. The yard steam whistle hadn't yet shouted out its 4:45 p.m. curtain call. With two hours to go, Dan readied himself for a little night action. In Dan's addled brain, he thought that just being hours away from Hump Day meant it was almost Thursday. *That means it's almost the weekend, so a little shot or four of Scotch whiskey will smooth things over nicely. Steel my nerves.*

His buddy, Dominic Sangria, a lanky Puerto Rican émigré with jet black hair, had offered to hook him up with some extra cash. When Dan asked him for a loan, Dominic had said, "Oh, man, you gotta meet my uncle, José Gutierrez. He's got an in with some money men who like to spot "guacamole" to our fellow yard workers in need. You know, when there's too much month at the end of the money." Dan loved that he got 500 smackers with just a handshake.

José, a bulldog of a man with the familial shock of black hair, had eyeballed Dan up and down, while Dominic espoused Dan's qualities. "Look, José, he's never borrowed off us before. I've worked with him for what, Dan, seven years? He's a stand-up guy—and he don't waste no money on the dog tracks. He ain't no bunny chaser like dem miserable greyhounds!"

"I get it, I get it," retorted José. "Lookey here, Dan, it's a 10% fee right off the top. You unnerstan what dat means? I han' you $500, you immediately owe me $550. Got it? Math's real simple. $50 a day gets tacked on, we tack it every day. We call it simple interest. This ain't no higher math outfit. Now, Dominic here tells me…" José started to rationalize as Dan stopped listening. His mind racing, he thought, *I need the cash bad. I can't wait till payday. I know I can hit it big tonight.* Dan kept nodding his assent to whatever José mouthed, acting all deferential and real polite like. *I can't believe this shmuck. He's wearing shinyl vinyl pants, white even! Black patent leather stiletto shoes and that Dippity-Do thing he's got going on top. The yard guys'd eat him for lunch, throw him back to the canteen truck and demand their money back!*

A street smart guy from way back, José formed part of a Puerto Rican "cultural organization" that, ironically enough, had its base of operations right in Dan's hometown of Fitchburg. Dan didn't have a clue about José and company, but soon would find out more than he ever cared to know, especially about their geographical reach. José studied guys like Dan all day long. He could have written a college psychology text on Dan's pedigree.

"Hey, Dan, looks like you left us for dreamsville. Whaddya plan on doing with this money? Dominic says you're in a spot till payday. You ain't gonna gamble it away on some sure thing at the track is ya?"

"No, no sir," Dan burped out, realizing Jose′ was playing *him*, not the other way around as he'd planned. "Like I told Dominic," who started nodding at Dan's explanation, "my mother-in-law's got this woman's thing down in her privates. I don't know all the what-fors, but her Doc wants $500 up front before he'll *exercise* it out of her female parts. Says it'll grow into cancer if he doesn't cut it out quick like. Ya know she's been bad sick awhile. Too old to work herself. So I figure it's the right thing to do. I mention my problem to Dominic here and lickety-split he hooks me up wit' you. I couldn't be more grateful."

"All right, but I got to warn ya. If me or my boys even hear you might have gambled it or pissed it away at the track, if you even show up at the track, then this is out of my hands. I'm a gentleman, but my business associates aren't, so what do we say Dominic, *comprende?*"

"I get it," Dan choked out. His breathing had become labored as if the Earth's percentage of oxygen had dropped. Starved for O_2, Dan felt like Jose′ had punched him in the gut. He coughed. "Like I said err, Mr. José, this gets the wife happy. She been worried sick. It'll make me out to be Prince Charming with the mother-in-law. No more Toadsville for me."

Cash in hand, Dan vaulted back to his welding area, masked up and hit a nice straight bead. Trouble was the welding rods, unbeknownst to Dan or the shipping industry, emitted manganese gas. Every time he'd light up an arc weld the rod smoked the gas right into his lungs. Manganese won't hurt people in small doses, but Dan and his colleagues got so much on a regular basis that the gas inexorably infected their brains. Slowed down their ability to think—polluted the synapses so they didn't fire like they used to. Not that Dan had a lot of those cranial connections to begin with. Later, class-action lawsuits would change the welding industry as much as the introduction of robotics. But for Dan, right now, manganese poisoning didn't even register, it just was part of the smells of the job.

There goes the whistle! Dan thought. *I gotta finish this bead line first though, before Connie 'The Bastard' Calhoun writes me up again.* Twenty minutes later, Dan was hightailing it to the craps game in Boston's Combat Zone on Washington Street, just between Boylston and Kneeland.

CHAPTER 9

Tuesday June 4, 1968—Night Owl Time
The North End—Boston's Italian Home Front

Like its Washington, D.C. cousin, Boston used to be a swamp with serpentine estuaries fingering the landscape. Once a swamp, always a swamp. At least from the perspective of the underground subcultures that thrived where lung fish once trod on to the shore. Dan pulled up to Antonio's Bar and Grille on Washington Street, handed his pickup keys to the bouncer—lien credit in case you got in over your head at craps—and passed through the front door. "Give me a Bud, Joey—and make sure it's a St. Looey, not one of dem Merrimack sewer specials." Joey Fenn, long-time Antonio's bartender, knew Dan as a regular. *A regular dork-mon-do that is,* Joey thought. "I never buy any Budweiser from the Merrimack, New Hampshire brewery Dan-O!" Joey yelled back.

Antonio had hired Joey as soon as he met him, even though he was short for a bartender. Five foot-two-inches wasn't going to intimidate anybody, especially a drunk with alcohol for blood. So Antonio constructed a special walkway behind the bar that elevated Joey so he looked like he was six feet at least. Joey knew that everyone who drank Bud hated Merrimack's. It was a point of honor in five of the six New England states. Bud in hand, Dan headed to the back hall and met the second bouncer, some Guido/Alphonse type with no neck. *What is it with these guys,* Dan wondered? Gaston gave Dan the once-over, a quick pat-down and let him pass to the inner sanctum.

"Man I can feel the action!" Dan whooped to no one in particular. "Someday the city fathers'll raid this place for sure. Antonio, better keep those skids greased—I ain't using any of these 500 smackers for bail!"

Antonio stayed in business precisely because he never stopped giving the politicos their cut, regular as the sunrise. And that's when the couriers showed up to stuff the take into their lockboxes. Best not wait to grab the prior night's haul, lest it get redistributed to other hungry mouths downstream. Dan swilled down his first Bud in five quick gulps, the better to embolden himself against the voice of conscience echoing in his chest.

Nobody appreciates my unique skill set, he mused as he gulped down the libation. Dan could open his throat and just pour the beer down his gullet, no swallowing. Another St. Looey quelled his guilt pangs, and Dan blew on the dice for his first throw. Two hours later he was up half again, holding $750 in his hands. "Exercise this, José!" he yelled as he threw the dice. Another winner. As Dan collected his take he looked up to see none other than José Gutierrez. The henchman beside Jose' all frowned in unison. José just shook his head real slow. Dan handed off the dice and ran over to José. "Mr. Gutierrez, this ain't your money, I swear! You'll...you'll get it all back next week, just like I said!" Dan felt his bowels loosening.

José shrugged his shoulders. "Dan, remember what I tol' you? Maybe not, when we talked earlier you seemed like you were on Mars or at Cape Kennedy—ready for launch. This is now out of my hands. Please join us outside in the back alley," José said, pointing toward a back door Dan had never before noticed.

Dan looked behind José to see his crew, all of whom wore dark sunglasses, like those rock stars who tired of the paparazzi forcing flashbulbs in their faces. Dan wondered how they could see in the dark bar at all. Maybe they found their way by sense of smell. Dan could feel his large colon gurgling. He prayed for stoppage: *God, please cork it, I can't show no fear!*

The group of new friends sauntered out the back door, which locked fast behind them. Can't have cops raiding the place—without bouncer Gaston's warning shout. Or was it Alphonse, Dan wondered. Dan heard the metal clank in three spots—one hell of a locking system, he thought. Clearly, no one got back into Antonio's through this door. The dumpster next to him spouted an unseemly effluent right out a rusty hole in the side. Dan swore he saw a rat scurry past when he first set foot in the alley. Dan realized in that microsecond that rats can survive anything—ship wrecks, poison, starvation, hell they can even flatten their bodies to squeeze under all manner of obstructions. "Oh, how I wished I had a rat's ability to survive," Dan whispered to himself.

José broke the silence. "Dan, I need to introduce you to some of my associates. This here's my cousin Pilar. He don't say much, but when he speaks guys like you usually listen. And don't be insulting him because he's got a girl's name. His momma, my aunt, was, ah, hoping for a *la hija*, comprende? Out pops Pilar and she liked the name so much she gave it to him. Only one bully ever made fun of Pilar. He ended up in the kid's ward missing his front teeth."

Street cred meant José already knew how this soap opera would play out. He grew up near the Green Street area of Fitchburg, a boundary between the Puerto Rican and African American ghettos. At age 13 he witnessed a loan shark overplay his hand by murdering his father. The goon only meant to maim his Dad. From that day forward, Jose´ hunkered down and vowed never to be in anyone's debt. He looked around and saw all the black-on-black violence and the 'Ricans killing each other over drug deals gone bad or stupid arguments over nothing. Across town he studied how the white men rolled up cash from their factories and paper mills. They'd got there with schooling and *connections*. He figured real fast that he could handle the schooling. The connections? Why, they'd come later. He turned the adrenaline from his grief toward self-betterment; albeit by stretching the law at certain pressure points.

José started his loan sharking with junior-high loans, buying and leveraging the free lunch tickets the poor kids got because their mammas were on AFDC, cutting nickel bags of dope, anything the other kids, and especially the white kids, wanted. As he learned the business ropes, he taught his cousins who joined him in his empire building. To a casual observer, Dan's loan probably seemed like so much chump change. But to Jose´ and company it meant getting a firmer foothold in the ship yard, its union and the *international* commerce that General Dynamics corralled.

As Dan suffered through this initial humiliation, he glanced back at Pilar. No neck, mostly bald, but favoring José in his facial features. Pilar had translucent brown eyes to José's black holes. They twinkled in the alley's spotlight as Pilar appraised Dan. Pilar sucker-punched Dan in the gut, his fist as hard as granite. Dan's knees buckled and he realized God had ignored the cork prayer. His bowels sluiced their day's intake. When Dan finally caught his breath he found his face lapping at the dumpster's garbage juice. He retched. Dan could smell the stale Budweiser and all manner of other festering waste. Pilar grabbed Dan's collar, hauling him to his feet as if Dan had helium for blood. Dan questioned the alleged inviolability of gravity.

Pilar stepped back and on came Ricardo, also of the species sans neck. Ricardo, José's other cousin, hit Dan's knee with one of those little toy baseball bats the Red Sox hand out on bat day. To Cub Scouts. Oh man, did it sting. Dan listened for the crunch of bone while he endured the 40 nanosecond delay of total debilitating pain that surely would follow. It did. Despite the welding gas's effect, his mind raced. The pain came crashing through. With its searing onslaught, Dan collapsed again. Ricardo stood over him smiling, three of his front teeth embroidered in gold plate. His dental work reminded Dan of someone. It didn't occur to Dan that he should be worried about the next hit. *Oh yeah,* Dan thought. *The big villain in the James Bond movies, Jaws. That guy's front teeth could bite through electric wire. What was his name? Richard Keil!* Dan realized that time had slowed way down. Time's relativity created a black hole where Dan could think about James Bond.

Ricardo now did the talking while José stepped back to roll a cigarette. He rolled it one-handed—a trick Dan never before had seen. José's other hand expertly sifted in the tobacco.

"Here's how it's going to play out. We're accelerating your debt. Tonight. Hey, that's what the bankers say: 'You're in default and we gotta foreclose. We no longer feel…secure with you as a debtor. The first time we use the Cub Scout bat 'cause we figure you're a risky investment, but an asset nonetheless," Ricardo advised.

Dan knew Ricardo was no banker, but kept the thought to himself. He appreciated Ricardo's ability to spout banking lingo like "default, accelerate, foreclosure, secure."

"Now, hand over your take, all of it. Give me the chit for your truck. Don't be surprised!" Ricardo scowled as he got in Dan's face. "We followed you over here. José saw your eyes glaze over and he knew, we knew, you're nothin' but a two-bit gambling addict. Love those dice—they're your friends. Seen it before. José, see, he wondered. But Dominic vouched for you, so now thanks to your stupidity, we got to visit Dominic too. You probably won't see him at work tomorrow."

"Don't hurt him! This wasn't his fault," Dan cried out.

"Hey, calm down already," José leaned back in as he flicked his cigarette butt. "Sangria don't owe us no money, so that's a different discussion. No Cub Scout bat. But still I need my nephew to know he's not to call on us again to help any of his so-called friends. I'm putting him on probation. For a whole year. You, my friend, are a different story. You lied to me, yes?"

"No, ahh, I didn't mean to," Dan yelped like so many addicts before him who promised family members they'd never use again.

On came Ricardo menacing. "I'm disappointed to hear that, Dan. Now you've lied twice, once to José and once to me. Counting the rest of the guys here, that's five lies in less than four hours."

Ricardo bored his fist into Dan's solar plexus, again. Dan didn't even stagger this time, landing up against the dumpster. It took a full minute for some precious O_2 to find its way into Dan's alveoli. Drowning in debt and shame.

Ricardo did his anti-gravity trick on Dan, levitating him up against the cold, dank dumpster. Dan's hands sought purchase on the sidewall. Time stopped. Random thoughts again cascaded through Dan's consciousness. *Who invented dumpsters? Ain't it a mob operation? They don't have dumpster washers do they, like car washes? They should! These suckers never get washed!* Manganese played tricks with Dan's ability to reason. He couldn't focus on the task at hand—surviving this skirmish. Instead, Dan recalled somehow that all local disposal companies off loaded their dumpster pickups in Saugus, off Route 1. His Uncle Howie made his living as a garbage hauler and regaled him with all kinds of trash stories. At family picnics, Howie would brag, "A good morning run for a city truck lands 18,000 pounds of trash. Anything less and the foreman takes us to task for slacking. You gotta hoof it to make nine tons by noon!"

Young Dan marveled at the stories, but wondered about the aura of garbage clinging to Howie like a saint's halo. Howie Brodie, all 5 foot, 8 inches of him, worked in the trade. He always smelled of Old Spice that barely masked his garbage bouquet. Good guy though, Dan remembered. Talked at family gatherings about the "choreography" between the truck driver and the two swing men out back feeding the hopper.

One time, Howie was holding court with the story of stories: "You guys ain't gonna believe dis! They hadda shut down the Saugus facility last Tuesday week. Police detectives, they be running around everywhere. They'd blocked the entrance. The crane driver thought he saw a body in all that mess a garbage. Can you believe it? Pulled the general alarm button. You know the big hole where we dump our loads…it's gotta be wide as half a football field. How that guy saw that body, I'll never unnerstan! Then the cops, they start walking the line a trucks. Ya know, they got to make their in-choir-ees! 'Hey Bozo, you see anything? You over dare, you notice any-ting?'" Then Howie caught his breath after a deep roaring laugh. He added the punch line: "Yes off-a-pisser, I saw dem gahbage trux!"

Back to reality with Ricardo mouthing his moralities. Dan caught that all his money had vanished, they'd "confiscated" his truck and "garnisheed" several upcoming paychecks. He now had to give Dominic the payments. Dominic shifted from friend and colleague to collections agent and part-time snitch for this august group. All thanks to Dan's five lies in four hours. And worse, Dominic didn't even know yet about Dan's stunt. Guess that was lie number six or seven. Dan cringed at the thought.

"It's not all bad news, Dan," Ricardo said as he peeled off a $5 bill from Dan's winnings. "First, you won tonight. Must be your once-every-two-years day, according to Joey.

So José once again is stepping up to cover your ass with a new loan. This here five dollar bill comes from our cultural association's benevolent fund—as a continuing investment in you, Mr. Dan. Take the train home tonight and back to work tomorrow. See, we want you to work, but for us now. Next week's check is ours and whaddya think ladies? *Hermanas?* We get half of each of your checks for the next five months. One month for each lie, Dan. Ya see, had you told the truth tonight, ya coulda loped off three whole months. Now get outta my sight. Remember all cash payments go through your new best enemy, Dominic, right? Am I right, Dan?"

Dan looked up and squeaked out a "yessir." He gave it all the feeling he had, not wanting to add yet another lie to the debt and hit six months or, hell, with five guys, one lie equaled 10 months total. He also thought better of pointing out the subway didn't get anywhere close to Fitchburg. Jeez, was Velma gonna go off on him tonight, assuming he made it home at all. "Shoot, what time does the dang T stop running anyway?" Dan asked the empty alleyway. "When's the last train run? And how do I get to Route 2? Who's going to pick up this piece of garbage?"

At 2:13 a.m., Dan finally made it home, some lonely old goat taking pity on him, driving Dan's same late model Chevy truck. A charity run. As Dan started to step into the passenger compartment the old man said, "Not so fast smelling like you do. Sorry, the missus uses this truck for grocery runs and such. Get your ass in the truck bed and have a lie down. The breeze'll blow off that damnable smell!"

"Sure, pardon me, mister. I shore appreciate the ride," Dan said as he eased into the truck bed, all his bones aching. As Dan staggered into the house banging around to keep his balance, he unwittingly woke up Velma from her perch on the couch. Sensing trouble, she came running. "Oh God, were you in an accident? What happened to your face? It's a mess of oil and Lord knows what else! And you stink something awful," Velma cried out.

As she cleaned up Dan's wounds, he decided lie #7 could wait for another day. "Velma baby, I had this feeling all day that it was my time with the dice. And it was, girl! I won $250 tonight before some mobsters had it in for me!"

Velma looked at Dan with measured sympathy, the kind only the best of un-recovering co-dependents lend their addicted spouses. "You went to Antonio's and you got robbed? Honey, I didn't hear you pull in, no gravel crunching! Where's the truck?" Velma asked as she looked out in the driveway.

"Baby, I'm not even sure where to start. I figured if I was going to hit it big then I needed a little extra cash. Ya know, a cushion. I told Dominic that your Mom had a cancer in her privates. Her doctor would cure it if we could cough up $500. Dominic has this in thing with these guys, locally, who help out yard workers sometimes. I've never asked him before. Next thing I know, after lunch break, he's introducing me to some Puerto Rican dude named José. Sure as I'm sitting here, José buys my story and lends me $500. On the spot!"

Velma turned five shades of purple. "You went to a loan shark! Are you nuts? Don't you know what these guys do to get their money back?"

"Velma, I know, I know. Believe you me, I know like I never knew before. José made me promise I weren't no gambler. That I'd really use the loan for your Mom."

"My Mom's been dead ten years for chrissakes! Cancer killed her. So you lied twice to this clown. He's a loan shark, for cryin' out loud!"

"That's funny!" Dan tried to laugh but he retched and quivered from the night's beating. Finally he spit out, "That's just what José said after he followed me to Antonio's: 'You lied twice to me.'"

"Dan that's no constipation! I mean consolation!"

"I get it, believe me, I get it. José introduced me to his, what did he call them? *Cultural Associates*. These guys were all muscle and no neck! This Ricardo guy got me out back in Antonio's alley—baby you should have heard that back door slam and lock tight. He really laid into me..."

"Dan, take off your pants..."

"Honey, I'm not up for gettin' laid right now!"

"No you dumb ass. Let me look at your knee."

As Dan struggled to pull off his pants, Velma squealed, "You shit your pants. Oh my God, Dan, is your knee broken? It's all purple. Let me get some gauze and wrap it. And here, take four of these aspirin."

Dan finished the story including the banking lingo style details and the loss of half of five months' worth of checks "garnisheed." While he spoke, Velma went into panic mode, at least under the surface. *What could they do to get out of this nightmare?* A moment later she thought of Jeremy. *How could they use his lottery-ticket brain? But what if those sharks got ahold of him? No telling what would happen to that precious PK.*

"Look, Dan, I may have some good news. But I'm not sure how to put this new tool to good use. You see, confidentially, Dr. Rebovitz has this new and amazing client, five years old, and the kid can flat out, no holds barred, no Barnum and Bailey magic act, *read people's minds!*"

Dan looked at her not fully registering what she was saying, like an eagle returning to its nest only to find that lightning toppled the host tree. "Wait a minute. This kid can mind read? What are you talking about?"

Velma got so excited she could hardly get her words out. "I heard it on Dr. Rebovitz's dictation. You got to call in sick tomorrow. The foreman will be OK—we'll tell him you hurt your knee in the shop here, whatever. We could grab this kid. I could offer to babysit. Maybe we could offer to take him to the museum for the day. I wonder if he can predict a dog race?"

"I don't get it. How could some kid read a dog's mind? Even the dogs don't know which one's going to win. They're just chasin' some damned rabbit—and it's as fake as the Chevy Truck in our driveway."

"Yup, you're right. We have got to get close to this kid. His dad is the minister at that big Rollstone Church on Main Street. Ya' know, near that Caroll's burger joint. I could tell him that I babysit on the side—might take a load off the missus. You could help him as a church fix-up guy."

"Babe, I don't need another job, 'specially one that don't pay crap."

"No, dummy, you don't. But you could get to know the family a bit. Gain their trust. Everyone loves a handyman. You can fix almost anything!"

"What? And then kidnap the kid? What's his name again?"

"Jeremy, Jeremy Hergenroeder."

"Hergen what? The hell kind ah name is that anyway?"

"German, I guess. It don't matter. We got to brainstorm. Remember what Dr. Rebovitz told me, those who fail to plan, plan to fail."

CHAPTER 10

Wednesday June 5, 1968—Just After Midnight
California—The Kennedy Campaign

Robert Francis "Bobby" Kennedy started his whirlwind Presidential campaign March 16th, 1968. Having been a successful New York Senator and a hard-nosed U.S. Attorney General from 1961 to 1964, a bid for the highest office in the land was a next logical step. He had the pedigree. After winning the California primary on Tuesday June 4, 1968, he needed to embrace the throng of supporters who'd gathered at Los Angeles's Ambassador Hotel. As June 4th turned into June 5th, the crowd grew. Back then, however, the Secret Service only protected sitting Presidents, not presidential candidates. His security team decided that, with the crush of the crowd, they should alter his egress plans. RFK would exit the hotel through the kitchen, rather than the mobbed main entrance. Unlike Jeremy, RFK's security contingent of former FBI Agent William Barry and two unofficial bodyguards could not feel the heads of would be evil-doers. That would have been a mission critical gift.

While the hotel's maître d', Karl Uecker, led RFK to the kitchen, Mr. Barry and the bodyguards in tandem kept on high alert, watching the facial expressions and body language of supporters, looking for bulges in clothing and other odd characteristics. Anybody's eyes darting around? Not so hard when you are looking at, say, a handful of people over discrete periods of time. Infinitely harder when hundreds of human beings have gathered. The presumption is that all are well-wishers except a few. That is the science of interdiction psychology. Stop the crime before the one with malice aforethought gets the opportunity. Imagine a security intervention on a would-be assassin like Mark David Chapman who, after he killed John Lennon, bragged that he had become as famous as the Beatles themselves.

But this early morning, Mr. Sirhan, a 24 year old immigrant of Palestinian/Jordanian heritage, stalked RFK. Awaiting his prey behind an ice machine, he found his mark in a passageway that fed off the hotel kitchen. With a mere twitch of his trigger finger, he shot RFK. Twice. Mr. Roosevelt "Rosey" Grier, an NFL football player, and others including writer George Plimpton, tackled Mr. Sirhan and crammed him against a steam table, even as he kept firing his gun. He shot five other people. Only RFK died. Some 26 hours after being shot. Perhaps Mr. Sirhan hadn't planned what his life would look like in the assassination aftermath. Just as for Dan Brodie, though, consequences would prove an invaluable teacher.

CHAPTER 11

Wednesday June 5, 1968—Morning
Shocking News Hits the Parsonage

As the early-bird Hergenroeders gathered at 5:30 a.m. for breakfast, Alex turned on the radio just as the DJ made a startling announcement. "At approximately 10 minutes past midnight last night at Los Angeles's Ambassador Hotel, right after greeting his supporters, and barely minutes after winning the California Democratic Primary, an assassin's bullet struck Bobby Kennedy."

While Alex and Jeremy sat in stunned silence, David jumped out of his chair, shut off the radio and urged the family into the TV room to hear updates. They caught a Walter Cronkite wannabe doing his best impression. "We know the attempted assassin's name is Sirhan Sirhan, and apparently he is from Jordan. Rosie Greer subdued Sirhan, making the tackle of his life, to which nothing from his NFL playing days could possibly compare. Bobby Kennedy is in critical condition at Good Samaritan Hospital."

After watching a few related interviews with talking heads, David ran to the TV and shut it off, astounded and frightened. "Can we all go sit at the kitchen table, please?" They found the dishes still caked from the remains of the breakfast Alex had prepared. She'd intended the meal as a celebration of Jeremy's mental health and his successful return to school that week—sweet rolls with a cherry compote on the side. She even had dishes of vanilla ice cream waiting in the freezer and hot fudge on standby. After the news, while the rest of America entered the shock and disbelief stages of grief, the Hergenroeders started a slightly different journey, one far less traveled. It soon would make all the difference in their young lives.

Jeremy felt the worry in his parents' viscera. "Jeremy, we need your help," David pleaded. "Do you remember our talk about the Democratic Primary in California last Friday?"

"Yes sir," Jeremy squeaked out. This was all the response he could muster, paralyzed by his gift. Muster is an interesting concept, which he might muse about in the years to come. If he lived and learned to keep his gift under wraps. Mustering involves the steps a ship's crew practices every day to get passengers safely *off* a foundering ship. Then, when their ship really is sinking, they work on pure muscle memory.

Alex leaned in and held Jeremy's hand. "Jeremy, you are special to us. We love you no matter what. Tell us, honey, what did you feel in that man's head last Friday?"

"I heard Dad talk about Robert Kennedy and California. I felt like I was flying. And under me I saw that man on TV loading his gun. He was imagining assinating Mr. Kennedy. I tried telling you, Mom!"

"I know, baby, believe me I know."

"Jeremy," David implored, "I don't understand your gift. You may not be ready to understand it yourself. But

Dr. R, as you call him, wants to help us. Alex, I don't know if we dare tell Dr. R this story. It's too alarming."

"I agree, David. Jeremy, tell me again what you felt please. And I apologize for saying 3,000 miles would make a difference. Please forgive me. Oh, and the correct word is 'assassinate,' not 'assinate.' Although I must say I feel like an *Ass*inate myself!"

"All right, Mom. It's like that first day of kindergarten last week. The other kids' heads jumped into mine. It scared me because all of them were scared about starting school. They wanted to be back home. Not at school. This Sir Hand man...he didn't seem scared to me. He was real mad though. He hated Mr. Kennedy. I guess. That's what he was feeling when he loaded his gun."

David reacted, "You know what this is like, Jeremy, this gift of yours? It's like that command scope Jimmy brought over. When you didn't hold up any fingers, he knew. He could see around that corner—and if you hadn't known he was there, he could have felt your head like you did with Mr. 'Sir Hand.'"

"How did you know I didn't hold up any fingers, Dad?"

"I'm sorry, I didn't mean to spy on you. But you know I love you and I sometimes watch you play just to make sure you are safe. It reminds me of when I was a boy. How come you didn't 'feel my head' watching you?"

Jeremy thought for a moment. "I don't know. Maybe 'cause I was feeling Jimmy's head, you know, trying to fool him."

Alex interjected, "Hey, I have an idea. I'm happy you didn't know Dad was watching! Maybe when someone is watching you out of love—your 'red alert,' like on Star

Trek, doesn't come on! Think about it—you feel heads when people are distressed or sad or when they're about to 'assinate.' You know, like at the funerals Dad does—your high beams come on, Jeremy, and you pick up thoughts and feelings. David, does that make sense to you?"

"I suppose. How do we get Dr. Rebovitz's advice and counsel if we can't tell him about Sirhan and Jeremy's 3,000-mile eye in the sky? This still shocks me. I just don't get it."

After clearing the breakfast table, David announced, "I think we must tell Dr. Rebovitz. Maybe he'll just think it's a fluke. Maybe not. What do you think?"

Alex looked up from her coffee. She always took it New England regular style, meaning cream and two sugars. "I haven't a clue, David. But listen, I did have this weird dream last night. It's been driving me crazy. So I see this man, he's standing on top of a mountain, maybe it was Mt. Washington in New Hampshire. Anyway, the wind's howling all around him. It was bitterly cold and he's standing on this sheet of ice wearing a three-piece suit. Wind's blowing his tie out past his neck. I know this will sound silly, but he had on black patent-leather shoes—not galoshes, and no crampons. But the wind didn't blow him over and he didn't slip on the ice. Just stood there ramrod style, like a soldier on sentry duty or something. Or maybe on watch, like some sort of mariner at night on the bow of a ship keeping his eyes peeled for icebergs or other vessels. Like the Titanic—you know, a moonless night. The sea was calm as glass—no waves. Then, all of a sudden, he jumps off the mountain, falling and falling, but not screaming like I would. And his life didn't pass before his eyes. He didn't fly down like Superman or Mighty Mouse might do. Anyway, he lands at a trail head and he's all dressed up like a hiker—nice boots, he's got an axe with him, a bed roll and a canteen. I awoke as he started down the trail. I have no idea what it means. Do you two?"

"I'm no Joseph the Technicolor Dream Coat interpreter, but I like how he was on watch at the highest point in New England. This is where America got its start, right?" David queried. "Maybe it's about Jeremy keeping watch over all of us with his gift. You know the part about being unmoved. That was compelling. I've heard they've clocked the winds up there at 200 miles per hour—broke the gauge, don't you know. So there's this guy, in a suit, tie flying, unmoved. At the top of the mountain—standing on hard packed snow and ice. Not slipping, right? OK, then he jumps, why I don't get. Done checking out the view? Which way was he looking?"

"East. And he never turned any other direction."

"So he's not looking west to St. Louis, say, the gateway to the West, or California—just east. Mecca—is that where he's looking—Saudi Arabia?"

"I don't know, Honey, I don't know."

"Fine, no pressure," said David. "Maybe it doesn't matter. Jeremy, what do you think?"

"Wow, Mom, I don't understand. So the guy sort of looked like a Boy Scout? After he landed?"

No one spoke for a minute.

"That's gotta be it!" shouted David. "Your dream is telling us to 'Be Prepared.' That's the Boy Scout motto. But how do we prepare? And what did the howling wind mean? Reminds me of Shakespeare's question for Juliet,

Wherefore art thou, Romeo? Let's call the guy Romeo—
'cause he's a hopeless romantic. I hate to interpret and run,
but I gotta get to church. OK if we talk about this later?
And by the way, Jeremy, I don't think it is wise for you to
go to school today. We need some time to sort things out.
Mom will send a note with you when you go back in a day
or two. We'll keep listening to the news and see if Mr.
Kennedy lives. He's hopefully getting the best medical care
there is."

CHAPTER 12

Wednesday June 5, 1968—Morning
After Breakfast

As they cleaned up from breakfast, Alex and David agreed that David would call Dr. Rebovitz's office and relay the RFK "Sir Hand" story. They figured that more data, not less, would help Dr. Rebovitz construct a filter for Jeremy, help him control his gift. They also decided, despite their avowed non-violence stance, that they would reallocate their budget to cover the cost of martial arts classes for Jeremy. They knew he'd soon be facing new enemies, whether on the school yard or elsewhere, and that they would not always be there to protect him. They had a beginning plan anyway.

David arrived at Rollstone just shy of 7:00 a.m. He stepped over two seemingly full, quart size, Miller beer bottles. The church's sexton, Roger Tomlinson, would get them later. Thugs liked to fill them with urine and get the drunks sick with "free beer." Pay it forward. Sow seeds of hate into the future, then sit back and watch them sprout.

As David entered his office the smell of the mimeograph machine greeted him. In the days before most churches could afford Xerox copiers, mimeographs were the cheapest machines for getting out large numbers of programs and flyers. It wasn't a bad smell, but it did get old and permeated the curtains and carpet. After brewing some coffee, he pulled out Dr. Rebovitz's card and placed the call hoping he'd catch the good doctor before he started his rounds. The church paid extra for a private line. No need to have party line voyeurs listening in on the foibles and woes of congregants and shut-ins who would foist their worries on David, morning, noon and night. A pastor's job never ended. Alex also had a full-time church operations position, unpaid of course. She managed the meetings, organized the potlucks, helped with the scout troops—all three, Cub, Webelos, and Boy Scouts. Not to mention the youth group lock-ins on Friday nights, oh, and the sock hops, too. Then she supervised the church auctions "to help make budget," which pleased church moderator Kurt Crider no end. Auctions took the form of a church-wide flea market where Kurt held court, and implored would-be bidders that this was an auction for Christ. Sometimes it motivated bidders and sometimes not.

"Dr. Rebovitz's office, this is Velma speaking, how may I help you?"

"Yes, Velma, I'm glad you all are in so early in the morning. This is Rev. David Hergenroeder. Could I please…?"

"Why, David," Velma gushed a little too enthusiastically. "How is Mr. Jeremy?"

"Good, thank you. I wondered if I might speak to your boss for a minute."

"I'm sorry, Dr. Rebovitz is already out on his rounds at Children's Hospital in Boston. I don't expect him back till 2:00 p.m. Is there something I could help you with?

You know, Dr. Rebovitz and I form a therapeutic team. No matter what, we always put our patients first. In fact, if there's anything I could do for you all, Alex, Jeremy and you, I'd love to help. By the way, my husband Dan is real handy. He can weld anything, fix stoves, engines, you name it. I know ministers don't make big bucks, so whatever. Also, I babysit my nieces and nephews all the time at our house. So if Alex ever needs a mother's day out, please call me. Just let me give you my home number: 555-8221."

Velma spoke in such a rapid-fire staccato style that it took David aback. "I see, um, thank you. I think we're fine at the house, though. Roger, our church sexton, is handy and fixes everything including at our parsonage. Our neighbors handle sitting chores." As David spoke, his Long Tom Commando scope radar registered a high alert. Velma's tone seemed a bit much. *What did she want? Of course! She transcribed the dictation! She'd have heard it all—including how Jeremy's gift could be used by manipulative evil doers. Oh God, what have I done to my son now? All I did was seek professional help. Once!*

"No, as I say, we are set. I've got your number, though." David tried to finish.

Velma caught David's reticence. "Oh, Reverend, I'm sorry. Sometimes I can be over enthusiastic about helping *our* patients. Dr. Rebovitz calls me a 'fixer' and I'm working on that issue. Again, my apologies. I know how busy you all are. Just trying to lend a hand. I'll be sure Dr. Rebovitz gets your message. I'll see that he calls you right back."

David rang off and sat back in his chair thinking he needed emotional judo lessons. He grabbed the Yellow Pages and looked up martial arts. Nothing. He found a heading called Karate/Judo and eyed a studio offering both styles and, best of all, it was right down the street. He'd never noticed the studio before. The ad even proclaimed, "Young children our prized specialty." David needed some fresh air and ran out the front door of the church. Roger had already picked up the beer bottles, thankfully.

As David walked to the dōjō center he thought about addictions and how long-term alcoholics contract something called wet brain. He also recalled from his pastoral care class in divinity school that it had a scientific name, some sort of syndrome named for an encephalopathy. "Winekey? No that isn't it. Wernicke's! I can't believe I remembered it!" David muttered to himself. "That's what these guys who drink that urine are suffering from. Heck, they drink long enough for decades and even if you could get one of them sober their only hope is a disability check. They could never really hold a job with any responsibility—their ability to reason is too far gone. Sad. That's what the thugs who peed in the quart bottles are banking on. A wet brain who'd lost the sense of time, space and the natural order of the universe," David whispered as he said a silent prayer.

Arriving at the studio, David saw an adult class in session. He quietly entered, but of course the door had a clanging bell that caught the class's attention. The instructor halted class and asked his students to spar for a minute with a partner. He hopped over to David. "Can I help you? My name is Mark Gallagher and I own this studio. Are you interested in karate?" Mark pronounced it 'carrot-tay.' He also noticed David's withered left arm and wondered how he managed.

David said, "No, not for me, I'm the minister down the street at Rollstone Congregational."

"Really? You know I've been meaning to try you all out sometime, but I get so busy and I do have a class on Sunday morning. Busy professionals, you know. They call themselves 'work-a-holics.' Never heard the phrase before, but it sure makes sense. And I guess I'm one, too!"

"Yes, thank you, Mr. Gallagher. Nice to make your acquaintance. And, of course, we'd love to have you join us for a service at Rollstone. Anyway I have a son, five years old, named Jeremy. I'm concerned about bullying, you know, and I was thinking it would be great if he could learn to defend himself, gain some confidence."

"I understand. Lots of parents come to me with the same concern. Really, many of them were bullied as kids, too. I'll tell you the consistent parental refrain my students got from their parents—'Ah, son, just ignore it. You'll be fine,' or worse yet, 'I'll call the bully's parents' or 'I'll call your teacher and get a meeting with the school principal.' Honestly, I've never seen those ideas work, particularly the 'just ignore it' line. Actually, that last one is a good start, but it has a critical component missing—a good defense when ignoring or 'non-engagement' as I call it fails. What I like to teach my younger students, and Jeremy may be a good candidate for this style, is judo. It's all based on using your opponent's force or strength against them. Watch."

Mark turned to his class and called out, "Arthur and Ted. Please come to the front. I want us to do a demonstration. Ted, you defend. Art, you attack—please use your judo skills Ted. Art, pretend you're a typical bully who's going to throw a round-house punch. Then try some other tactics we've practiced."

Ted and Art bowed to each other and yelled to empty their lungs of dead air. Art took a swing at Ted who slipped out of the way—the same direction as Art's round-house punch. Art kept going and nearly fell over. Ted waited and did not attack.

Mark said, "Good. Keep at it, Art. Now, Rev. Hergenroeder, watch Ted. You see how he doesn't attack—but just lets Art run out of steam? There's a crescendo, of course, as Art the bully gets more frustrated and lets his anger get the best of him."

Art tried to sucker-punch Ted in the gut, but before Art could connect, Ted grabbed Art's fist, pulled him forward, fell and rolled back while placing his bare foot in Art's gut. Ted threw Art head over heels. Art rolled with the throw—safety first, and Mark said, "Now, most bullies would have had enough by now. You also can see how Art knew how to land like a cat. We mimic nature in many ways. As civilization has developed over the millennia, we've lost our ability to defend ourselves. Our brains get in the way. We practice habits here, Reverend. Is this what you are looking for?"

"Yes, a most impressive display. Please do call me David."

"And you must call me Mark."

David nodded and turned to the combatants. "Thank you, Art and Ted. I'll know to give each of you a wide berth in the grocery store aisle or on the street." The young men bowed to David and ran back toward their classmates to practice sparring. "This was ideal, Mark. I'm most appreciative. Do you have classes for kindergarteners?"

"Yes. This class here is for young adults and runs from 7:00-8:00 a.m. The students can get in, practice, shower and get to work by 8:30 a.m. It's a real satisfier for this group. I do have a class for four- to five-year-olds on Mondays, Wednesdays and Fridays starting at 2:30 p.m. It's a two-hour class, $4.00 per session."

"Great, I'll bring Jeremy by tomorrow for an introduction. Will that work?"

"Yes. Should I be aware of any special concerns you have? Lack of motor skills, for example, or anger issues? Is Jeremy fully ambulatory? No handicaps or disabilities of a mental, spiritual or physical nature?"

"Wow," David remarked. "He's pretty much a normal kid, active imagination. He's just started a kindergarten class—accelerated version at Fitchburg Teacher's College. His first day was a bit wild and I had to pull him out since he seemed traumatized. But I took him back on Monday, and he's been doing fine. Kept him out today, though."

"I see," said Mark. "So it's a confidence issue then?"

"Maybe, but I don't want you to pre-judge. I do want this to be collaborative. So if you see things we could work on at home, please call me or mention it when my wife, Alex, or I pick him up. Here's my card. I'll write my home number on the back." They shook hands and David headed back to Rollstone, picked up yesterday's mail and drove home. For ministers a day off really was all about running errands, not resting up. That's the price for working six days a week and most evenings.

CHAPTER 13

Wednesday June 5, 1968
After Lunch

Dr. Rebovitz finished his rounds early at Boston Children's Hospital. Hospitals always had trouble recruiting enough psychiatrists. Like most states, Massachusetts had the same problem. There were not enough psychiatrists in the United States to address just one state's mental health issues. Supply and demand gone haywire. In the meantime, other professions filled the gaps without the benefit of the prescription writing capacities MD psychiatrists enjoyed: clinical psychologists, social workers, and therapists of every stripe. The Hergenroeders had been extremely lucky in being able to see Dr. Rebovitz on such short notice, since his new patient wait-time for a first appointment could be four months or more. And Dr. Rebovitz had not yet grasped how young Jeremy using his gift would eventually save the good doctor's life.

As he drove back from Boston up Route 2 to Fitchburg, Dr. Rebovitz admired the early summer sunshine. *I can't wait to start tending my garden and spending July and August at the lake house on Winnipesaukee. Wake up to the call of those loons.* The lake was just as beautiful, if not more so, than what Hollywood would depict decades later in Henry Fonda's last motion picture, *On Golden Pond.*

Dr. Rebovitz loved the autumn, too, with the brilliant leaves. He recalled his botany professor in college, Dr. Lucius Mikula, advising students on numerous field trips in the back woods of Defiance College in Ohio that the trees were always displaying those brilliant reds and yellows. The problem was that the trees' chlorophyll blocked the colors. It was how the trees ate sunshine and converted that energy to sugar for their sustenance.

Route 2 winds through central Massachusetts as a life-giving ribbon both for the towns along the way and the Ft. Devens military base. It feeds into Fitchburg, which is where Dr. Rebovitz happily exited. He padded into his office to find Velma brimming with a big smile and a fresh pot of coffee. "To what do I owe the pleasure of your good-natured smile today, Ms. Velma?'

"Oh, Dr. Rebovitz, I just love my job and I got all of your dictation and filing done. It helped a great deal my working Saturday, too. I do appreciate the overtime. You know, Dan's salary just doesn't seem to stretch as far as it used to."

"Really? I thought General Dynamics paid well. Or, well enough?"

"Oh yes, but it's those darned union dues. They just find new ways to stick it to the working man. And you know no union, no job—so we pay the dues and all the other fees they seem to come up with every month. Before I forget, Rev. David Hergenroeder called you early this morning. Sounded urgent."

"You should have paged me at Boston Children's, Velma. This is a new patient who's in quite a vulnerable state."

"I'm so sorry. You're right, I should have called. David, err Rev. Hergenroeder, seemed OK with your calling him at 2:00 p.m. when I thought you'd get back. I listened with interest to his son's diagnosis."

Shaking his head Dr. Rebovitz responded, "I don't have any kind of diagnosis yet, but we'll see if further tests will help."

"But I thought Mrs. Hergenroeder didn't want any newfangled brain scans!" Velma said a little too excitedly.

Dr. Rebovitz's eyebrow rose as he gazed at Velma.

Velma caught the tell and again realized that twice today she'd overstepped her boundaries. If she lost this job, she and Dan would really be in a pickle. She quickly recovered, "I just thought that Jeremy was cute as a minute. Can we help him, do you think?"

Dr. Rebovitz just nodded and padded into his office, shutting the sound-proof door for good measure. His last secretary had been a bit too nosey and he started worrying that Velma appeared headed down a similarly voyeuristic path. He picked up the phone and dialed Rollstone. No one answered, so he called the Hergenroeder residence.

Alex answered, "I'm so glad you called. Here, let me get David out of the yard—he's mowing the lawn."

David came in all sweaty and grabbed the phone. "Hello, Dr. Rebovitz! Thanks so much for tracking me down at home. Did you call the church?"

"Yes, but I'm glad I found you at home. Is something the matter?"

"I'm sure you heard about RFK getting shot just after midnight?"

"Of course. It's been all over the news. I understand RFK's still hanging on by a thread at the hospital. Does this have anything to do with Jeremy? Is he taking it badly?"

David thought for a moment, "No and yes. It was something he said to us, actually several statements over the last few days. Alex and I believe, I don't even know how to say this, Jeremy somehow got into the head of the would-be assassin, Sirhan Sirhan!"

Dr. Rebovitz sat in stunned silence. "I don't understand. That man was 3,000 miles away—on the west coast of the United States. I get that Jeremy picks up signals from you two and his classmates. Me, even. But you're saying he predicted the shooting?"

"Yes that's exactly what I'm saying. It started on the drive home from your office last Friday. Alex and I were discussing the election, or Jeremy and I were. I can't remember precisely. My head is spinning. I tried explaining to Jeremy how we elected Presidents—you know, primaries first, then a general election second. I talked about Robert Kennedy, how he was running, was JFK's brother, and Jeremy says he was worried or something. Alex kidded him, saying just what you did—nobody can 'feel the head' of someone 3,000 miles away. It just defies logic. And, don't you know, this morning during breakfast we caught the UPI report on the radio. News…Jeremy usually finds pretty boring with a capital B. Lo and behold, the announcer comes on and…"

"Yes, yes, David I heard the broadcast too. What did Jeremy intimate?"

"He didn't intimate anything! He flat out told us he felt the head of "Sir Hand" as he called him. Saw him loading his gun—preparing to shoot RFK. Even said he watched him or felt him in the future crowd at the assassination site. He didn't know, of course, the name of the Ambassador Hotel in L.A. But I'm telling you he was right there—in the kitchen with that Sirhan guy just after midnight. From what I understand, RFK and his entourage planned to leave the hotel out the front door for some sort of press briefing since he just won the California primary. Everyone was excited. But a last-minute change in plans had him exiting through the passageway leading off the hotel kitchen. That's where Sirhan shot him. It was like Jeremy was some sort of eye in the sky like on the pyramid on the one-dollar bill."

"I don't know what to say, David. I've heard of psychics before, soothsayers and the like, seen it depicted on film—the stuff of suspense novels, for crying out loud. You're telling me that five days before Sirhan gunned down RFK your son hinted that an assassination might take place in California?"

"Yes. I hate to ask this, Dr. Rebovitz, and this may sound paranoid and a complete non sequitur—but does your secretary Velma type up all of your dictation?"

"Absolutely. She's a fast typist. Works all the hours in a week and then asks for more. Why?" Dr. Rebovitz already feared the answer and realized he should have paid more attention to the little voice in his gut at the point of hire. *What was Velma up to?*

"When I called your office first thing this morning, I asked to speak to you. She said you were out and asked if she could help. She said you and she were quote unquote a therapeutic team, and she does whatever she can to help your patients. Then she offered to have her husband Dan do odd jobs at the parsonage, I guess for free and, oh, she wanted to babysit Jeremy. Said she babysits all her nieces and nephews, happy to help, that sort of thing. More like aggressively happy to help. She gave me the creeps."

"I'm sorry. She was way out of bounds. I'll speak to her."

"No, please don't!" David said more loudly than he intended to. "I don't want to make a stink or let on. I have a big favor to ask and I know it's unorthodox. I can say that since I'm a pastor." Dr. Rebovitz laughed, which helped break the tension, or some of it. "Please, no more dictation—no more records. I really need you to burn any records you've created. Jeremy's gift is too explosive. Even ordinary people like Velma might want to use him for God knows what. Alex and I are firm on this point, Dr. Rebovitz. I must insist."

Dr. Rebovitz considered David's request for a moment. The silence seemed to David to last an eternity. But, five seconds later, Dr. Rebovitz approved. "I could not agree more. I'll not only burn the records, which is crazy from a medical malpractice defense posture—in fact, my malpractice carrier might drop me as uninsurable if they found out. You know, it's all about loss prevention—if you didn't document patient care, it never happened. But this may be just the time to *not* document! I'm going to further suggest we no longer meet in my office at all. I won't even calendar you, or Jeremy, that is. I'll tell Velma that we've severed the doctor-patient relationship because your child does not have an illness that insurance will pay me to treat.

That at least is a plausible explanation. How does that sound, David?"

"I could not have asked for more. I'm most grateful. Alex will be too. This gift of Jeremy's is a living nightmare. I don't know what we should do. Actually, as I say that, I have a potential ally in my church. A retired military man who may know a thing or two about how we should protect Jeremy, what steps we should take."

"David, whatever you decide, I'll support you every way I can. That's odd for a psychiatrist to let the patient dictate the course of treatment. Do you agree I still have a role in helping Jeremy build a filter—learn to turn off and on his gift, or at least keep it to himself?"

"Yes, Dr. Rebovitz. I almost forgot. The three of us discovered something last Friday about the gift. Apparently as they say, love really is blind. Jeremy was out in the yard playing with a neighbor boy, Jimmy. He showed up just as we were finishing lunch and had some new-fangled toy with him, a right-angle military scope. You look through one end and the telescopic feature allows you to see around corners. Anyway, Jeremy tested Jimmy by holding up his fingers, while Jimmy called out the count. I watched him from the window. Later we realized he didn't know I was watching—didn't 'feel my head.' Alex and I were shocked—after all that had happened over the last few hours, our discussions with you. Our takeaway lesson was that Jeremy gets to feel people's heads—empathize and read their minds when they get distressed, angry, or any of a number of hard-edged emotions. But not love. So we were watching him out of admiration. He is God's gift to us; we've always felt that way. Maybe when he feels safe, his 'eagle eye' lens switches off."

"OK. That's certainly a great working theory, as we medical professionals like to say. We almost need a differential diagnosis of this gift. When does it manifest? Why? Are there bio-chemical markers we can tag or trace? I keep thinking about Mass General's ability to test a patient's brain or scan it somehow. The FDA hasn't approved their scanner yet. It's such new technology, mostly untested, which carries its own set of risks, some unknown. So let's consider it as a placeholder. I do need to work one on one with Jeremy if I'm going to help him build his filter. I've been thinking. What if I met with him before your church services—early Sunday morning? I'm guessing you're the first one to get to your church. Does Alex go with you or does she arrive just before the services?"

David considered the question. "Oh, she goes later, but drops me off first. She runs back home to get all gussied up—you know, the preacher's wife and all. Plus, Jeremy sometimes needs her booster-rocket coaching to get a move on."

"Good. Then if he and I worked from 7:00 a.m. to 9:00 a.m. at my house, not my office, Alex could swing by and grab him with no one the wiser."

"Yes, I'll need to discuss this with Alex, get her take. We're putting a lot of trust in you and we've only known you for a hair's breadth period of time. Alex is not the people person I am. She needs time to bond with ideas and people. Let me get back with you."

CHAPTER 14

Wednesday June 5, 1968--Midafternoon
Accosting the Pastor

After hanging up, David decided he needed to run back to the church. The radio announced that RFK was still in serious condition and not expected to live. When David arrived, he was pleased to see that no more beer bottles had been laid out for the homeless men. Either Roger scared off the thugs or the thugs moved on to greener pastures. They say bullies act out of a deep sense of fear. David speculated on what that meant. *How would bullies hold up in Vietnam? Would they be stand-up guys, or the first to run? How bullies cope with fear, maladaptive as those mechanisms are, might also be a key to Jeremy's vision and gift. Was Jeremy tapping into something primal? What would one of these untested brain scans show? Would the scan tell us something new—help Alex and me connect the dots? What are the dots, I'm not even sure I know.*

As David walked up the steps, he saw a man sitting on the rail eyeballing him. "Hello Reverend. My name is Dan Brodie. Velma may have mentioned me to you when you called the office?"

Dan caught David off guard. David thought: *I'm the one that needs the judo lessons. This guy could fold me up like a pretzel, shake my pockets clean of loose change and drop kick me to the curb.* "Yes, she did mention you and that you're quite handy. I'm sorry. I told her we're all set here at the church and the parsonage as well for maintenance work. In fact, our church sexton is a jack of all trades—and a master of quite a few as well. Roger is a great guy," David finished, as the hairs rose up on the back of his neck.

"Oh yeah, Preacher, my Velma, she's not always good with details. Anyway, we have a saying in the shipyard: Jack may not master *any* of the trades he touches. That's what I figured with this Roger friend of yours. Even if he's as good as you say I bet he needs help now and again, and I could sure use the work."

As David listened, he couldn't help noticing that Dan was wearing shorts and that his knee was all taped up. It looked like a home doctoring job, not anything that a real physician would do unless he'd been drunk as a seaman on shore leave.

"Like I say, we're pretty much set, but I'll call Velma if Roger ever needs an extra hand. Say, looks like you banged up your knee pretty bad. What happened?"

"Ah, Preacher, you don't miss a trick. Yeah. I hurt it yesterday at the yard. Some fool swung a monkey wrench at a frozen bolt trying to loosen the damn thing. Don't you know he lost his grip and the wrench flew right into my knee. I'll be awright. Boss gave me the rest of the week off. That's why I came by. Can't lift a lot but I'm great with my hands. Also I can help babysit your kid if your missus, you know, needs one of them, whaddya call it, 'mother's days off?'

"'Mother's Day Out,' is what we call it here. My wife uses the service exclusively. Once again, I think we are all set, Mr. Brodie. I really have to get to work now so, if you'll excuse me, I have to run. Nice to meet you." David tried to gently exit.

"No, the pleasure's all mine, Preacher," Dan said with a tinge of derision. "I can tell I'm holding you up."

David, sensing the opening, said, "It's not that, I've just got to get on my visitation rounds."

CHAPTER 15

Thursday June 6, 1968--Morning
Taking Matters to the Dōjō

David got up early again and arrived at the karate/judo studio at 8:00 a.m. During breakfast, he and Alex had heard the final devastating news that RFK had died during the night. They sat in silence and then started reviewing the Velma/Dan problem. As they planned, Dr. Rebovitz called to say he had deleted the Dictaphone recording of Jeremy's chart entry and pulled the hard file from the cabinet. He assured Alex and David that he burned the paper record as kindling, which made for a cozy blaze in his living-room fireplace. "My wife was none the wiser," Dr. R pointed out. "That's part of our marital covenant—she knows not to invade my patient documentation. She's good that way, and it helps me keep my license and sense of ethics. I shredded the record ahead of time."

David thanked Dr. R for his discretion and then told him the story of Dan showing up in the afternoon at the church just yesterday, complete with a wounded knee.

"You mean he took the day off from the shipyard? Velma's always telling me they're hard up for money. Why would he skip work? This can't be good. They must be hatching a plan!"

"Maybe. Anyway, I'm scared enough now that *both* Jeremy and I are taking martial arts classes. Alex, too. I've started wondering if I need a gun! I wouldn't even know how to load one, let alone what kind to buy. I feel like I'm suddenly living in a parallel universe. Last night I dreamed that RFK and two Secret Service agents forced their way into our house, threw Alex and me in the basement after taping our mouths shut and handcuffing us, and then interrogated Jeremy on why he didn't call them with a warning. Like a five year old would know how to reach them, or that it was his duty as a U.S. citizen! I woke up in a cold sweat! And I must say that, now that RFK has died, there are lots of evil men out there who could manipulate Jeremy's gift."

"Oh, my," said Dr. R. as they ended the call.

****

David entered the dōjō and saw Mark doing paperwork in the adjoining office. Mark signaled for him to have a seat. "Can I get you some coffee? Grind the beans myself!"

"That sounds great, Mark. When you said you grind the beans, all I could think of was how you black-belt types break boards in half. Please tell me you use some sort of grinder."

"Funny guy. Yeah, that other stuff's just for show. No, I have this hand grinder. Takes a minute and makes a heck of a racket, but it really unlocks the beans' full flavor. My former master Sergeant, Chuck Ames, lives in Hawaii—on the big island, near Kona. Sends me the best beans in the world at cost. Great guy. Here, try a cup and don't be a wussy—no cream and sugar shall dilute this here nectar!"

David took one sip and some neuron in his brain fired telling him that, a.) this coffee was world class and, b.) maybe Mark could be trusted after all.

"So, why I came in…Let me get right to the point."

"Always a good place to start. You seem like a bottom-line guy."

"Yup, I try not to mince words. That's what Vanderbilt Divinity School does to you. Dismantles the "house of authority" and its cadre of Christian myths and half-truths, and then lays you bereft of all hope at the foot of the Cross."

"My, my, profundities this early. It's gotta be that Kona coffee kicking in, Preacher!"

"Yeah, sorry about that. I'm not here to convert you."

"Damn. I hoped you might take a shot. Maybe teach me a wee bit of theology in trade for your son's class fee. What do they pay you, Revy Baby, $8K a year?"

"Actually that's spot on, but they throw in the parsonage. Jeez, you're good."

"Accounting gene skipped a generation. When your parents are clueless on numbers, first-born son must step up."

"Any-who, back to the chase. Literally. What's the fastest you could teach someone like me, a half-wit with only one good arm, to defend myself in a street fight?"

"Slow down Revvy. Can I call you Revvy? Just kidding. Humor me. Tell everything to Sgt. Mark here, reverse priest/penitent privilege. What's said or done in this studio stays in this dōjō. Consider your whole family as part of our studio family. Really. I smell your fear and it ain't pretty, David."

"I'm not sure where to begin."

"Just start talking. I used to be an MP—you know, Military Police. I know how to interrogate. You just keep asking the same question over and over. "Did you murder Suzy Q? Did you murder Suzy Q?' Everyone or most everyone wants to tell the truth. Or, should I say, they don't want to lie—goes way back to their childhood. Guilt formation and that sort of thing. They'll say anything to avoid a direct lie, which brings in all sorts of tells. How often have you heard a politician, some arrestee or, say, a state senator, when the reporter asks, 'Did you embezzle that $50,000 from the Girl Scout Cookie fund?,' retort, 'I can't believe you'd ask me, a six-term senator with an unblemished record, such a hateful and biased question!' Then the reporter doesn't follow up. Let's the scumbag off the hook."

Dang, David thought. It would have been sport, good sport, to sic MP and black belt Mark on Dan and Velma. "No, my wife Alex and I are quite scared. I guess we are still in a state of shock, too. You'll be only the second person on God's green earth who has heard about 'the gift.' I'm not convinced it is a gift like your Kona coffee. Need another cup by the way. Good stuff."

As Mark poured and passed, David told Jeremy's story, his feeling heads gift, how Jeremy hadn't noticed David admiring his play with Jimmy and the combat scope, the thunder clap of RFK and "Sir Hand," along with Velma and Dan. Mark maintained eye contact and David could tell he had a remarkable capacity to focus. A discipline. *Guess that's part of the key that separates a good from a great interrogator.*

Mark took another sip from his second cup of coffee and remarked, "If this is all true and it appears to my MP ears that you're not holding back, *we've* got a pickle on our hands. You know the game of pickle, David?"

"You mean that base path game—two bases, two guys with gloves—runner trying to beat the throws?"

"Exactly. That's what we've got here only Jeremy's the ball and you and Alex are at home plate—you want to make the catch—save Jeremy and kill the runner!"

"I don't like the sound of this at all—*kill the runner!*" David said shaking his head.

"OK, let's backtrack. When I was in the military we cherished inside Intel. World War Two—the enigma machine. You've heard of it?"

David thought for a minute and then said, "Yes. The signal machine the Nazis used to encrypt the mission orders for their U-Boats. I'm a history buff, by the way."

Mark nodded. "Good. Jeremy has all the code books ever devised by any military power in history. He's fluent in simple languages from Morse code, and I emphasize code, to crypto graphics. It doesn't matter that our military could come up with some unbreakable code. *Someone* has to receive and *understand/decipher* the coded message. Are you following me?"

"Yup, but I feel great trepidation."

"I'm glad. I want you scared. First, I'm not going to tell anyone. Second, let's trade your theology for my defense and intel."

David thought for a minute. The dōjō smelled of sweat and something else—angst maybe? "I can't help but think that theology lessons aren't valuable enough to repay your confidence and training."

"That's the beauty of it. Two guys making a deal, each gets what they want out of the bargain. I believe lawyers, the death knell of all of us, call it consideration. We'll need to do some accelerated work with you three. Ever boxed before, David?"

"No. Of course my bout with polio kept me away from that sport, and my pacifism meant I'd never volunteer for Vietnam. I've never been a fighter. I gotta tell you though, I'm struggling to figure out what Gandhi would have done in my place!"

"I can work with that. You thought I'd call you a pansy or at least think it, right?"

David reflected a moment before responding. "If the shoe fits...."

"Come to class with Jeremy this afternoon and bring Alex if she's free. Just spectate. You'll be surprised what you can drink in just by watching my ten to twelve year old students practice. They are young and supple, bendable—as my mom liked to say. Malleable might be a better word. Young minds and bodies not fully formed. You, on the other hand, like most adults, untrained, are full of bad habits. You mentioned that House of Authority your Vaaahnnnderbilt professors destroyed for you. The bedrock of your old beliefs. That's what I'm going to do for you, Part II. Better yet, let's get started right now. First, take off your shoes and socks. You've heard of stop, drop and roll when you're on fire? That's good wisdom. Second, when most people are punched, particularly in the head, they not only stop, they drop and do not get back up. I want you to focus on your Chi—your heart and power center—it flows from just above your hip. In a fight, your stance is everything. It's what centers you and drives your defense. That's what I'll teach you—a defense or a set of defenses. We don't have time for you to learn offense—except a wee bit of Krav Maga. Ever heard of it?"

"No. It sounds other worldly," David said.

"The Israeli military uses it—sort of their specialty," Mark pointed out. "Some guy named Imi Lichtenfeld invented it. He was some sort of boxer and wrestler combined, of the Hungarian persuasion, I think. The reason it works so well for the Israelis is that it's not all about fancy theories. It aims to teach soldiers how to fight in real-world situations. The techniques are brutal. You neutralize the threat and get away from the danger immediately. Live to fight another day. If need be, you go on offense and try to cripple your opponent with anything at hand, a pen for example, or a brick—then aim for the eyes, groin, neck, the gut, or if you get the chance, break fingers and smash a knee. Yes, I can break boards and Bric-O-Blocks. But that's after years, years mind you, of daily practice, three to four hours a day. Takes about 10,000 hours to reach my level. If what you've described is true, we have maybe 30 hours at most to get you ready. But that's good. We have a timeline, a set of deliverable objectives and a weapon no one else has: Jeremy."

"What do you mean? Jeremy's no more a weapon than I am, or Alex, at least without a gun."

Mark chuckled at the misplaced sentiment. "True, true, but think of Jeremy in the contexts of martial arts and military tactical orthodoxy. We're blitzing those houses of authority. For unlike you and me, Jeremy can see your enemies coming and tell you their plans! Apparently, from three-thousand miles away."

For the next 25 minutes before the next class started, Mark put David through some basic paces. "You're making some progress. Now clear on outta here before my next class starts. See you this afternoon at 2:30 p.m."

CHAPTER 16

Thursday June 6, 1968--Afternoon
Mark's Studio

David, Alex and Jeremy arrived promptly at 2:25 p.m. for their lesson. Mark greeted them and fitted each with the white karategi or "GI" uniform. The rest of the class was already sparring, with most students arriving 15 minutes early. Mark invited Jeremy to join the other students and offered the Hergenroeders chairs off to the side. He took the class through its paces—offering Jeremy a bit of extra help. Halfway through the session, Mark asked Matthew Hannah, a more advanced student, to spar with Jeremy. As the group watched, Matthew tagged Jeremy a few times, gently. But, as they continued sparring, something strange and wonderful began to happen. While Matthew attempted various fakes and parries, Jeremy soon met each one with a clumsy, indelicate block.

David and Alex nodded, appreciating that Jeremy was feeling the head of Matthew with each parry. Mark, in turn, was struck by Jeremy's remarkable strength. Jeremy easily stood his ground—much more so than Mark had ever seen in a five year old. Soon Mark intervened when the boys' sparring moved toward a stalemate. He then spent the remaining time teaching the whole class the art of falling.

After class everyone but the Hergenroeders departed. Mark suggested they sit in the middle of the studio on the mats.

"Jeremy, why are you here?" Mark asked.

"Because my parents are scared of me?" Jeremy offered. "Or, not afraid of me, but scared of what I might tell them I feel in other people's heads?"

Mark knew immediately that this child had a serious gift. "Jeremy, your Dad visited with me earlier today and told me of your secret talent. You seem like a nice boy to me. Have you ever heard the saying, 'Nice guys finish last'?"

"No sir."

"OK, well sometimes it's true. Nice guys, polite people, often let other people take advantage of them. Why do you suppose that is?"

Jeremy scrunched up his face as he thought for a minute. "I don't know, sir."

"Well, I do," Mark remarked quietly. Jeremy sensed quietude in Mark's mind and spirit. Mark continued, "They don't want to hurt other people's feelings. They let themselves get taken advantage of, get bullied. They hand over their time, talent and treasure and hurt themselves in the process. They'll do anything to avoid conflict. Do you understand?"

"Maybe," Jeremy offered sheepishly.

"I put you in front of the class with Matthew today to teach you something."

"Yes sir."

"Do you know what the lesson was?"

Jeremy looked around the dōjō for a moment pondering the query. "Yes, the only person who can defend me is me?"

"Bingo! I was proud of you because you learned quickly. You adapted and my, you're remarkably strong for your age. Those other people I'm talking about give free rent in their heads to people who bully them. They feel like they're responsible for how those bullies...manipulators, feel. That's way too much responsibility—all you can manage is taking responsibility for yourself. Do you know what the scariest thing in the world is, Jeremy?" Mark turned to Jeremy's parents. "Do you, Alex? David?"

The family all looked at him awaiting the answer. David wanted to offer up fear, but was unsure. Jeremy felt David's head and then Mark's, but still didn't understand the point.

"No answer?" Mark grinned sympathetically. "Most of my adult students say fear, but fear is a good thing if and when you harness its energy. No, it's sound. Sound is all around us even when we're still in the womb. But then we're birthed only to get slammed with an entire world's white noise, unfiltered by our mother's protective belly. Imagine you are out in the wilderness, camping as a family. Let's even pretend you are in, say, Yellowstone National Park or some wild place where there are mountain lions and bears. We all know those animals are afraid of us, yet they have the teeth and claws that can rip us apart in seconds. We know this—have all heard the stories. You know what they did to Mt. Monadnock in New Hampshire several decades ago?"

As the Hergenroeders shook their heads, Mark continued. "Everyone in the late 1800s was sick and tired of the wolves decimating their livestock. Wolves hunt in packs and make a frightful yelping noise that carries over the wind for miles. Think about it. There you are in your tent, absorbing the call of the unseen wolves. They send a wrenching chill down your spine. You'd feel the same effect after hearing the growl of a cougar or a bear, or some predator cracking a stick a few feet from your tent. What creature is out there hunting nearby, trampling sticks? Our imagination runs wild."

"Back to Monadnock. Our forefathers decided to kill off the wolf population by setting fires all around the mountain. The flames roared toward the summit and Lord knows how much other wildlife burned alive. Not just the wolves. I tell you that story to remind you of two things—your family is a wolf pack, a small one yes, but a strong and smart one. You've been smart enough to know there are twigs breaking just outside your line of sight. Most folks would cower. You, however, have reached out for help. I'm going to teach you to make your own sound. Great warriors bellow when they are attacking, yes? Ever heard of the Rebel yell from the Civil War? Imagine you are encamped at night—and through the woods you hear scores of enemy soldiers yelling as they attack you from all directions. That's the image I need you to understand and turn to your advantage. First, you must yell back—from your Chi center, your strength, and rage a scream from those depths. Second, most of your enemies need quiet and stealth to destroy you. You counter with that rage—but only when you can't run. That's right, run. Live to fight another day."

The Hergenroeders took a collective deep breath. The dōjō's walls seemed to close in on them as they felt their fear rise in their throats. Jeremy, especially, felt his parents' deep-seated anxiety.

Sensing everyone's angst, Mark quietly said, "OK, let's practice a Rebel yell, shall we? I'll start. Close your eyes and listen; not with your ears but with your rage."

He let out a scream that shook David and Alex to their core. Jeremy, expecting it, feeling it, put his hands over his ears. "Jeremy, I need you to unblock your ears when I do it again!" shouted Mark. "I know it's hard, but just 'feel my head' as I do it. Get inside my mind—use your gift and tell me what you experience."

Mark roared again. Jeremy entered Mark's head, saw Vietnam, a wide open jungle, steamy after a long spell of rain. Mark was on night patrol, lying in wait, but starting to doze off. As his buddy, Chuck Ames, kept watch he clutched at Mark who had relaxed beside a swollen log. The crickets had stopped chirping as if their chief predator, the mossy tree frog, was hunting with night-vision goggles. "Hey, dude, wake the hell up," Chuck whispered. "Wake up the guys down the line." As Mark did so, he heard the Viet Cong bellow as they started racing towards the platoon's position, holding their fire until the last minute. But Master Sergeant Chuck, a Kansas farm boy, had taught his unit to feel sound in a new way—draw composure and energy from the fear. Like sunshine feeding the tobacco broadleaf.

As the Viet Cong raiding party launched their assault, Chuck said, "Wait, wait...now!" At that moment the unit roared back, louder than the approaching enemy, using and refocusing the VC's measure to push back. Caught off guard by the raging nemesis that used sound as their primary weapon, the VC soldiers stopped in their tracks, trying to make sense of what they were experiencing. Chuck's unit formed a semi-circle to start encroaching toward the VC. Their guns and voices suddenly silenced the VC who turned and ran for their lives, making easy pickings for Mark and his comrades.

"Jeremy what did you feel in my head?"

"You were in Vietnam, sir. I think in the jungle. Then your sergeant friend, Chuck...why did you call him 'gunny'—did he like guns?" Jeremy asked.

"Yes, Jeremy, he liked guns. He learned to shoot squirrels when he was your age. But let's not worry about farm boy Chuck. What else did you feel?"

"Sergeant Ames taught you to shout back louder than your enemy, but to wait and do it all at once. You waited, until those other guys were almost on top of you. I thought you might die!"

Mark smiled, "We thought so, too, and I'm glad you said that. Repeat after me, 'Today is a good day to die.'"

The Hergenroeders formed an impromptu choir and said in an academic monotone "Today is a good day to die."

"No!" shouted Mark. "Say it like you mean it." They tried again.

"Today is a good day to die!"

"Almost. You've almost got it. Again!"

"TODAY IS A GOOD DAY TO DIE!" the family screamed.

"You've almost got me convinced. One more time!" Mark implored them.

"But I don't want to die!" Jeremy shouted back.

"Good boy, Jeremy. That's what I need you three to understand. Today is *not* a good day to die. But you missed what we had learned about shouting when the Viet Cong soldiers ambushed us. Running away when your enemy has you in his gun sight brings certain death. We shouted instead just what I need you to rage for me. The VC didn't speak English. They didn't know what we were saying. But they sure felt it and our shouting scared them no end. It turned their world upside down. Suddenly the attacker was under attack. Your enemies will ambush you—when you see them coming through Jeremy's gift, wait, *wait,* then do what we did. Turn the tables. Now shout it out like you really feel it deep down. I'll join you. Ready, One, Two Three: *"Today Is A Good Day To Die!"*

Everyone caught their breath, the insight settling into their collective consciousness. "You did it," Mark declared. "There's one more element, one more lesson here. When you shout that line 'like you feel it' you're telling your soul that there's nothing left to lose. You're as good as dead anyway—so fight back with everything you've got. It's like the old saying about not going after a cornered animal. They've got nothing to lose, either. Make sense?"

"And David, I'll cancel my Sunday morning class in a couple of weeks and attend your service. Then I'll remind you in the receiving line what Christ's message was to Pilate: "Go ahead, do it, I'm not going to waste my breath on you. You've won this battle. Kill me and you've lost the war."

David thought for a moment. "I've never thought about the crucifixion that way, Mark. You've helped me find some courage. I'm grateful."

Next, Mark and the Hergenroeders worked on offensive Krav Maga maneuvers. Every move dirtier than the next, all unfair, but all guaranteed to shock their enemies. "And Rule Number One, run when you can so you can live to fight another day." Mark's rejoinder left the Hergenroeders brooding over how many more days they had left.

CHAPTER 17

Thursday June 6, 1968—Late Afternoon
Velma Reevaluates the Importance of Voice Tone

Earlier that same day, things were quiet in Dr. Rebovitz's office. As Velma busied herself with paperwork, the phone rang. "Dr. Rebovitz's office, Velma speaking, how may I help you?" As she rescheduled the patient, Velma felt pride in her welcoming voice. She knew she could soothe the most distressed and even psychotic patients. She believed she could channel healing powers through the phone lines, a vestige from her nursing avocation. Velma had attended a scripting class where she learned how important her word choices were. Scripting made all kinds of sense until she met a teacher in the grocery aisle one day. They got to chatting by the canned soups, comparing recipes, when the teacher, Paula Lovejoy, asked her if she worked outside the home. Paula had platinum-blonde hair in a pert haircut style that adorned her accouterments. She taught fifth grade at Edgerly Elementary, the same school that Jeremy was attending. Velma found her charming face and searching eyes bewitching.

"I'm the office manager for Dr. Rebovitz. He's a psychiatrist in solo practice, and specializes in pediatric problems."

Paula laughed warmly and said she really was in pediatric medicine too, only she specialized in mental and emotional development. "I teach at Edgerly Elementary, across town. Have for several years."

Not to be outdone, Velma announced, "I just finished my second scripting class—what to say to distressed patients. Quite insightful."

Paula paused for a moment and unwittingly gutted the whole class's purpose. "That's interesting. You know, I could say to my Edgerly students the most hateful things in a sweet tone, or vice versa, and combine my statements with nonverbal cues that would rock their worlds. I find nonverbal posturing to mean everything. I've got to run. Nice meeting you, Velma. How's that for tone—and all without a script!"

After paying for her groceries, Velma remembered something her grandfather told her when she was a little girl. "My lawyer could tell you how to go to hell in such a way that you'd look forward to making the trip!" As Velma left the store, she reached into her ample purse, grabbed the CEU training manual entitled *Scripting for Patient Success and Increased Practice Revenue*, and hooked it into the nearest trash bin.

CHAPTER 18

Friday June 7, 1968; 3:30 p.m.
Office Politics: A Mobster Needs a Helping Hand

S haken out of her reverie while typing up a chart, Velma answered the line and heard the caller say, "Yo, Velma, this is José. We gotta talk." Velma shuddered. *Could this be the same José who beat up Dan and stole his winnings? Oh God, not more crap. Dan would be the death of her yet!*

"I'm sorry. I don't show a José as one of Dr. Rebovitz's patients. Would you like to make an appointment, sir?" Velma tried her best to sound sincere and clueless at the same time.

"Velma, honey, I'm just down the street at a pay phone and you're wasting my dime. My new business partner Dan ain't showed up to work in three days," José chirped. "What's even worse, I gave him money for a train ticket. He owes me. What say you?" José dripped out his sarcasm like maple syrup on blueberry pancakes.

"Oh, he called in sick. He gets sick pay, so he'll still be good for the debt he owes you, Mr. José, is it? Do you have a last name?" Velma asked as she started choking on her own stupidity. *Why did I ask that? He'll know I'm trying to get him in trouble with the cops!*

"Listen lady, I didn't just get off the Greyhound from pickin' apples at some outta town orchard. It ain't even apple season. In fact, why don't I just c'mon over and pay you and Dr. Vicks-Vapo-Rub a visit? Right now. I bet I could scare you all up some business, help with the collections activity. Got any deadbeats owing you? You toten' the note for any a dem psychos?" Maple syrup again, sarcastic flavor.

Velma hung up and then realized that was a mistake too. The phone rang again and she picked up the receiver saying, "Look, Mr. José, I'm sure Dan will make things square with you. In fact we have a little secret of our own that might help you with your collections…" Velma's voice trailed off in fear.

All Velma heard was static. Then, of all people, David spoke. "I'm sorry, Mrs. Brodie, I must have caught you at a bad time or we had a funny connection. This is David. Reverend Hergenroeder. I just needed to let Dr. Rebovitz know I had a great visit with his mom at Pinehurst. I found Mrs. Rebovitz alert and engaging."

Tone is everything, but Velma forgot in her shock. "Err, oh my yes, um, Reverend Hergenroeder, I *am* sorry. Yes, of course, I'll get the message to Dr. Rebovitz as soon as he gets back to the office. He's at juvenile court testifying in a case. Thank you for calling."

She hung up abruptly and missed cradling the phone as her hands shook uncontrollably. Her paranoia kicked in: Did David hear what I said about collections? About the secret? Oh my God. I should pull Jeremy's file to hide it from this José character. She ran to the cabinet and looked at the tabs, L, M, N, here it is, O, but no file! *I swear I put*

it in there the other day—made a new label and everything.
What happened to it?

The phone rang louder than it ever had before. Velma grabbed it. "Hello, this is…"

"Cut the crap lady. Nice play keeping the phone off the hook. You're really getting on my last nerve," José asserted, the maple syrup now a thing of the past. "Now where might I find Mr. Dan *right* now? I need to meet with him ASAP and he ain't at your house. I checked and, yes, your back door is in sudden need of repair."

"Jeez, Sir, I, um, don't know where Dan is. I thought he was at home resting his sore knees," Velma said, trying her best to ingratiate herself with José.

"Ma'am, Ma'am," José said in a caustically sweet voice. Velma realized again how spot on Paula Lovejoy had been. Tone also could scare the bejesus out of anyone.

"I don't mean to pry, but Danny ole boy better reach out to me and fast. As his creditors, my cultural associates and I deem ourselves unsecured. We must have our security. Tell him to join us for a party *tonight* at the batting practice cages in North Boston! Then, after our workout, we'll hit Antonio's in the Combat Zone!"

Nothing Dr. Rebovitz had taught Velma about psychotic or neurotic patients had prepared her for José. He exuded pure evil—like a sociopath, lots of charisma and a magnetic personality, but evil through and through. "Oh God, please don't hurt my Dan. He's all I got. Look, we have something cooking that we think will make you a pot of money. Forget Dan's salary for five months—that's small change. Enough to pay off Dan's debt with interest a hundred times over."

"I'm all ears, lady. I've heard lots of hare-brained schemes before and I don't even like the Easter Bunny, you got that? Just what in hell's name are you saying?"

Velma tried mightily to control her breathing. "OK, OK, well Dr. Rebovitz has this special patient…"

Before Velma could spit out the next sentence in walked Dr. Rebovitz. "I'll have to call you back Sir, the Doctor's…" Velma couldn't get a word in edgewise with José screaming at the top of his lungs "Don't you hang up on me…!"

"Who was that, Velma? I thought I heard shouting," Dr. Rebovitz queried. When psychiatrists ask patients questions, they exercised great restraint in awaiting an answer, as they'd learned to do in residency training. Silence often is their best tool. And most people hate silence—they'll fill it with all manner of drivel. Velma was no different.

"Oh, ah, it's just, no, they weren't screaming ah, it was the, ah, mechanic at the Getty station trying to stick us for a warranty repair. No way I'm taking my car to that clown for repairs." Velma marveled at her ability to lie in the clutch. Just like the holiday cartoon about the Grinch who stole Christmas. Velma took lying to a whole new level.

"All right," Dr. Rebovitz responded. Velma thought she caught some of José's maple syrup in his voice. She was still shaking, which Dr. Rebovitz registered on his medical radar. Velma found David's message on the floor under her typewriter stand. "Sir, Rev. Hergenroeder called. He just wanted you to know he had a good visit with your mother. Said she was lucid."

"Perfect. He'll help keep her mind supple and active. Nothing like engaging social discourse. David has such a healing presence. I picked up on it immediately."

"Sir, I meant to ask you." Velma started, "I was doing routine filing and sent a bill to Mrs. Foster Nelson for her son Jason. And I noticed the Hergenroeder boy's file was missing."

Dr. Rebovitz gave Velma a confounding look. "Yes, I decided it was not worth pursuing. Boy's fine. Healthy and wise, if not wealthy. No need for a file. Plus, I don't want a psychiatric record buried in the boy's past if we can help it. In fact, I'm advising David to consider the whole matter as a fact-finding visit concerning generic issues related to normal pediatric development and cognition. No worries."

"Thank you for clarifying. I was afraid I misfiled it. Looked everywhere. Sir, would it be OK if I leave a few minutes early today? I forgot I have a 4:30 p.m. appointment at Mindy's Hair Salon in Cleghorn. A bit of a drive with rush hour approaching and all," Velma asked hopefully.

Relieved to have her leave the office, Dr. Rebovitz said, "Sure, go ahead." His gut told him that his trusted secretary was up to no good. And that screaming on the phone as he arrived. *Her car is so past its warranty period the vehicle qualifies as a jalopy.* On a lark and just to satisfy his curiosity, he phoned the Getty station to ask about her car. No, the mechanic said, no one brought in a Dodge Coronet Lancer today. The attendant said, "I'd have paid attention to that car with those monster tail fins. They don't make 'em like that anymore!"

Dr. R said, "Must have been the dealer then, sorry to bother."

Just down the street from the Rebovitz office, José and Ricardo played stakeout. Sure enough, they saw Velma emerge in a frenzied run to her car. Ricardo chuckled, "Man, Dude, you sure put the fear ah God into her. What the hell did you say to her from that pay phone?"

"I tol' her, a.) We need assurances about our money, and b.) We're inviting Dan to join us at the batting cages in the North End. We'll take Dan-O out on the town. He's gonna make partner someday. Soon as he pays his dues. He's in a new union where we weld everyone's mouth shut. That way, we keep things in the family. Ciao!"

Ricardo pulled in behind Velma as she drove. She made an easy mark, always signaling way ahead of every turn, even braking for a bull pigeon trying to ply his wares on a would-be mate.

"Hey José! Check it out up ahead. That bad boy pigeon tryin' to woo the ladies—in the middle of the street. Dude, get with the program. All the blood's drained from your head!" Ricardo announced to José's guffaws. "Frickin' pigeon's about to get crushed."

"Yessirree," answered José. "Won't even know what's hit him."

"He forgot his aftershave man! All the ladies is runnin' away!" Ricardo roared.

José laughed so hard he almost spit up his meatball sub sandwich. Ricardo just shook his head.

Velma pulled into the Brodie's matchbox house neighborhood. Her home had "deferred maintenance" and "fixer upper" scrawled all over the roof and siding. When the family's whole focus is on gambling, like the pigeon to his quarry, they tend to lose perspective. A car will run over the strutting pigeon. The mob will get its due from the unlucky gambler.

As Velma got out of her Coronet, Ricardo pulled in three inches shy of her bumper. The big Caddy dieseled a bit before the engine finally quit. José said to Ricardo, "I thought I tol' you to pour some a dat Marvel Mystery Oil down the carburetor. Free up dem stickin' valves for chrissakes. Least that's what our Rican boys is always telling me. Lessons from their shop class."

"Yeah, yeah," answered Ricardo. "You're keeping the lady waiting in a cold sweat."

José jumped out of the car. "Velma, Velma, Velma! We finally meet in person. No sense getting out your keys. Back door's wide open!" José pointed.

Just then Dan hobbled out of the garage, shock registering on his face. Every part of him radiated his desire to turn tail and run. Except his right knee locked up instantly. Dan fell to the ground in pain and Velma ran to help him up. Now she was spitting angry, her good-sense governor turned down to its lowest setting. "You SOBs did this to him and you wonder why he didn't go hit the shipyard the last three days. Great strategy on handling your accounts," Velma said, spewing venom.

For not the first time today, Velma immediately regretted her outburst. The compelling rebuttal came in the form of Ricardo's meat hook doing his anti-gravity trick on 96-pound Velma. She thrashed at him, to no avail, as he held her away and pointed. "Yo, José, check out the female clown! She wants to defend Dan. Does a better job of it than he done for his own self Tuesday night."

Ricardo let go. Velma dropped to the pavement, scraping her right knee and both hands. She turned her ankle when she reached to massage her limbs to salve the cascading pain. She started bawling softly.

"All right you two get up and inna da house. Velma, dahlink, go make us a high ball or a Manhattan and let's hear all about your little secret." José prided himself on articulating so well and even made the quote signs, pitching Ricardo into stitches.

****

Dr. Rebovitz pulled out David's Rollstone number and called.

"Rollstone Church," said Linda Dunn, the secretary.

"Yes, I'm trying to reach David. This is Dr. Rebovitz. He and I are friends and I wondered if I might speak with him."

Linda, ever cautious about "friends' seeking money or a hand-out, doctor or not, hesitantly replied, "No, I'm sorry Doctor, he's been out all day. You might try him at home. I'm not allowed to give out that number, though."

"Of course, I understand. I never give out my home number either. You never know with patients. I'm guessing it's the same with all manner of church callers. I have the number and will try him there. If I do miss him, would you please tell him I called anyway?"

"Will do, sir." Linda wrote the note but realized she forgot to get Dr. Rebovitz's number. She liked to be thorough, since David had so many meetings including all the pressure of getting the confirmation class ready for their big Sunday presentment in two weeks. Biggest class yet of sixth graders, not to mention proud parents.

Dr. Rebovitz called the Hergenroeder's parsonage. "Hello, this is Jeremy Hergenroeder speaking. May I help you?" Unbeknownst to Dr. R, Alex and David finally had to give up trying to stop Jeremy from answering the phone. They compromised by teaching him to answer in a professional manner.

"Oh good, Jeremy, this is Dr. R. How are you?"

"I'm fine. We took judsu today."

"Do you mean judo?"

"Yes, judo, that's it. And we learned to scream that this is a good day to die!'"

"That's good, Jeremy. Not something you want to tell anyone but your psychiatrist, OK?"

"Huh"? Jeremy said, confused. Not used to adults other than his grandmother spending time talking to him on the phone, Jeremy asked, "Do you need my Dad? I'm not really supposed to talk too much on the phone to church folk."

"Yes, please get your dad," Dr. R said while suppressing a Santa-sized chuckle. Don't want to embarrass a young patient. Not good bedside manner. "Jeremy, don't worry about me. I don't go to your church."

"Dad!" Jeremy yelled with the phone a bit too close to his mouth. "Phone's for you. It's Dr. R!"

"Hello, Dr. R., this is David. How are you?"

"Please call me Azriel."

"OK, Azriel it is."

"Listen, I hate to say this, but Velma's up to no good. She found out that Jeremy's file was missing," Dr. R warned. "I explained that, after consulting with you, we decided Jeremy didn't need psyche help after all and it was just a developmental advisory on a matter of cognition. Not sure she bought it or understood my jargon. The worst part is that, as I arrived at the office, she was fighting with someone on the phone."

David caught the alarm in Dr. R's voice. "Yeah, I've got another piece to the Velma puzzle. Two pieces actually," David offered. "I called your office earlier to speak with you. When I called, Velma obviously thought I was someone else—maybe the person she was fighting with. She got quite a start when she realized *I* was on the line and not the other caller. I covered the issue by saying I was following up to let you know I visited your mother. By the way, what time did you show up at the office?"

"Three-thirty."

"I called just before then. Anyway, she answered the phone by saying she and Dan were prepared to 'make things square' with a José person and they had a 'little secret' that would help José with his 'collections.' I guess the second puzzle piece is that I stumbled on Dan waiting on the church step for me on my day off, Wednesday. I just happened to go in to the office. Anyway, he got all gooey friendly in an aggressive way trying to sell me on his handyman services for the church and parsonage. When I demurred, saying Roger, our sexton, handled everything, he switched tactics and offered Velma's babysitting services. Does she have a babysitting sideline or something?"

"Not that I'm aware of," said Dr. R.

David pressed on. "Dan's face looked bruised—like he ran into the business end of a cement mixer. And he had a pronounced limp, with a piss-poor gauze job on his right knee. Put two and two together, add in José and collections, and I get Dan over his head in a gambling debt or something with the Puerto Rican mob."

"Oh God," said Dr. R. "That all makes sense. Velma left early, allegedly for a hair appointment. She claimed the José caller at 3:30 p.m. involved an argument over warranty service at the Getty station for her Dodge Coronet Lancer. I called Getty and confirmed she was lying. I didn't think Getty Oil provided warranty service for Dodge cars. I'm sure hers is a 1958 model. And when did Dodge start giving warranties that extend ten years? Sell 'em before they hit 75,000 miles, my Dad always said—a rule I still live by, FYI."

As he mulled Azriel's information, David looked out his back window to the hill behind the house. The wild raspberry patch that stretched for a good half acre would soon deliver its fruit. Alex made a fine jam out of the fruit—it lasted well into the winter months. Great with toast complemented by morning coffee—Chock Full O Nuts, the heavenly coffee. "What should we do Azriel? Or, what should I do?"

"Hell if I know. We can't call the police. It would make no sense unless we told the truth, the whole truth and nothing but. Including the RFK prediction."

CHAPTER 19

Friday June 7, 1968—Late Afternoon
Back at the Brodie House

José waited for his cocktail expectantly. He lounged on the Brodie couch, noting how the middle cushion had worn thin from Dan-O lounging as he watched the idiot box. The floral patterns of the fabric were pock-marked with odd brown spots. The house smelled a tad musty, testament in José's mind that Velma couldn't work full time, clean house and cover Dan's gambling. Supergirl would have had trouble with that task list. Meanwhile, Ricardo watched Velma make the whiskey sours, with a powder mix. Dan came out of the bathroom with a new knee wrap. He was wearing a sleeveless t-shirt and still had on the plaid shorts that only served to highlight his knee wrap. His demeanor failed to intimidate. Welding was hard work and Dan had the muscle pedigree to show for it. He knew he was no match for the neckless cultural associates, however.

Dan slipped quietly into the living room. José said nothing, letting the silence and his unwelcome countenance do his menacing. José knew he had Dan for life, a modern-day version of indentured servitude. He guffawed about his five-lie insight. Sometimes his brain surprised even him.

"Dan, you want a whiskey sour?" asked Velma from the kitchen.

"Sure, make it a double."

José laughed again. Velma brought in the drinks, sat down and waited. Ricardo sat his big frame on the love seat, no love emanating from his visage. He scratched what for anyone else would have been his neck. No neck, just torso extension. José continued his silent routine. Prime negotiating strategy. Hell, they weren't negotiating. They'd give up their little secret and soon.

"Awright…Velllllmmmmaaaah! Like I said on da phone, d'hell's dis package, yo little secret?"

Dan started to speak and Ricardo slapped the side of his head. "Shut up, bub. Let's not add any more lies to your extended line of credit."

Dan cowered into his chair. He belted down the double in three loud gulps. Now his knee hurt worse than ever.

Velma shouted, "OK, we need some consideration. I could lose my job for handing this client, this patient, over to you. Dan and I need you out of our lives. Tonight."

"Fat chance, lady. If I like what this secret is, and *if* I think we can use it, and *if* it works, and *if* I don't draw jail time for using it, and Ricardo comes out clean, along with my other colleagues, then and only then might I let you and Dan live. Got it? Now, spill before I ask Ricardo to help with this deposition. You are under oath…now where's the family Bible?" Amused at José's linkage of scripture to this legal proceeding, the men laughed so hard they started hacking.

"I see your point, José. You're calling the shots. I'd hoped to grab this kid's file today but it seems the good doctor ran off with it and I didn't make a carbon copy. I honestly didn't understand the importance of this patient's amazing power until I'd nearly finished the dictation."

"All right...out with it," José barked. "We got a little Clark Kent here, or what?"

Velma twitched. "This kid's better than Superman. He reads people's minds and they don't have a clue. He's only five, innocent as the baby Jesus himself. Truly, this kid's got the winning lottery ticket, the Olympic Gold Medal in the downhill. Actually, in every event."

José let out a deep breath. He reflected a moment. "You're telling me this kid, standing right here in front of us, could tell me what's going through Dan's pea brain right now? That's no trick. I know Dan wants to kill me *and* Ricardo. He thinks we're 'over bearing,' right Dan?"

Everyone looked at Dan and saw that José had nailed it. Dan's eyes darkened, his hatred conflicting with his fear. He didn't utter a word.

"Awright, who is this kid? What's his name, Puddin' Tane, and where's he live?"

Velma crossed the point of no return. "His name is Jeremy N. Hergenroeder. His dad is David, the minister at Rollstone Church—right on Main Street. Named for the big rock overlooking the city."

Ricardo reacted. "I get it, he's a PK—usually the wildest hellion in any church. Holier than thou when the adults are looking, regular El Diablo when they ain't. So, how does he read minds?"

"I don't know," Velma answered. "The doctor was going to help him 'filter' his talent. Best I can tell, Dr. Rebovitz and Jeremy's parents wanted to teach him not to blurt out what folks are thinking—'cause it scares the heck out of them—and to use his gift sparingly."

"I gotta think about this!" José announced. "What are you thinking he can do for us, pick the winner every time at Wonderland Greyhound Park, Suffolk Downs maybe or, hell, better yet, screw with the minds of one of those Yankee pitchers like Mel Stottlemyer? Could he get into the heads of our beloved Red Sox—we lost last year to the Cards in seven games. We'll boost old Jim Lonborg I tell you. Get Yaz to win the Triple Crown again!"

Velma's temper flared. "No, you're not listening, José!"

"Watch your tone with me, missy. My patience has worn as threadbare as this here couch."

There I did it again, Velma realized. *My tone getting me in trouble. Paula, where are you when I need you?* "My apologies. This kid is five years old. He's just a baby practically. Completely innocent. He doesn't understand the gift any more than his parents do. That's why they came to our office. Get a handle on it. Focus it. But protect the family at all costs. Think of using the gift in a grandmaster chess tournament. Imagine whispering into the ear of your guy to tell him the opponent's next move. No, not the next move—the next four moves!"

"Chess, there ain't no money in chess. That's just stupid," Ricardo said dripping his macho sarcasm. "She's wasting our time, José!"

"No, please listen," Velma begged. "Imagine getting him into a casino or some situation where you've got to know what some guy, some enemy of yours is thinking. Presto chang-o, just ask Jeremy. He's a funny kid. Says he 'feels other people's heads.'"

"You mean he has to touch their heads to tune in his special radio station?" José asked incredulously.

"No, that's just what he calls it. 'Feeling heads.' He's really smart. Feels other people's vibes—like he's reading a radar screen of your thoughts. Problem is he's only five. You can't take him into Antonio's, I guess. Or maybe you could. Get him in front of the blackjack dealer. But the pit boss might catch on fast. I don't know. I'm not a criminal, that's your specialty."

José did not suffer insults any better than he did fools. But this time he decided he'd make an exception. Just this once. He'd hold off jack-slapping Velma into the next town for now. His stock in trade was providing needy clients the services they couldn't get themselves. José thrived as a connector—resources meet needs, for a price. And this Jeremy character might just be his ticket to a really big score where he'd take down his competition once and for all.

CHAPTER 20

Friday June 7, 1968
The Cultural Associates, Fitchburg High School and a Barkeep Named Trixie Calls the Police Department

What José affectionately called his "cultural associates" really had matured into an organized crime outfit called the "Rican Rangers." He named their group "rangers" to match the unintended insult found in the name of the Lone Ranger's sidekick, Tonto, which means stupid in Spanish. Rather than a special handshake, they shared that common joke. They'd yell "Tonto" after most big jobs and guffaw at their brilliance. Best of all, hardly anyone outside the Rangers spoke Spanish so they could communicate right in front of their marks with no consequences. They'd infiltrated local trucking firms, the lifeblood of American commerce. It proved a great choice, given the demise of the railways. Once President Eisenhower opened up the U.S. Interstate System, following the General's awe at the efficiency of Germany's Autobahn, America's destiny manifested through individual conveyances. America's arterial crime network naturally followed the new pathways.

While José, a founding member, often appeared to be a micromanager—showing up at Antonio's to hound Dan about a petty $500 loan—it was this leadership characteristic that drove his 'Rican Ranger' army's success. He and his cousins, Ricardo and Pilar, not only grew up in the Puerto Rican ghetto of small-time Fitchburg, they ingratiated themselves into the community like David did with his congregation. This intimacy belied their delight that small potatoes Fitchburg seemed too out of the way to ever fall onto law enforcement's radar. Nothing of significance ever happened in Fitchburg. Nor did José or Ricardo, or eventually the younger Pilar, care that, thanks to city fathers filing a robust entry in a national competition, the National Civic League declared Fitchburg an "All American City."

José, Ricardo and Pilar spent their childhood honing their ability to assess weaknesses and opportunities in their peers and the local constabulary. This ability later flowed to their considering how to defy or avoid altogether other local criminal elements. Their practiced talent finally led them to figure out an in with local and regional trucking firms. Never attack directly—always outflank your competition! Ever the envy of local youth, the threesome made their move by recruiting only the best and brightest to learn auto diesel mechanics.

The Puerto Rican teens they enlisted soon became expert big-rig mechanics and drivers. Ironically, Fitchburg High School's auto mechanics instructor, Ray Peterson, was only too happy to accommodate the Puerto Rican students' sudden interest in his classes. Often thought of as troublemakers from broken homes, the "PR" students excelled at their studies, all under the watchful eye of...José. In order to get his or her weekly stipend, each student had to route all grade cards and teachers' notes through José and Ricardo. They reviewed them and tracked progress as well as any IBM mainframe could. Students who fell off the wagon were still supported in José's "corporation." As José's grandmother Daniella taught him, "many hands make light the work."

As the years unfolded, these PR graduates, with their close-cropped haircuts and pressed clothing, made quite an impression on the trucking firms' HR leadership. Rather than discriminate by excluding these Rangers, the companies held quarterly calls with Ray Peterson and the school's principal. "Send us more of these graduates please! We cannot get enough of them. Not only are they hard workers and safe drivers, they can repair their own rigs! Do you have any idea how much the money that saves us?"

Ray and the principal, Dr. Alfred Gonyer, a mouse of a man at 5-foot-3 inches tall at high tide, just beamed. Even the School Board showered accolades and awards on the school. Tonto.

****

Detective Rodney McNamara, the third generation of Irish émigré parents, joined the Fitchburg Police Department right out of Leominster High School. Leominster borders Fitchburg to the south and made for a great rivalry with school sports. McNamara was a wily student of game theory, long before game theory hit the popular lexicon. He didn't even know his special aptitude had a famous underlying theory. He just studied people, other cops, his kids, the local priest—whose 12-minute homilies he admired for their theological economy—and, above all, the local hoodlums. His concentrating ability could match any chess grand master, only he didn't play the game.

What surprised everyone who met Rod was his shock of electric red hair that rocketed into view when he took off his cap. Especially at high noon, full sun. His wife Agnes, also of the Irish bloodline, brooked no criticism from Rod on how their home operated. After the first two weeks of their 18-year marriage, he offered none. For her part, Agnes liked to advise Rod on his case work—but only when he was inclined to include her on his schemes and theories. He got his detective shield the old-fashioned way; he studied hard and aced the exam. Most other FPD detectives had not had the same temerity. What they lacked in aptitude, however, they more than made up for in political connections.

The Police Department must be funded. That meant guns, cars, foot patrols and above all else, pensions—which kick in when officers hit the magic age of 55. These expenditures required real tax revenue. When Mayor Sean Fitzpatrick called Chief Tim Tolliver about a detective candidate, Chief Tim took the hint and greased the applicant's file. It's the way of the world, heralded as graft, or mutual back scratching, or the Peter Principle. No matter, when the incompetent detritus flowed downstream, it just meant Rod had to rely on his wits instead of his compadres from the Keystone Cops. To some of them,

"Lock and Load" meant burning through a fifth of vodka after their shift ended.

Rod was doing game theory at his desk on Friday morning, enjoying his cup of java when the phone rang. A local barkeep named Trixie McLoughlin, also of the Irish red vintage, offered a tip. "Listen, detective, you didn't hear it from me, but there's some smuggling outfit called the 'Rican Rangers' moving in for the kill." That's all she said, except out of habit she gave him her first name. She warned him not to track her down or ever ask for any more tips. "I gave you their name and they are into trucking, big time. Good-bye!"

"Trucking?" Rod said to himself. *What in hell's name is going on with a smuggling operation that only a barkeep knows about? This is beyond bizarre*, Rod thought, not yet realizing that his twin sons might help him find the answer.

His boys, Rodney Jr., and Conor (who liked to call himself "Conor the First") were 15 years old and fascinated, not with girls, but auto mechanics. They could do anything to a car and it was Rod's own dang fault. He liked to tinker with his 1958 Ford F-150 pickup and they, at first, liked to watch. The truck was a monster. Ford dubbed the model "Super Duty" equipping it with a huge V-8 engine that boasted a whopping 534 cubic inches of power displacement.

"Mom, we're going out to the garage to help Dad tune the truck!" was the twins' popular refrain, starting at age four. "OK, Mom?" Agnes would just wince. "You boys did that last Saturday. Why is it out of tune already? Leave your father be!" she'd implore to an empty kitchen. "Ah,

Ma, the points...they're off a tad!" This from youngsters whose future probably would depart from the college track. They definitely would play a role, however, in whether their father could help Jeremy live.

CHAPTER 21

Saturday June 8, 1968—Morning
Fitchburg High's Auto Mechanics Program and Musings in the McNamara Garage

Rod Jr. and Conor had taken an immediate liking their sophomore year to the mechanic's teacher, Mr. Ray Peterson. The mechanics program was a crown jewel in the curriculum at Fitchburg High, and not because of the PR influx. Ray looked the part of the absent-minded professor: round glasses always about to slide off his face, ruddy complexion, and a purple veined, bulbous nose, though not from imbibing alcohol thank you, and a white handkerchief, grease spotted, a constant appendage from his pants' pocket. When students in shop class asked Ray a question, he'd often say, "Humph, that's a good one. Now let me t'ink a bit. Anyone help an old codger like me with a theory? Yes? Then speak up or forever hold your man wrench!" The all-male class would cackle and roar their approval. To the chagrin of the Ranger corps cadets, however, Rod Jr. or Conor usually had the answer first.

Ray always started class with a group question. Friday's query: "Awright men, what are the four strokes of an internal combustion engine?"

"1.) Intake; 2.) Compression; 3.) Power; and, 4.) Exhaust!" the student choir would howl back.

"Yes, and what do those strokes tell us?" Ray taught his students to focus their differential auto diagnoses on those strokes. "Any one of them goes wrong and you know where to look! Intake problems—check the carburetor and manifold. Car's got to breathe just like you! Compression—how do my cylinders work today, are my valves a-leakin,' rings worn down? Power! You got to get your date home—are those plugs clean? Is the battery juicing you? Fuel line OK? How about that little ole fuel filter? Clogged? Something caught in your throat? Same principle! Suppose the motor's fine, now it revs, but you ain't moving! Work your way back. Transmission gears worn out or slippin? Don't forget your belts, boys. And, lastly, exhaust. Is it blue and stinky? Check your rings again. Foul and black?" And on it went, like an attending physician pushing a new group of medical students. Drill, drill, drill, every day. Rote memorization worked.

As Rod Jr. and Conor headed to the garage for their ritual Saturday session with Pops, they could hear him musing to himself under the hood of the family's truck, which only served to amplify his thoughts. "Alright, Trixie, just what in blazes you sayin'? Hi, ho Silver—the Rangers. Trucks! What do Puerto Ricans have to do with trucks? What do trucks have to do with Puerto Ricans? Who gives a rip? R.I.P., rest in peace my ass. What kind of game is she playing? Oh, and then she has the gall to say, don't call me about this. No questions! No-sir-ee and…Oh, hi boys. Just your old man a-tinkering and a-noodling. Hand me that timing light and start her up."

Conor found the Craftsman deluxe timing light, which looked more like a ray gun that an alien had left behind than a light tool. Rod Jr. started up the truck. "Dad, let me do it—you can supervise!" Conor begged. Rod Sr. stepped back and soon enough the bruiser of an engine purred like a tiger cub hungry for its momma's milk. Rod Jr. shut off the motor and Pops dropped the hood.

Conor spoke up. "Couldn't help over hearing you, Dad. Who's this Trixie person? You fixin' to bust her?"

Rod Sr. looked at Conor with a twinkle in his eye. "Nah, you know boys, this is police business and, remember, what you hear in the garage, stays in the garage, right?"

"Show 'nuff," said Rod Jr. "But ya know Dad, there's rumors at school about some group called the 'Rican Rangers.' I've seen that name graffiti'd on the bathroom stall."

"Yeah," said Conor. "It's some sort of culture club or something. Not what I would think of as gangland stuff, though."

"You know the guys who are Puerto Rican in our shop class really toe the line. Never late, never cutting class, no long hair, no smoking. They're almost goody two shoes. But they always have cold hard cash on them. I'm envious of the cash, at least. Say Pops, how's about bumping up our allowance as a finder's fee? Me and Rod could go all Sherlock Holmes on these guys. What say?" begged Conor.

Rod Jr. chimed in. "Yeah, Dad. Put us on the case. Let the negotiations begin," Rod Jr. used his best auctioneer voice.

"Look you two. I appreciate the mechanical help here. I really do. The last thing I need or the Chief needs are my boys on the prowl for trouble."

Conor busted out, "This goes all the way to the Chief? Dad, we had no idea!"

"Stop that right now. You overheard your old man chewing on a stupid tip from some hussy named Trixie. The Chief hasn't a clue about this. Jeez, ya' see how rumors get started? Oh man! Now let's put the tools back where they belong and see if your mom has worked up some lunch. I'm starved."

As the three McNamaras cleaned up, Rod Sr. started forming a working theory about these so-called Rangers. *Was it a perfect foil—train them young, mentor the kids, help them get decent jobs, then move in for the pay-off? Trucking firms.* He had heard these firms loved the high school's vocational grads. Couldn't get enough of them. *Were these kids plants or sleepers like the Ruskies supposedly had all across the U.S. of A? How do you activate them? Suppose you do, what freight are they moving and how could the trucking firms not know? All the loads are sealed tight, right? Maybe not all loads. Are they moving drugs? Stolen property? High-end art thefts? What's the old saying,* Rod struggled to recall—*follow the money? Well how the heck is the local police department gonna undertake that kind of forensic analysis? If it's interstate commerce, then any case I'd build, the Fibbies would just swallow whole.* He'd heard it before, "Thanks

Detective, we'll take it from here. Too complex for your department without our nationwide resources and ability to drag net." Rod felt baffled for the moment and then heard Agnes yell, "Time for lunch, boys!" *Something had to break this log jam, though.* He could sense it breaking his way and soon.

CHAPTER 22

A Day in the Life of a Police Detective

After lunch with Agnes and the boys, Rod got the itch to head to the station house. After arriving, he fidgeted at his detective's desk, still pondering how he could crack the Rican Ranger case. *Was it even a case?* His backlog of burglaries, a couple of sexual assaults, and a wave of juvenile vandalism could keep him busy for weeks. In popular culture, everyone assumed that cases unfolded for detectives just like on TV dramas. In 1968, the Police and the D.A.'s office still had the upper hand in prosecuting defendants. Forensic scientists hadn't yet figured out how to tap into the wealth of information DNA testing could provide. For now, they could only dream about it. Decades later the balance of power would shift to defense attorneys, who merely had to plant the CSI question in juror's minds: Why didn't the DA offer any *DNA evidence* I ask you, ladies and gentlemen of the jury?

For now, though, Rod had to build a case from the ground up. Rarely would eyewitnesses open up without real motivation. *Why not start at Fitchburg High, as his sons had suggested? It would be easy to visit Ray Peterson.* Rod realized he could use the pretext of Rod Jr.'s and Conor's future in the mechanical field—or engineering maybe. Rod Sr. knew his sons should go to a college of some sort. The long term math for salaried high school grads versus college grads made that a no brainer. But the boys had tasted of the paradise apple—with engine repair, seeing how their hands and brains could combine to make machinery hum—just like the engineers designed it. And, the gratitude factor was never to be underestimated. Nothing matched the ability of his sons to help other people in need—getting their conveyances back on the road. Not to mention the hapless neighbors who couldn't afford market prices for a tune-up or an oil change. The widow next door paid Conor and Rod Jr. in pies and ice cream, and a two-dollar tip for good measure. The boys even bought the parts at wholesale, thanks to Ray's connections with auto suppliers.

On a whim, Rod pulled out the phone book and called Ray's home number.

"Hello," Ray answered.

"Ah, yes, Mr. Peterson? This is Detective Rod McNamara."

"Oh my," interjected Ray in a worried tone. "From the Police Department?'

Rod, sensing Ray's concern, quickly said, "No, I mean, yes. This is not official police business. I was just working the swing shift today at the precinct and hoped I might reach you. I hear great things about your classes from my boys, Rod Jr. and Conor."

"OK, I thought your name sounded familiar. I've read about your crime detection exploits in the *Sentinel*. You're really something. I loved that story last year about how you single-handedly solved that fraud scheme those n'er-do-wells foisted on elderly folks, going door to door. Great scam—offer a free roof inspection, then find all kinds of code violations, and calmly advise the homeowner that, as upstanding licensed roofers, they'd be duty-bound to turn in the luckless homeowner to the authorities, who'd then condemn the property. Oh, and they just happened to have a pallet of roof tiles on the truck ready to offload. Hard sell away we go: 'Listen lady, I can keep you out of real hot water with the codes inspectors—but I need $500 cash today. As long as we have a repair contract all signed, I don't have to turn you in!' What a racket. I heard they almost got away with something north of $40,000—never doing more than two houses on any given street."

"Yeah, that was my case. The figure actually topped $100,000 because the ring had a whole crew canvassing several locales each week. We only reported part of the take because we didn't want to encourage copycats. You know they made it look good—dropping off the pallet of roof tiles one day and then coming by two nights later with a tow motor to haul them off. They'd tell the homeowners that they just noticed that the tiles were defective—and had checked with the manufacturer for a warranty replacement. That line just built more confidence—and time. 'We'll be back in two weeks. Your tiles are on back order. They've adjusted the assembly line process to remove the defect. You're lucky we got word to the company before we did the install, Ma'am!'"

"So, how can I help you, Detective?"

"Please call me Rod. I already feel like I owe you a favor. Two in fact, you know—for encouraging my twins.

They are so much handier than I am. My Dad was all thumbs—I had to learn auto mechanics by trial and error. Lots of errors! I should tell you a quick story. I got cocky while courting my future wife, Agnes. I offered to tune up her father's Chevy. He was thrilled of course—free labor from a young man high on his own testosterone. So I got all my tools lined up and started into replacing the points. One of the damn screw bolts fell down into the distributor. Without thinking, I pulled the whole distributor worm assembly out of its shaft. Found the bolt, of course. It just never occurred to me that the teeth of the worm gear shaft had to be placed exactly in the same location in its hold. Not only would the car not start, Agnes's old man had to get the damned thing towed to the shop where a real mechanic could fix it!"

"Yup," Ray laughed. "Rookie mistake!"

"Yeah, we weren't even engaged yet. Plus, I added insult to injury later that evening when I asked her Mom to get me some ketchup as a garnish to her roast beast. The silence—just deafening! You'd have thought I had called the Pope a philanderer or something. I broke an unwritten rule. Months later they deigned to allow me to keep the ketchup by my chair—on the floor. Then, after we got married, we showed up one day for dinner and there sat the ketchup bottle plain as you like, right next to the salt and pepper shakers. Like it belonged there. I suppose that's when Agnes's family accepted me, warts and all."

"I get it. I'm a ketchup man, too. It's an underrated sauce for any beef dish," Ray guffawed, using his best French chef accent.

"I wondered," Rod went on, "if I might stop by sometime to see your auto mechanics' facilities, maybe even pick your brain on future career moves for Conor and Rod Jr. You know—college ain't in the cards for those two, best I can tell. Unless, of course, *we* can steer them towards mechanical engineering or design. Get them thinking—wave of the future stuff. Maybe they can draft plans for a flying car or something. Plus, I don't want them getting sucked into this damned war. You know there's all kinda talk about how the all-volunteer Army ain't cutting it numbers wise."

Ray picked up on the "we" can steer them notion. "Oh, sure, Detective," Ray said smiling. "We rarely get parents like you who are interested in their kids' education. Methinks teenagers, especially teen boys, are so busy raging, rebelling, and conniving, that their parents are all too happy to be rid of them five days a week. When would you like to drop by?"

Rod sat back in his squeaky squad-room chair, the noise heading back to Ray through the phone line. "How does Monday afternoon sound—or you tell me. When is there a break for you during the day? A study hall slot or something. I could bring us some lunch, or do you prefer the school cafeteria fare? Please do call me Rod."

"OK," Ray intoned, "But you're not the detective I assumed you were if you think I enjoy cafeteria food—starch for the masses. Does my gut no good! How about 11:00 a.m. Monday? I have a break then. Actually, I'm on cafeteria duty, but a few of my colleagues owe me so I could switch days with one of them. And, please, call me Ray."

"Fantastic. And thanks for taking my call…Ray."

"Sure. One more thing, Rod. Do you want me to line up a couple of my other star students to help with the tour? I'm guessing your sons might be embarrassed to have you around. They might think you're checking up on them."

"Wow. That hadn't occurred to me—a student-led tour, I mean. I could buy the four of us lunch—bring several sub sandwiches from Giuseppe's Pizzeria. How many would we need?" Rod asked, thinking about how much food Rod Jr. and Conor could eat at a sitting. Hollow leg syndrome and all.

Ray thought for a moment, admiring the mental image of his spit-shined shop. His kids really did take pride in their mechanics facilities, almost counterintuitive for teen boys. Good thing their mothers didn't see how they could police up an area. Ray bet that most of their bedrooms were piled high with dirty clothes, their beds unkempt and unmade for weeks at a time. Dust bunnies the size of volleyballs whisking around under their beds. Ray's office chair squeaked just like Rod's. Old as dirt, it was.

"If I got Julio Mendez and his cousin Cordero Díaz to walk us through their paces that might just be the ticket. They have an appetite on them. I'm betting they could each wolf down a large sub, a side of chips, and a large drink. They are two of my star students—one's a junior and the other's a senior, and both of them already have job offers from USA Truck Lines, if you can believe it. It's good you called, since summer break is almost upon us."

Not believing his luck, all without prompting, Rod said, "I couldn't have hoped for more, Ray. You're most gracious. Do you think we could de-emphasize that I'm a cop? I mean…maybe just say, I don't know, that I'm an interested member of the community or something? I hate for kids to get scared, think I'm there to snoop around, look for drugs or some such nonsense. Are Julio and Cordero of the Puerto Rican persuasion? Only reason I ask is because that community has not always had the best relationship with Fitchburg's finest. And that's partly our own fault, at my end."

"Hmmm," muttered Ray. "Let me noodle on the best approach. These students are as clean-cut and studious as they come. They ace every exam I throw at them. Never miss class. But they're not gunners either—trying to lord it over their classmates. Real humble bumbles. They go out of their way to help everyone in class. It's quite heartening to watch."

Rod leaned forward in his chair thinking about cracking this stupid case. "Great, and thank you. I'll see you Monday. I appreciate your time, Ray." He rang off not believing how forthcoming Ray had been. *Obviously, Ray hadn't a clue about any trucking scams. That Trixie, what a name. What kind of mother would announce to her attending OB nurses that, yes, Pops and I have decided on a name after giving it much thought. Trixie! So was ole Trix just full of crap? Why call me at all? What's in it for her? She is just some upstanding bar keep who wants to help out the police. Right. Did they wrong her in some way? Short one of her liquor orders? Threaten her if she ratted them out?*

Rod realized he'd have to play things close to the vest come Monday. He'd fight off his natural tendency to want to interrogate Julio and Cordero. At least not anything overt. Rod leaned back in his chair and lit up a pipe crammed full of cherry-flavored Borkum Riff. He needed some more background information on this operation and his sons could provide it, he mused—maybe tomorrow whilst I'm tinkering with the truck.

CHAPTER 23

Saturday June 8, 1958—Afternoon
Jeremy Meets Eva

"**H**ey Jeremy? Come down from your room, please," David yelled.

Jeremy romped down the stairs wearing a smile. David had finished a working draft of tomorrow's homily and needed an outing. "How'd you like to go meet Dr. R's mother?

"Sure, what's her name, Dad?"

"Eva. But we'll just call her Mrs. Rebovitz, OK?"

"Yes, Dad. Where does she live?"

"Pinehurst Nursing Home. You've been there before with me, remember? Big long hill, curvy drive, lots of squirrels."

They hopped in the VW Beetle and headed across town. Sure enough the squirrel brigades marched all over, foraging in earnest. Jeremy marveled at how they all stopped grazing in unified panic as a red-tailed hawk descended out of nowhere to feast on one of their slower cousins. He remembered a Jacques Cousteau special where the narrator explained why fish swam in schools. Those school members on the outer quadrants battled to get back into the safe middle where the sharks and barracudas couldn't get at them.

Jeremy and David entered the main administration building and Amy Quinn's smile greeted them. "Reverend Hergenroeder and...don't tell me, Mr. Jerry, no, Jeremy!" Jeremy blushed, but was smitten that Amy remembered his name from prior visits. He noticed he could not feel her head, which he now understood meant she felt some love for him and his Dad. "Welcome back to Pinehurst. We're so glad to have visitors."

"Thank you, Miss Quinn," Jeremy replied.

David spoke up, "We're here to visit Eva Rebovitz."

"Yes, you visited her last time. I suppose you know the way. It's a pleasure to have you return. And Mrs. Rebovitz, I'm sure, will be pleased as well. I'll take care of signing you in."

David and Jeremy left Amy's warm embrace and stepped down the hall to find Eva's door. They knocked and Eva asked them to enter. As they passed the threshold, she exclaimed, "Well, to what do I owe the honor, Reverend, and who is this fine handsome prince who's with you?" Oddly, Jeremy could feel Eva's head and sensed her feeling of relief at their company.

"We were coming over to this side of town, Mrs. Rebovitz, and I wanted Jeremy to meet you. He's my one and only son, all of five years old."

"Nice to make your acquaintance, Jeremy. You know, when you get to be my age and come to live in a rest home like Pinehurst, most of your visitors are nurses and aides. All I have to do is press this red call button and, presto, they'll come running. So tell me, are you starting kindergarten next fall?"

"No, Ma'am, I just started this week. My first day was last week but I got scared. Dad took me right home. Then we saw Dr. Rebovitz and he helped me with my head problem. So I got to go back Monday."

"Head problem you say? Well, that is my son's specialty. I don't let him near my head, I'll tell you. That's a mother's prerogative! Another benefit of reaching my age! Do tell me about yourself, Jeremy. I know your Dad's a nice man and I'm guessing you didn't fall far from his tree."

"Yes, Ma'am. I like my Dad a lot. He lets me collect Matchbox cars. I have 27 already. I save up my allowance every week."

"You do? How much does a Matchbox car cost these days?"

"Fifty cents. For the big ones it's a dollar. That takes me four weeks to buy one of those. Last week I bought a Mercedes ambulance. All the doors open—even the back one for the patient!" As Jeremy answered he could feel Eva's head and realized she was thinking about giving him a coin.

"Jeremy, honey, please reach into that top drawer beside my bed. There's a Kennedy half-dollar in there that I just don't know how to spend. I'm hoping you can help me solve that problem. I can't use it in the vending machines here to buy a soda. They only take quarters, dimes and nickels. It's too big to fit in the slot. I was afraid I'd have to throw it away." Eva looked on Jeremy with the soft eyes of a loving grandmother.

"Dad, may I have the coin?"

"That's up to Mrs. Rebovitz, Jeremy."

"You just grab it out of that drawer, Mr. Hergenroeder," Eva pointed to Jeremy.

Jeremy realized no one had ever called him Mr. Hergenroeder before. He'd heard "Mr. Jeremy," but never his last name. He pocketed the coin after marveling at President Kennedy's likeness on its shiny heads-up face. It felt so big in his hand. "Thank you, Ma'am. That's two week's allowance!"

"So it is. You're good at math, too, Jeremy, aren't you?"

"Sort of, Ma'am. My Mom has me count her change after we go grocery shopping every Saturday. We sit and go through the stuff on her receipt."

"Yes," offered David. "Alex is big on numbers. She'd count off his fingers and toes every night before bed almost from the moment she brought him home from the hospital."

Just then visions of 1930s Germany flooded into Jeremy's head. He saw Mrs. Rebovitz as a mother worrying about her 12-year-old son, whom Jeremy realized was Dr. Rebovitz. He was tall even back then. As they stood in front of their hat shop, they watched a large crowd marauding down the street. The raging mob threw rocks, smashed windows, and then set most of the stores on fire. Jeremy could feel the family's fear. He saw them run to the back of their shop and out into the alley.

"Jeremy!" David implored. "You left us during one of your daydreams. That's not polite. What do you say to Mrs. Rebovitz, for her gift?"

"Oh, I'm sorry…." Jeremy started to whisper.

Before Jeremy could say thank you, Eva sat bolt upright in her bed, a look of shock on her wizened face. "Jeremy, what were you doing just now? You looked like you got stuck in the cosmos for a minute."

"Nothing, Ma'am. I just daydream a lot. Like my Dad said."

"OK, son. We've talked about your paying attention to what adults have to say to you. It's just good manners, remember?"

Before Jeremy could answer his father, Eva chimed in with a story. "Jeremy, when I was a little girl growing up outside Munich, Germany, I had a dear friend named Helga Shivitz. She and I played together all the time. We had a guessing game we invented—we called it, 'Guess what I'm thinking.' Sort of like charades—only no hints. We were just five years old like you. Helga got real good at guessing my thoughts. In fact, she never missed once, as I recall. But, you know what happened, Jeremy?"

"No Ma'am," Jeremy lied. He realized Eva, too, had a gift as did Helga. Maybe a little like his. Or a lot like his! Did it get them in trouble, too, he wondered?

"Even though I was quite young, Jeremy, and I've never told my son, your doctor, this insight, I could feel Helga searching around in my head! I thought she was cheating. I didn't invite her into my head, after all. It was just a silly game. But the more we played, the more we realized something was going on that we just didn't understand. How could anyone read another person's thoughts? We kept our startling discovery a secret— girlfriends' honor code. Are you wondering why I'm telling you this story, Jeremy?"

David sat transfixed. His thoughts arced across the Atlantic to the time in Germany before the World Wars. The first one was the war to end all wars. It didn't, as history proved many times over. David looked at his son, amazed again.

"Yes, Ma'am, I think I understand your game."

"It's not a game, Jeremy. I could feel you reading my thoughts. For one as young as we were, you happened on some horrific images in Germany. I want you to understand a bit about what you just saw."

David interrupted. "Mrs. Rebovitz, I'm sorry about this…."

Eva didn't let David interrupt. "Jeremy, unlike you, I can't see into other people's heads or read their thoughts. My gift, such as it is, finds me realizing when someone like you is reading my thoughts. I knew when Helga was doing it, could feel her searching my mind and I suddenly felt you doing it too. You're looking for answers. It's completely innocent except when you see horrible thoughts and memories, traumas even. I want you to promise me you'll try not to read my thoughts again. Helga and I never got to really take our game to the next level. She and her family moved off to Dusseldorf and then, in 1911, they moved to America after her father took a job with a firm called the Computing-Tabulating-Recording Company. It was some sort of three company merger. Anyway, later it became IBM. Helga and I wrote to each other for a while, but then we lost touch—the wars taking their toll."

"Mrs. Rebovitz, I'm worried about where this conversation is headed. Jeremy's been through a lot the past few days. It's why we took him to see your son. He calls his gift 'feeling people's head'."

"Yes, David, I understand. And I'm hoping my son can help you both. I'm a big believer in helping children understand the world around them. 'Old enough to ask is old enough to know' is a saying I believe in. Please let me explain what Jeremy saw happening to my family. You can help, David. I don't want him leaving here wondering. Is that OK?"

"I suppose," David shuddered. "Let's ask Jeremy what he saw. He calls it feeling people's heads. Jeremy?"

"Dad, I saw Mrs. Rebovitz, another man, and Dr. Rebovitz when he was a twelve-year-old boy. They ran a hat shop. The night I felt had lots of broken glass. It was everywhere. There were mobs of people shouting, yelling, and using sticks and rocks to break windows."

"Oh gosh. OK, so you saw Mrs. R in what's called 'Kristallnacht,' the night of the broken glass. That was a tragic event in German history."

"What do you mean 'German,' Dad? Aren't we German?"

"Yes, Jeremy, we're German."

"Were you in Germany Dad—back then?"

"No, son. My great-grandfather, your double great grandpa, came to America long before then."

"That's good, right Dad?"

"Yes I suppose so. But that night was horrific. Many people, many Jewish people, died for no reason. The mobs ran them out of their shops. They lost everything—especially the ones whose homes sat atop or behind their stores. It was beyond criminal."

"Jeremy I just want to caution you about, what do you call it, 'feeling people's heads'?" Eva's steely blue eyes stayed softly focused on Jeremy's countenance. "It can get you into trouble—I never realized it until today. Helga may have gotten into trouble when she used her gift. To us it was just play. I could feel her in my head—like she had a flashlight in there—searching around in a dark, dank cave. Bats flying around. Only the cave was my mind. I felt your flashlight, Jeremy. I don't know why I was thinking about that night in Germany. That may not have been fair to you. I apologize," Eva finished as her eyes filled with tears.

For a moment, the three new friends let the room's silence wash over them. Everything seemed new and old to each of them. Jeremy smelled the room's scents. He recognized the cleaner Roger used at the church. Only it wasn't as pungent. He thought of it as less stinky. Mrs. R. smelled like flowers. He wondered if Dr. R. bought her that big bottle of gold liquid for her birthday sitting on her table, just like the brand that Dad bought Mom. It had the name "toilet" on it, and two words Jeremy didn't understand, "Eau" and "De." *Dad said it meant fresh smelling. But how could toilet water smell good? Why bathe in toilet water? What did the factory put in toilet water to get Dad to buy it? Must be good—it smells good.* "It's romantic, Jeremy," his Dad had told him. "When you have a wife someday, you'll buy her 'Eau de Toilet' too!" Mom pronounced it "Oh" and "Twa-Let," sort of like the moist towelettes they carried around in the VW's glove box. They used them when they picnicked on the Mohican Trail with the youth groups. Everyone had canteens and peanut butter and marshmallow spread sandwiches. That was a

Massachusetts specialty—called a "Fluffernutter." And Hershey Bars—boy were those good, Jeremy recalled.

Dad would take the Rollstone youth group on long hikes. The kids were nice to Jeremy, mostly. He could feel their heads and knew that they were confused and seemed to have crushes on each other. His Dad called it "puppy love" when Jeremy asked him about it. *They sure seemed to think about it all the time. Puppy love sounded like something that wouldn't last. Like my parents' love for each other. Did that start as puppy love?* Jeremy wondered.

Eva spoke up just then, breaking Jeremy's reverie. "Jeremy, is my son helping you with your gift?"

"Yes Ma'am. I think he's figuring out a way I can turn it off."

"Good. When do you see him next?"

David interceded. "We're trying to make it Sunday mornings—sort of a secret so no one knows about him. He won't be showing up at Dr. Rebovitz's office. We'll arrange to take Jeremy to Dr. Rebovitz's home, then pick him up on the way to church."

"Sounds like you three have thought it through. I wish I had your wisdom back in Germany when I was a little girl. Maybe I could have warned Helga that it wasn't a game after all. Life's full of regrets, of course, but you can't focus on the past—it will suck your soul dry, leaving you spiritually bereft. I did teach my son that piece of wisdom, however."

Jeremy interjected, "What's bee-firt" mean?

"I'm sorry, Jeremy. That's one of those sixty-four-thousand-dollar words. Bereft just means empty."

Jeremy imagined a big hole in the sand, like at Craigville Beach on Cape Cod where the Hergenroeders often vacationed. He never felt like his mind was empty. From the minute he'd awaken each morning, his thought floodgates opened. Sometimes he could feel the heads of neighbors rushing off to work early, or others scattering to do morning errands. Some were happy with their day all planned out—he could feel their warmth and their peaceful bliss. Others had headaches or were stewing about fellow workers whom they despised, or who had crossed them for scores of reasons. It felt just like the mental cacophony at church. Everyone *seemed* to be paying attention to his Dad or the choir. But they were far off on cloud nine, as his Dad would say. Jeremy also had started teaching himself a game—one he'd soon tell Dr. Rebovitz—one that might help him with that big electrical switch his folks hoped he'd create. He found that if he held his breath and concentrated only on holding the air deep in his lungs, he could ignore the thoughts of other people. It didn't work all the time, but it seemed to work once in a while.

"Jeremy," Eva motioned, "I hope you'll come see me again soon. I want you to tell my son to take good care of you. He loves children, you know. Especially the real smart ones like you. Will you do that for me? Tell him, I mean?"

"Sure Ma'am. He does seem to be very nice. I like him."

The three new friends said their good-byes after David announced it was sermon-polishing time. David and Jeremy fired up the VW and headed back down Pinehurst's long drive.

CHAPTER 24

Saturday June 8, 1968—Afternoon
Rican Ranger Research Mission

José and Ricardo had left the Brodies to their own devices and now had finished researching the Hergenroeder family. It didn't take long, thanks to a quick trip to the library to look at old *Fitchburg Sentinel* newspapers on microfiche, the librarian only too happy to oblige them as they scanned for local ecclesial leadership highlights. Their story about wanting to help a nephew with some background for an essay on the subject turned out to be all the cover they needed. After all, who goes to the library for criminal enterprise research—when that enterprise is their own?

The Reverend David Hergenroeder had received his BA in Divinity in 1959 from Vanderbilt Divinity School in Nashville. This bachelor's degree (now a standard Master's degree or "M-Div.") followed a religious studies degree from NYU in 1956. Hergenroeder's first church had been a congregational post in New Bedford, Massachusetts, former whaling capital of the world. The same seaport from which, a century or so before, Ishmael of Moby Dick fame had set sail on the whaling ship Pequod under the fateful direction of Captain Ahab. As they read more, José and

Ricardo took copious notes—almost as if they really were trying to help a young mind. Just not for their nephew.

Later, looking for the parsonage, they drove up Pearl Hill Road. Crossing the bridge that ran over Putts Pond, the pair saw a grade school class walking its perimeter in search of aquatic fauna and flora. Pearl Hill also traversed passed a handful of old apple orchards, mostly abandoned, except someone forgot to tell the apple trees, whose blossoms had just now transitioned into baby apples. Every house appeared to have a good half-acre of land adjoining it. All the yards were well manicured. They slowed as they came to number 123 and marveled at how big a home it was, never realizing that it was a parsonage—on loan from Rollstone to the current occupants. "Dang, this minister must have something going on the side to be able to afford that mini-mansion!" Ricardo exclaimed.

"Yeah, dude, there may be more to this family than meets the eye. How could they afford to send their kid to some shrink? That don't come cheap!" José thought out loud.

None of the neighbors seemed to take note of their passing, except a couple of dogs, one of whom chased the car for 50 yards aiming to capture their right front tire for dinner. Ricardo chuckled at the dog's plans. "What, you're going to bite our tire? Sure you want to do that, Tonto?"

Ignoring the canine, José said, "Now that we've got Dan and a few of his yard mates in our camp, I wanna use them to hook up our trucking operations to the docks—we've got to penetrate those longshoreman facilities. Get us a foothold in the main union. They'll get us right past Customs—or better yet, get us prime influence with the

Mass. Port Authority. Clearly, the Port Authority needs the efficient help and direction that only our Rican Rangers can provide. Just think—all those freighters waiting to be loaded and unloaded. We'll become international importers and exporters! Pier Rican Rangers—no more Pier 1!" José schemed.

"First, we gotta snatch and grab this Jeremy kid. But we gotta do it right. Imagine if *his* kindergarten class had been at Putts Pond on that field trip. Quick diversion—throw the teacher off, and we coulda nabbed him right then. I'm thinking about a subtle approach. You know how little kids think older kids are gods? Maybe we get one of our Rangers to pal around with Jeremy, you know, befriend him? Maybe Julio, for example, just happens to fend off a bully in Jeremy's neighborhood. We could set it up all easy and nice. Have one of our younger Ranger trainees act the bully, get what I'm sayin?' Scare the kid, then save him—all in one fell swoop."

Ricardo just shook his head. "Nah, that ain't gonna work. This kid will see right through the fake bully immediately. Hell, maybe before he even shows up to beat up Jeremy. Remember José—mind reader."

José appeared flummoxed. "Of course. We've got to think three or four steps ahead of this kid. I bet we could get one of those kids who's been begging to join the Rangers to bully him, and ask another one of our rangers to watch out for bullying in general. This is just so damn confusing. It's too complicated. We might just need to grab the kid, period. Watch his patterns—school, church, play time—that kinda shit," José said.

Ricardo started shaking his head again.

"Awright, I know what you're going to say. He'll know we're watchin' him. So what do *you* suggest?" José demanded.

"I don't know. All's I know is we need this kid for the really big job—getting into the minds of those longshoremen and their union bosses, maybe even the Port Authority bosses. We might only get to use him once or twice. Maybe we grab the parents while he's away at school, then tell him as he walks home. Thing of it is, how do we know he's not 'feeling our heads' right now?"

José ignored the question. "Don't you suppose his mom or dad picks him up after school? Are you saying we grab the two of them in the driveway say, as they get home?"

"Let me give it a think!" pleaded Ricardo. "There's too many angles here. Maybe Dan and Velma—we use them to make the grab. Keeps us out of the immediate vicinity. Anyway maybe we bide our time—for the right grab opportunity and the right job to use the kid on."

José and Ricardo sat for a while hoping the light at the end of the tunnel wasn't a train. Their next flash of insight would arrive soon enough.

CHAPTER 25

Monday June 10, 1968--10:30 a.m.
Trixie's Unveiling and a Visit to Fitchburg High School

Det. McNamara hopped in his unmarked squad car and tooled on over to Giuseppe's Pizzeria. He'd wisely called in his order ahead of time. The pizzeria was a mom-and-pop affair that had long ago gained a reputation for great Italian food. Mom insisted on the freshest ingredients, meaning that Giuseppe, "Pop" for short, had to drive into Boston a couple days a week at 3:00 a.m. to Haymarket Square. There, he'd battle with all the local chefs for the freshest basil, oregano, tomatoes, onions, not to mention the choicest sausage, pepperoni and mozzarella. The savvier chefs had learned to suck up to Pop because, having hailed from northern Italy and with little prompting, he'd radiate the old-world wisdom for creating the best red sauces. It was a two-way deal, however, as the chefs would have to cough up their secrets as well. No harm to Boston area competition since those restaurateurs had nothing to fear from a Fitchburg pizza parlor 90 minutes west with but fifteen tables.

As Rod Sr. pulled into the Pizzeria lot, he noticed a bar two doors down and wondered if Trixie held court there. He saw a few cars out front already that had delivered the early liquid-lunch crowd—the business doppelgangers that needed steeling up for the rest of the workday. After parking his car a discreet distance from the bar, he ambled on over. Sharp folks and especially drug dealers could spot his unmarked vehicle since it lacked whitewall tires and, of course, was all black. Rod Sr. enforced the drug laws long before the U.S. government declared its war on drugs, meaning he had no real seizure powers. Oh, sure, he could confiscate drugs out of a house or a car, but he lacked the statutory authority to seize the conveyance or the home. The future war had a unique feature—a self-fulfilling prophecy so to speak: the more property the DEA and local constabularies seized from drug defendants, the more they could line their coffers with the proceeds. All funds then went to hire ever more cops and prosecutors. No one later would pay any meaningful attention to the inherent conflict of interest that kept the war raging on. It buttressed many a capital budget across the U.S.

Rod slipped into the bar and let his senses adjust to the smoky mix of dark paneling and stale beer. He strolled up to the bar and signaled the female barkeep. Trixie started to smile at her new customer. Her smile vanished when she recognized famous Rod Sr. from his PR picture in the paper, following his roofing-contractor takedown. She gulped hard and pretended she didn't recognize him. Wisely, he stood at the far corner of the bar. The bar owner kept the jukebox's volume turned down low to accommodate the business lunch crowd. "I hope this guy's subtle," Trixie said to no one.

"What can I get you, sir?" Trixie asked.

"Well Ma'am, I think we both know what I'm here for," Rod whispered. "I'm into trucking and was hoping for more information after you called me. You didn't reeeeaaallllly think I'd stay away, did you?"

"Sir, forgive me, but I've got other customers I have to wait on. I'm thinking you're looking for someone else," Trixie said, forgetting for just a millisecond that her prominent name tag matched the name she gave Rod when she called him. Name tags also encouraged customer tips. But with that sudden realization, Rod noted that she'd aged 10 years in 10 seconds.

Seeing an easy mark, Rod decided to take a conciliatory tone. "Look, I need only five or six minutes, lady. You called me and used the name on your name tag. I'm guessing these 'RRs' you mentioned may even be bilking your bar somehow. Why else call me? You strike me as a concerned citizen, or have I missed something?"

Trixie leaned in and said, "Yeah, OK, I called you. A few of my customers are local truckers who have gotten laid off because they're too old and it's easy to replace them with cheap labor right out of Fitchburg High. To a man they all say the same thing. Those 'Rican Rangers,' as they secretly call themselves, have some sort of side line going with lots of their transports. It's how the trucking companies can hire them cheap—they never complain, never strike, never call in sick. You know, model citizens. Except for some reason they don't join the Chamber of Commerce! I don't know what exactly they're up to, but one trucker who got his walking papers said he noticed that one of his trailer rigs had two false gas tanks and a four-foot false front at the head of the trailer. It was some sort of storage compartment with a neat-as-you please welding job on all sides. He was about to open it—was trying to figure out how to get into it, when a couple of these young honchos caught him in the act. They beat him up pretty bad and drove him home in his car. The guy got the message— we know where you live Dude, so watch your step. I think he skipped town with his wife and kids, got some long-haul trucking job with an Arizona outfit. Drives the I-10 corridor exclusively, Florida to California. Got as far away from Fitchburg as he could get. Now, I need you to skedaddle before one of their henchmen recognizes you and connects the dots to ole Trixie here. Got it?"

Rod nodded, thanked her discreetly and left. He moved on to the pizzeria just as Pops pulled up from running an errand. Rod picked up his assortment of subs and headed to Fitchburg High. After swinging into the lone remaining space in the teacher's lot he snuck in the back door, ignoring the sign warning all visitors to check in at the principal's office. Rod had a vague idea where Ray held his classes—had to be near an open garage door to get the cars in for practice repairs. He jumped down two flights of stairs and out a back door, scaring three students sharing a smoke. Eyeballing them, he moved around their scattering circle toward the sound of a pneumatic wrench tearing off some car's lug nuts. The boys working the air compressor gave him the once over as he slid by. Sure enough, he found Ray on his hands and knees pointing out to a student how a brake caliper worked.

"Mr. Peterson?"

"Who goes there?" Ray asked as he stumbled to his feet, his arthritic knees cracking in protest at the sudden elevation.

"Ah, yes, my name is Jim Smith, and I called the other day hoping for a tour."

"Of course. You're the guy from...don't tell me...Chelmsford!" Ray exclaimed, concocting the subterfuge Rod had hoped he'd create. "You wanted your local high school to open up a mechanic's shop like we have here. Didn't you say something about needing a soup-to-nuts overview of our operations?" Ray smiled and winked, wiping the sweat from his brow with his omnipresent hanky.

"Yes, please, and like you suggested I brought a mess of sub sandwiches, ten in all, as payment in kind for the tour and the chance to pick your brain a bit."

"Sure. Tell you what. I gave a heads-up to a couple of my students, Julio Mendez and Cordero Díaz. Told them to be ready to give the tour—sort of like museum guides. I mentioned a free lunch and that got their attention. I see you went to Mom and Pops. My favorite."

Ray shouted across the shop floor for the two students. In seconds, Rod faced two young men who appeared as coiffed and clean-shaven as graduating ROTC students. No wonder trucking firms liked these kids. No hippie or druggie visage here.

Rod held out his hand and introduced himself. "Gentlemen, my name is Jim Smith. I'm from the Chelmsford, Massachusetts PTA. A pleasure to make your acquaintance."

Julio and Cordero snapped to attention and gave Rod a firm handshake, but not too firm. The kind of greeting you'd want at the start of a job interview. Make a good first impression—leave the interviewer wanting more.

"All right gentlemen," Ray interjected, "Mr. Smith wants to lobby, that's the right word Mr. Smith, isn't it, his local school board in Chelmsford for a shop program. Like the one we have. I told him you two could showcase our operations." Ray pronounced Chelmsford like the locals: Chemsfa, no hard R or D.

Julio stepped up. "Come right this way Mr. Smith. The first thing we want you to see is how clean our shop is. Mr. Peterson insists on polish and sparkle. Why, you might ask? Because it reduces the chance of hazards. You know, falls, slipping, lost parts, etc. Also it makes a good impression."

"That's right, Julio," Ray proudly declared. "My boys make great employees—companies and mechanic shops don't have to teach them to clean up after themselves. Nothing's worse than losing an expensive part. Use the wrong special order bolt for an engine rebuild and you're back to square one. Also means the customer has to wait longer—an extra day or two. What are they going to do for transport then—for the two whole days after their promised delivery date?"

Rod was bemused. "You guys sure are detail oriented. I'd love to have you come speak to the naysayers at my school board meetings. Please continue."

Cordero spoke up next. "Mr. Smith, I want you to see the actual engine mockup we have on the stand over here. It has four cut-away cylinders so you can get a window into how all the engine parts work-together. There's a hand crank on the front—please turn it for me."

Rod dutifully turned the crank, surprised at how easy it was.

"I noticed your surprise Mr. Smith. We re-bored the cylinders a couple micrometers to reduce the compression. Now, a real engine would take the two of us to turn it like you just did with one hand."

"Nice," Rod said.

Julio pointed, "Look up at the ceiling. We have big air pipes that feed outside the school—to carry the cars' exhaust away from us in here. It's a vacuum system. You know, we get some real clunkers in here—blue smokers. But we have to start them up to begin to get an idea of what we have to repair."

The tour went on for 20 more minutes and the boys impressed Rod, no acting needed. "Gentlemen, I thank you. Now, I'm hungry. Anyone else? I brought plates and napkins. Right over here," Rod gestured, hoping to start the real interrogation post-haste.

As the boys dug into their food, "Mr. Smith" aimed his questions at Ray. "OK, Mr. Peterson, great shop and clearly your students are proud of their work. But isn't it a tight job market out there these days? Shouldn't we be directing these bright minds toward a college degree?"

"Oh my, and put me out of business..." Ray started to ask.

Julio jumped in as he finished a bite of his meatball sub. "No sir, not at all. Shop class prepares you for college— learning how businesses operate, not to mention machinery. Most of us have job offers before we even graduate!"

"Really," said Rod, "I don't see how that's possible."

Cordero broke in. "Yup, thanks to Mr. Peterson's connections we got lotsa recruiters come by here every month."

"Recruiters?" Mr. Smith asked. "I didn't realize your average mechanic shop had recruiters show up."

"No, you're right, they don't," offered Cordero. "But the big national trucking firms do! They love us."

"That's true," said Ray. "The firms teach these kids how to drive the big rigs—double clutch and all. But our kids, our graduates, come gift-wrapped and pre-assembled. All ready to repair the trucks they drive. Do you have any idea how much overhead that saves those companies, not to mention towing charges?" Ray insisted.

"I never thought of it that way. So what you're saying is that by hiring a driver who's also a mechanic, the long-haul companies get a two-for-one deal?"

"Yes," Julio replied, enthusiastically.

"So you guys ever hear from prior graduates, how they're doing?" Rod asked.

All of a sudden the shop got quiet. Rod used the silence to his advantage. He raised his eyebrows and waited expectantly. As he suspected, the boys soon felt like they needed to fill the silence.

"You know, most graduates never look back or come visit us underlings," Julio offered.

"Underlings? I'm not sure what that means," Rod said, barely hiding his glee at the obvious nexus to the wider Rican Rangers group. "So you never see them again? That's sad," Rod pressed.

"No, we see them, ya know, on weekends maybe. They tell us it's great out on the open road. Wind at their backs. Dropping off loads here and there, sometimes to rail yards even," Julio noted.

At the mention of rail yards, Cordero visibly stiffened. Rod saw the tell.

"Geez, I had no idea you'd drop off a load at, say, a Piggly Wiggly, and then drop a second load at a rail yard. How does that work exactly? Isn't it one load per customer?"

Julio and Cordero exchanged glances and fidgeted in their seats.

"Mostly it's taking a load from one shipper to one distribution point or one customer. But carriers are getting more sophisticated. Logistics," Julio pointed out, hoping to end Rod's line of inquiry.

Rod said, "Logistics? I've never heard that word. What's it mean? By the way how's your sub?"

Cordero coughed and then said, "Logistics is like a chess match. You've got to move your pieces around, get them in the best position to do the most good. Watch out for the competition."

Rod changed tacks thanks to Trixie. "Do you guys learn welding?"

"Oh yeah," said Julio. "We do spot welding, practicing our seams. Use acetylene torches. Cut through metal—and weld it back together again."

"Why would you cut something just to put it back together again?" Rod asked, realizing instantly that he'd struck a nerve. Or, had he hit the Mother Lode? No one answered.

Rod moved on. "I suppose practice is a good reason. But do trucking firms ever ask welders to break something open with an oxyacetylene torch, say, and then ask them to weld it back?" Rod's question met only silence. Rod realized that this was one way the Rican Rangers might smuggle and hide their contraband. *Weld everything shut in a metal compartment so that no scent emanated or, if it did, an investigator would meet only a metal wall and assume the product had vamoosed from the rig. It'd be just like that scared trucker told Trixie before he vamoosed to Florida.* He thought to ask one more question. Or two.

"I'm fascinated by the welding-shop idea. Welders make good money, particularly in shipping. Welding barges for example—they're really just big iron bathtubs aren't they? Any of your graduates work the rivers or help build barges?"

"No, but we'd like to!" Julio said, too excited. Cordero eyed Julio with utter contempt. Julio cowered into his chair, the last of his meatball sub retching back up his throat.

Rod said, "Well, I know they make barges in Nashville. Big company called Ingram Barge. I've had friends watch from the far banks of the Cumberland River when they'd slide one of those puppies off the construction dock into the drink. They say you can feel the spray all the way across the river—about 500 feet. Quite a sight indeed. So one more question and I'll get out of your hair, gentlemen. When these big rig firms come a-courtin' you, do they ask if you are good at welding? I mean, are they recruiting welders to drive trucks?"

The boys' silence answered the question for him. He'd follow up with Rod Jr. and Conor tonight at dinner.

Ray interceded. "You know, come to think of it, the trucking companies never ask about welding skills. Why would they? They don't need or use that skill set, do they, boys?"

"No, sir," Julio and Cordero whispered.

"Gentlemen, I ask for your prayers," Rod quipped, trying to close his undercover sale. "Pray with me that the Chelmsford School Board votes to add mechanics and welding to our high-school curriculum! Many thanks for your time and if you're ever in Chelmsford, look me up or come by our mechanic shop next school year!"

The boys nodded their assent and jumped off their seats to head for the exit. Rod followed surreptitiously and they paid him handsomely for his deceit. "You stupid ass, Julio," Rod heard Cordero say. "What in blazes did you tell that guy we needed welding for? Or that we oxyacetylene stuff apart and weld it back together? Why even say our guys drop off a second load at a rail yard for chrissakes? You better warn José, Ricardo or Pilar, one!" advised Cordero.

Julio said nothing, but Rod could see the back of his neck and ears burning a bright crimson. Finally Julio spoke up—"The guy's a frickin school board flunky from Chelmsford, of all places. Who gives a rat's ass about Chelmsford? Our truck guys don't go near the place. It's not like he's a cop. I ain't sayin' nuthin' to José, Pilar or Ricardo. And you better not, either!"

Rod caught all this excited talk before they turned the corner. He whipped out his notebook and wrote down the names José (*wasn't that a name he'd heard before around mob activity?*), Pilar and Ricardo.

Rod walked back to thank Ray Peterson. "Man, Ray, thanks so much. It was an education. I'm glad my boys have you as their teacher and mentor. With your permission, I'd like to write a parental note of gratitude to your principal and copy the superintendent of schools. Great tour, great program—all deserving of continued budgetary support."

For a second, Ray looked perplexed because the tour seemed to have turned into some sort of extended interrogation. He also couldn't understand Julio's and Cordero's obvious reticence in answering Rod's questions. *And why did he seem to sneak after them down the hallway? Our mechanic's program has nothing to hide, so why did the boys cower in Rod's presence?* Ray snapped out of his stupor. "My, of course, a reference letter would mean a great deal to me and our program."

"Well then, I'll check in with the principal on my way out. Mention I was running late—ask his forgiveness for not following school policy by signing in. I'll send you a carbon copy of the letter—that way it won't look like you put me up to it or that I'm sucking up for better grades for my boys. I'll use Police Department letterhead if that's OK."

"Sure. I'm in your debt. I still don't get why those two boys got queasy with some of your questions."

"Queasy? I didn't notice," Ray demurred. "Maybe it was an adult—kid embarrassment thing. No worries," Rod offered as he padded back towards the hallway.

CHAPTER 26

Tuesday June 11, 1968; 4:00 a.m.
The Brodie Household Tension Meter Redlines

*T*hose *damn neckless wonders! Love to see them actually fix something themselves!* Dan mused silently as he looked over his fix-it job on the backdoor. *Took me almost the whole day Sunday to rebuild the jam and rehang the door. Well, at least it works like it should. Thank heavens I've been dumpster diving all these years at every construction site I pass. Those contractors don't want the stuff anyway,* Dan thought as he looked out through the garage to make sure the door held fast.

He marveled at the bins over flowing with nuts, bolts, pieces of metal scrap, 2x4s, and plywood. His garage was filled to the brim with the stuff. A passerby might have assumed Dan lived as an OCD packrat—worshipping every odd thing that came into his possession. Dan never hoarded, however. He recognized the value of construction scrap—and the back door repair proved his spot on wisdom. When every spare dollar goes to cover gambling losses and debts, construction effluvium gains an intrinsic value.

Dan hobbled back upstairs, showered and limped to the mirror. "Thumbing back and forth to Quincy again today will be the death of me yet," he grumbled. His legs and knees ached from all the walking and thumbing to and from work on Monday. He'd learned in high school to carry a cardboard sign that said "Please" whenever he thumbed. Worked well most of the time, but Monday's rain wilted the sign in the first half hour. Wiping away the steam sheen, he saw his face looking back at him. The specter sent a shudder down his spine. *What the hell have I become? Velma's right. I've put our very lives at risk. How in tarnation do we escape this slavery?*

Despite Dan's fading mental capacity, his spark of insight proved revelatory. They say alcoholics have to get sick and tired of being sick and tired. Only then do they take the first step towards sobriety. Same principle applies to compulsive gamblers. Dan slapped on some Old Spice, its mild burn sealing the start to his recovery. As the street light spilled through the blinds, Dan somehow felt today might be a good day after all. It was the first day of the rest of his life. 4:30 a.m.—time for coffee and hitting the road to the shipyard. First things first, though, he needed to negotiate with Velma on borrowing the Dodge—couldn't stomach thumbing both ways again. He struggled down the stairs to find ever faithful Velma making coffee and filling his cereal bowl with the store brand version of corn flakes—Velma always bought them to save a few cents at the Piggly Wiggly. Sometimes as the flakes got soggy in the milk it reminded him of his financial demise.

"Velma, I've come to a decision. I ain't gonna gamble no more. I saw this sign at work about some sort of support group for gamblers. Thought I'd give it a try today. They meet for 45 minutes after the lunch whistle blows."

"Yeah, right, Dan. I'm so done covering for you. I've heard all this before—shame on me for believing it. Believing in you."

Humiliation cascaded down Dan's neck, through his gut, all the way to his toes. Rather than fight Velma, Dan had a new-found wisdom. "You're wise not to believe me, Velma. Why should you? I barely believe it myself. Hell, I've lied to both of us so much I'm not sure life's even worth living. Without you, I mean. Gambling's destroying me and my future. Our future."

Velma thought for just a second that she'd just heard a faint wisp of new insight. She couldn't believe her ears, though. "Dan, what a load of crap you're feeding me. And at the crack of dawn. I'm not buying what you're selling. I want you out of this house and my life. *Today*."

"Oh my God, Velma," Dan choked out. He collapsed, sobbing—struggling for air. Dan's heaving and wracking flowed from his throat, choking out the oxygen. "Baby I don't blame you. I deserve everything you can dish out and more."

Velma, fooled and played the fool for so long, still doubted Dan's sincerity. But he wasn't arguing with her, conning her. Something had changed, even the air felt different. *I'll push him harder, she thought, test him and get 'Dan the bullshitter' to re-emerge—just like always.*

"Dan, gimme a break. I'm not falling for this act. I slept nary a wink last night and realized you've seen me as nothing more than a means to your gambling habit. I'm done. I'll help you pack."

"Sure," Dan said, broken. "Makes perfect sense."

"Whaddya mean it makes perfect sense?"

"Everything you just said. You've been a fool to stick with me all these years. I've lost everything you've ever earned. Everything we've earned. I hit rock bottom at Antonio's with my face pressed up against that dumpster. The guy who gave me a ride home wouldn't even let me sit in the cab of his truck, I stunk so bad. I lost our truck. I'm about to lose my job if I don't get into work today. What then? I'd kill myself but General Dynamics's life insurance policy don't pay off for suicides. Now we're helping some Puerto Rican gang kidnap a frickin' five year old. How low can I get? I'm so down and out even the sewer is outta my sight."

Velma paused. She'd never heard Dan talk like this. It reminded her of the charming Dan she met in high school. All piss, vinegar, muscle and charisma. "Well, I don't want you to lose your job. I'll need the alimony."

Dan spouted out, "It's yours, all yours, with interest. I'm like that Scrooge character. Or his partner, Jacob Marley—with all those chains tying me down. Down in Hell. I don't even know where to start. We've got no friends. Who would I turn to? I better hit the road and start thumbing to Quincy—if I'm going to make it to work on time—to beat the whistle. I barely made it on time yesterday." Dan shrugged his shoulders in defeat.

Dan got up to leave, skulking through the kitchen to the back door, his uneaten corn flakes wilting in the bowl and his coffee now cold. But like the resurrected Grinch, Velma's heart grew three sizes. She thought it had died, snuffed out—like the flame she used to hold for Dan. Ideal Dan, not actual Dan.

"Wait a minute," Velma exclaimed.

"What? I gotta go. I'll move out this weekend. Maybe I can rent a room near the Yard. Go to the Y or something."

Velma shook her head. "Look, I may regret this, but I've never heard you talk like this. You seem humble. Broken. Like some of Dr. Rebovitz's patients. I still think we need to follow through on this Jeremy thing. How else are we going to pay off José?"

Dan rolled his eyes, then said, "You think *those clowns* are gonna let us live after we get them Jeremy all gift wrapped? They'll keep that kid hogtied for months. Use him every chance they get and then get rid of him, too, when the cops start to close in!"

Velma sat back down. "God, Dan, I'm not even sure we can get away with it anyway. I'm betting Dr. Rebovitz thinks *I'm* up to no good."

"You, no we, need you to keep that job, Velma! Don't screw that up."

"Well then, if I'm gonna keep my job I'll have to come clean with him—ask for his help!"

"We gotta turn things around Velma. Save that kid. I could never live with myself if those neckless bastards get a-holt of him. He's so damned innocent!" Dan sat back down, vanquished.

"Well, how do we play it?" Velma asked.

"I dunno. I gotta get to work. If José finds out I've skipped work again, I've written my own death warrant!"

"Take the car. I'll ride the bus today. You're gonna be late. I'll grab an extra cup of coffee at the diner near the office. Think things through. We might have to go to the cops, you know."

Dan got a worried look on his face. Then he caught a spark. It replaced the death pallor of shame he exuded when he showed up for breakfast. "What if José has contacts at the police department? We'd be signing the contract José would take out on us!"

"I don't know. Let me talk to Dr. R. He's got to help us. He has all those military contacts. He'll be motivated to save Jeremy."

"Can we trust him?" Dan asked aloud.

"Do we have a choice? He may know some folks at the Police Department as well. He testifies for them a lot. You know, with commitment cases. Getting the walking wounded off the streets. He always steps up to help the cops get physically abusive parents away from their kids, especially when those children are his patients. Just go now. We'll talk later tonight."

"Does this mean I still live here for the next twenty-four hours at least?"

"One day at a time Dan. If I see the old Dan show back up at this doorstep all bets are off! I'm the one who's gambling now. And don't tell me how to roll the dice. You never had that skill to begin with."

Dan grabbed the keys to the Dodge and hauled ass to Quincy. Velma quick cleaned the kitchen and showered. After toweling off and gussying up, she gathered her purse and strode to the bus stop.

CHAPTER 27

Tuesday June 11, 1968, 7:45 a.m.
The Reverse Confessional

A cross town, David chugged the VW down to Rollstone Church and filled his tank at the Getty station for 35 cents a gallon. Little did he know that the VW Beetle was a death trap. Ralph Nader and his Raiders only focused on the Chevy Corvair. David did like to brag that Beetles could float for 17 minutes—should he ever drive one into a lake. Volkswagen finished off Beetles with a solid undercarriage that was semi-impervious to water, at least for the first 15 minutes out of 17. Nice feature compared to most other cars that had their guts, transmission, fuel lines, brake lines, exhaust, all on display for any mechanic to view when he put them up on the lift.

Getty's worker bee filled the tank and then asked David for $2.25 for the gas. David paid him and headed back across Main Street to the church parking lot. Alighting on the second floor office suite, he put the coffee pot on and settled into his office chair. Time to call Col. Edward McPherson and get his advice. David pulled out the church directory and dialed. Col. McPherson answered on the second ring.

"Good morning, McPherson residence. Who's calling and how are you on this glorious day?" the Colonel asked in a pleasant tone.

"Colonel, hello, its David Hergenroeder."

"Well how–dee–do, Reverend. What's on your mind, and to what do I owe the pleasure of an early morning pastoral call?"

"I need your help, Colonel," David said as he burst into tears.

"Whoa, big guy. Catch your breath, please. This sounds deadly serious. Are you OK?"

David couldn't speak, paralyzed by fear and grief all at once. He had a catch in his throat and spilled out, "Please, give me a minute to collect myself."

"Of course. Are you in the office? How's about if I come pay *you* a pastoral call?"

"No…. Well OK, sure. Not clear I'm fit to speak at the moment."

"Be right there," Col. McPherson said and rang off.

Just then Linda Dunn came into the church office to find David with red eyes, blowing his nose.

"I see you put the coffee on and, oh my, are you OK?"

Tears filled David's eyes. Again. He thought, *This is ridiculous. I've got to get hold of myself.*

"Yes, I'm OK. Just need some advice. Listen, Col. McPherson will be here in about 20 minutes. Can you bring in our coffee service with some cream and sugar?"

Linda said, "Of course. I'll show him in as soon as he gets here. But I bet that military man takes his coffee black."

Linda turned and headed back to her office gently closing David's door. Before she crossed the threshold, David caught his breath, composed himself, chuckled, and thanked her. A few minutes later, Linda returned with a tray, a plate of gingersnaps, and some leftover donut holes that the volunteers had wrapped up following Sunday's coffee hour. Somehow she had managed to put the refreshments on one of the church's antique silver trays.

"I'll close your door until Col. McPherson gets here," Linda said compassionately. She wondered what happened to upset David so. He was great about holding his emotions in check during church functions, especially with funeral services for beloved parishioners. She sensed, though, that something else was afoot as she softly closed the door.

David leaned over and put his face in his hands. He felt broken, helpless. Karate…. He'd fool no one! He was the bullied one growing up. Always chosen last for pickup games. Here he found himself again—chosen last—needing some protector to step in and save him *and* his family. *Today might be a good day to die—but only for me, not Alex and Jeremy.* He felt a trance overtake him as he wondered how he got here, to this office, the leader of this flock. They chose him on the basis of one candidate sermon. The Rollstone United Church of Christ Search Committee coming to his Peabody UCC church to hear him preach, get the feel of the man, drink in how his flock responded to him. *What a funny way to interview for a job—a command performance. But, they liked my message. Liked me, and Alex and little Jeremy.*

Linda gently knocked on his door. "Come on in. Please," David responded. Linda opened the door, announced Col. McPherson and discreetly closed the door.

"Well, preacher—always a pleasure! Two days in one week in fact. I feel one step closer to heaven already!" McPherson bragged, his steely blue eyes sparkling, a contrast to his blond butch cut.

"Thank you for coming. Please sit. Have a cup of coffee. I'll pour—you take it jet black, right?"

"Just so, Reverend."

"Please call me David."

"Sure, what's got you so upset?"

"Not sure where to jump off. I believe my family's in danger and I'm not sure what to do. I may need to borrow a gun."

"Whoa Nelly, David! Slow down a minute. Guns can make a big difference and I'm a fan, as you know. Of you...not guns. Most folks think guns solve problems. Have you ever even fired a gun?"

"No," David eked out.

"Before we even get to the reason or reasons you feel you need a gun—and the need may be justified—I gotta warn you that aiming, firing and actually hitting your target are incredibly difficult. We'll address those problems later if we cross that Rubicon. Let's start with a simple example. I want to tell you about my favorite gun, the 1911 Colt 45. Sounds like that malt liquor, doesn't it? This is one badass gun. A real marksman practices firing several hours a week and still will miss his target. You have to strengthen your fingers—because when you go to fire, your three fingers that aren't on the trigger will pull the gun down or to the side. And this is when you are taking your sweet time at the gun range—no pressure—just you and the target. OK, enough lecturing. What in hell's name has got you so scared that you need a gun?"

"A couple of weeks ago Alex and I took Jeremy to see a psychiatrist. A child specialist here in town, Dr. Azriel Rebovitz."

"Oh really? I know him well. He's treated many of my comrades, helped them get over their sense of shell shock—battle fatigue. Quite effective. He gave up that part of his practice though, a real disappointment to me. I think all that battle fatigue rubbed off on him. Can't say I blame him though. Listening to all those war stories. My word!"

"Yes, we were lucky to get in to see him on such short notice. He had a last-minute cancellation. I had taken Jeremy to his first day of kindergarten the day before the appointment."

"Kindergarten? Doesn't that usually start after Labor Day?"

"Yes, usually. But we applied for him to get into a special accelerated program. Fifteen students— Fitchburg State put it together. Jeremy tested out at a fourth grade level."

"Fourth grade! Holy shit! Pardon my French, that's military speak for hot damn. I'm surprised."

"Anyway, I took him to class the first day. Almost from the minute we arrived, he started bawling. His teacher, Mrs. Murphy, tried to console him, and then told him a little white lie about how she, too, cried on her first day of class years ago at Farnsworth Elementary in Peabody where she apparently grew up."

"You don't say. So did that assuage Jeremy?"

"No, it made it worse. He knew she was lying. I don't know how best to say this. Jeremy has a gift which may be a real curse. He can read people's minds. Sees into their heads—like some sort of radar or TV show he watches and sees what they're thinking, even what their memories are, as they themselves replay them in their heads."

"I'll be damned. Now that you mention it, I have heard talk about Jeremy making comments to some of the ladies in church. They'll say one thing—trying to be polite and he'll jump in and catch them in a lie, or mention some part of a story they were leaving out intentionally. Thought it was a fluke—you know—like he'd heard them say something else another time and he just had a good memory. OK, so why do *we* need a gun?" Col. McPherson asked as he took in the scent of his coffee tinged with mimeograph ink vapor. He reflected on the idea of a minister's office. *Must be a funny place—a bit like my old military office. Lots of secrets here, lots of confessions.* Like David, he had heard all manner of soldiers' and officers' confessions—then interpreted reality for them, dishing out advice and counsel, some of it sound, some not so much.

David was shaking his head. "The real trouble started when we visited Dr. Rebovitz. He met with Jeremy and, of course, saw right through our worries over early childhood schizophrenia. He recognized Jeremy's gift and tried to calm our fears. He offered to help Jeremy learn to filter his 'outbursts' of insight into what other folks were thinking."

"Sounds like a good plan to me," Col. McPherson exclaimed.

"It would have been, or is, except Dr. Rebovitz's secretary, Velma Brodie, transcribed the dictation the next day and suddenly she's calling us wanting to babysit and have her welder husband, Dan, come do odd jobs at the parsonage and here at Rollstone."

"Brodie. I know that name. I know Dan's dad. Stand-up guy. Butch Brodie, used to serve with him years ago. I've heard, too, that son Dan didn't get his dad's stalwart nature. No wonder you're worried. I wouldn't be too afraid of Dan—he's more bark than bite. I could talk to Butch and get him to clip back Dan's ears."

"No, please, it only gets worse. I called Dr. R's office the other day to ask him a follow-up question. Velma answered the phone, thinking I was someone else. She's all, 'We'll pay you back... We're good for Dan's debt. In fact we have a little secret to tell you that'll fix this problem.... Blah, blah, blah.' Then she realizes I'm not the prior caller who must have hung up on her.

"She finally figures out it's me. So I changed tactics. In between her stuttering, I mentioned that I just wanted to let her know that I'd visited Dr. R's mother and the visit went well. It was a plausible line, since his mom is at Pinehurst and he'd asked me to visit her—a little pastoral care. It was a trade, a barter of sorts, since we couldn't afford his hundred-dollar-per-hour rates."

"Jesus, that's rich! That's $200,000 a year in salary. Sorry, got off track. David, that whole Lord's name in vain thing. My apologies. I'm a vulgar man."

"Don't worry about it."

"God bless America. So the little secret you're thinking is Jeremy? What's the debt? Oh don't tell me, gambling?

Holy cow. Dan's in with loan sharks and gamblers. The mob? No wonder you want a gun, preacher!"

"Yes, even Dr. Rebovitz is convinced Velma and Dan are up to no good. They might view Jeremy as some sort of winning lottery ticket."

"He can predict lottery winners, too?" Edward asked, incredulous.

"No, sorry, figure of speech. And that's not the worst of it. Jeremy flat out saw through his mind's eye Sirhan Sirhan preparing, no making preparations, to kill Robert Kennedy, one week early."

Outside the office Linda noticed that an eerie quiet had descended on the second floor of Rollstone. She thought, *Upset preacher, upset church.*

CHAPTER 28

Tuesday June 11, 1968—8:45 a.m.
Rollstone Church Office

"**T**hanks for the impromptu counseling session, Preacher!" Col. Ed McPherson said, as David opened his office door and Ed hugged him.

Linda couldn't help notice the hug—it was way out of character for the stern military man she had come to know at church. She asked, "Did you two get everything settled in there—all the problems of church and society?"

Appreciating Linda's presence of mind, Ed laughed. "Oh yeah, church is fine and all squared away Linda. Society, I'm not so sure about."

Ed turned back to David. "Listen, come on out to my place later this morning around, say, ten a.m. I've got a couple of errands to run in town. I'll swing back by and you can follow me out there. I'll go over the particulars we discussed. David, I really appreciate your wise counsel. The good old military could use some of that tried-and-true Vanderbilt Divinity training. Heck, wasn't Vanderbilt some sort of Commodore? He shoulda been with a first name like Cornelius!" Ed laughed as he stalked off.

"Linda," David said, "I'm going to need some calendar flexibility over the next two weeks. Jeremy's needing a lot more emotional support and physical presence from me and Alex these first several days of this advanced kindergarten. More than we anticipated. Will you listen to me—I make it sound like MIT or Harvard. I know it's not, but still..." David's voice trailed off.

"Well, believe it or not, the Conrads canceled their counseling sessions with you Wednesday and Thursday— something about an out-of-state family issue they had to attend to. Her side, I think. Postponed, I should say. I rescheduled them for late June, since they were vague on their return date. You've also got that ecumenical service tomorrow. Remember—the Episcopal Bishop wanted you to provide the invocational prayer. Do you want me to advise Bishop Montgomery's secretary that you've had a family illness and can't attend?"

"Please. Great thinking. Kevin owes me, anyway. All the favors I've done for him including getting him out of a sticky wicket with that last civil rights march. You remember. The organizers scheduled him to give the invocation. Last-minute thing and fortunately I was available. Mark me down for Edward from ten to one p.m. today. But the rest of the week I'm unavailable except for emergencies. Make sense?"

"Absolutely, boss. Please take care of your family. You're no good to any of us if they are struggling."

CHAPTER 29

Tuesday June 11, 1968—6:59 a.m.
Quincy—General Dynamics Shipyard;
Electric Boat Division
12 Step Introductions—Salvation on Earth

"**B**est to have the work whistle at your back," Dan said aloud, as he made it through the front gate with minutes to spare. "Can I avoid Dominic again today?" he mumbled to himself, or so he thought, until another co-worker, Jeff Pelletier, overheard him.

"You lookin' for Dominic?" Jeff asked, eyeing Dan. Short and stout, Jeff looked the part of an old boson's mate.

"No, just wondered why I missed seeing him yesterday," Dan said, with surprise written all over his face.

"Yeah, he's been out a couple of days. Someone said he's got the flu bug or something," Jeff offered kindly as he moved on toward his worksite. Then he added, "I'll tell him you're looking for him!"

Dan thought to say "No!" but held his breath, as Jeff moved on. "Damn, got to learn to keep my mouth shut," Dan mumbled to himself. "I can't even talk to myself without getting in trouble. I'll just focus on my welding work to get through the day," he mused as he wondered when he'd next see José and Company. *Would they be waiting at the gate at the end of his shift?* Dan envisioned Velma at her desk transcribing dictation. *I just don't know if she'll stick with me. Would I stick with me? Would I stay with her if she'd gambled away everything we ever owned? After all those broken promises—all the thousands of dollars pissed away chasing dice. I'm a frickin' loser!* Dan recalled someone telling him that despair is a good thing, a great teacher. Well, Dan thought, I'm a frickin' PhD at despair. P.H.D…piled higher and deeper!

Dan's thoughts turned to welding and he moved across the seams like an automaton. Three hours passed like they were 20 minutes and Dan heard the lunch whistle blow. He hightailed it to the canteen truck and bought a cheese sandwich, cheapest item on the menu. Dan headed back to the main facility and found the "GA" room with a sign on the door that said, "Friends of Bill W." He knew GA stood for Gamblers Anonymous. He stepped inside and got a start as he eyed 25 other guys all standing around drinking coffee and smoking cigarettes. Some guy named Mike something or other called everyone to order from a makeshift podium. The men all took seats, classroom style.

"OK, welcome everyone. My name is Mike and I'm a compulsive gambler."

"Hello, Mike!" The crowd yelled, startling Dan. Twenty-five guys made quite a choir when they sang out in unison.

"For you first timers and I see a couple, this here's a Twelve-Step group. Everything we say here is anonymous and confidential. That's why we don't use last names and don't talk about each other outside the confines of this group. This is what we call a speaker's meeting. We do this a couple times a month. So for you first timers, I say again, welcome. Usually, we sit in a circle and anyone who wants to share, can. We learn from each other. You've likely taken the first step—getting past your denial that you've got a gambling problem. Pretty soon you'll get to the rest of the steps. We take things one day at a time. That gets too tough, well then, one hour at a time, or one minute at a time. You'll get out of this Twelve-Step group exactly what you put into it and maybe more. Hey, get yourself a sponsor, too. A bunch of us old-timers with some long-term sobriety can mentor you. I sponsor about five guys, some here and some back home in Lawrence. OK, enough of me babbling on. Steve, come on up here and give us the good news."

Dan looked around the room and noted the stale cigarette smell. He realized that hundreds of meetings had been held in this room and there must be something special going on here. As Steve made his way to the podium, Dan had a sudden feeling of compassion for himself. Looking around at all the guys struggling with gambling—his problem, their problem—struck him as a hopeful thing. He was no longer alone! *I gotta get a sponsor—someone who's been down this path....*

"All right, my name is Steve and I'm a compulsive gambler."

"Hello Steve!" The crowd and Dan chanted back. Dan felt a stirring from these other guys, most of whom he'd never even glanced at in the yard. His one and only group experience came from his teammates on the high school football team—where everyone pulled together. "Not sure I trust these guys," Dan muttered to himself.

Steve took a deep breath and launched into his talk. "I lost my first marriage to gambling. And my second marriage. My drug of choice? Blackjack, poker—cards, baby. Oh man, when I'd win, I was king of the world. It's like golf—drive for show, putt for dough. I was a great driver. Just didn't have a putter. I borrowed money from everybody I knew just to feed my beast. I lied, cheated, anything that'd get me back in the game. I couldn't live without it. Three years ago when I hit the bottom of a box canyon, Mike here found me and offered a dose of hope. He got me this job—a real job. I'd been driving trucks, short-haul loads—short so I didn't get too far away from gaming. I finally borrowed money from some guy I shouldn't have touched with a ten-foot pole. Interest racked up fast and next came the beatings—never enough to kill me or make it so I couldn't work—but shit, I hurt. Bad and often. So, here I am, three years into sobriety, doing my fearless moral and financial inventory, Step Four."

The other compulsive gamblers nodded their support for Steve. "If you want to gamble, that's your business. I made it through the first three steps, admitted I was powerless over gambling. I couldn't manage my life. I found a power greater than myself who could and would pull me back from the brink. God got me thinking right again. I couldn't do it myself. It's like that definition of insanity: I kept doing the same thing year after year, expecting different results. Man, that's when I finally turned everything over to God. You don't have to use God, but you've gotta find something bigger than yourself— some spiritual power. Call it whatever you want. But then I slammed into Step Four. Had to take a long look at myself—take a financial inventory. That part was easy—I ain't got shit for finances. But the moral part—I'm struggling to be honest with myself. It's funny, Step Five is easier and I'm doing it now. Admitting to you guys the exact nature of my wrongs. I'm a liar and a cheat, or I used to be, and could be again in a heartbeat.

"I've been asking God to remove those defects. For you first timers, that's Step Seven. So for me, these Twelve Steps are a bit circular. I do one, move on to the next, then double back to one I've done before—'cause I found more shit in my personal history and current way of thinking. I feel the pull of those card games the mob runs, all behind closed doors off of dank alleys, and oh man, I'm tempted. But when that happens, I pick up the phone and call my sponsor—he pulls me out of the abyss. Thank you!"

The crowd warbled, "Thank you, Steve!" As Dan joined in, too, he started to sense that he may have found some comrades who might have been down the same path. Steve's story struck a nerve in Dan that had long ago atrophied. As they adjourned, Dan bolted to the podium. "Steve, thank you. We've never met. My name is Dan Brodie. Say, would you mind giving me a coupla minutes after shift. Some of what you were saying made some sense. I'd *shore* 'preciate it."

"Walk with me. I can steal a few minutes. Let's grab a coffee at the diner across the street from the entrance. Nothin' too long, 'cause I gotta get home and run some errands. Sound OK?"

"Great. Means a lot to me. See you after shift, Steve," Dan offered as Steve bolted for the door.

Dan felt like the last man standing. The room had cleared as everyone beat a hasty retreat to get back on their jobs. As Dan stepped out the door, Dominic jumped out in front of him.

"What did you do to me, Dan? You lied like a pro—had me fooled bad with that cock and bull cancer story. I vouched for you. I figured we were buddies!" Dominic raged, two inches from Dan's face.

Just then from across the yard, Connie Calhoun, the foreman yelled, "Hey Danno. Take your thumb outta your ass and get back to it!"

"Yes, Connie. My bad. I'm there already." Dan started to hustle back to his welding spot.

Spitting venom, Dan whispered to Dominic, "Yeah, some favor. You set me up all right. Set me up to fail. Loan sharks—I owe those guys five month's salary *and* they took my truck. You stay away from me!" Dan pushed past, hoping to avoid Dominic for the rest of the day.

"We ain't through Dan. Not by a long shot. I got consequences, too—and you're gonna make me whole. Hole in one, damn it!" Dominic hollered to the wind, kicking up gravel as he turned back to his yard area.

****

The End of the Shift

After the whistle blew, Dan found Steve smoking a cigar by the security gate. Dan parked Velma's car adjacent to the shipyard security fence, hopped out and lumbered over to Steve. "Geez, thanks again Steve, I'm glad for your time. Coffee's on me."

"OK, Dan. Let's snap to it." Steve exuded a military air about him, having served a tour in Vietnam and in his last few months of service in 1965 was promoted to the officer in charge of a *Patrol Craft Fast* or PCF, later dubbed a Swift boat. It was that tour that got Steve interested in shipbuilding, after learning how to service every inch of the PCF's 50-foot aluminum hull. It's one thing to do shipbuilding as a job, quite another to service a boat so it saves your own life in battle. Dan and Steve angled toward the cross walk. The security guard eyeballed them as he stopped traffic so they could cross.

They entered the diner and were greeted with the aroma of steaks, mashed potatoes and steaming corn on the cob. Working man's food with lots of hot black coffee flowing from two bottomless urns. Dan entered with his head down, realizing that some of his yard mates made the diner their regular dinner stop and might wonder why he and Steve were together. Steve nodded to a few of his mates as the waitress pointed them to an open booth.

"I'll give you a half hour, then I gotta head for home, Dan," Steve said under his breath. "So before you get started with some line of bullshit about how you found Jesus at our meeting today, I gotta tell you I've had lots of first timers race up to me claiming they were ready for a change. Next thing you know they've lost their jobs from the gambling bug. Let me tell you something else, I'm guessing you fit that mold. So how are you different? Prove me wrong."

Dan got another catch in his throat before he warbled, "I'm in deep trouble." Then he stopped talking.

Steve looked him over, and then said, "You gotta do better than that, for chrissakes. Every guy in the yard's got trouble of one sort or another."

Forgetting where he was, Dan half-shouted, "Please, Steve! I need help, bad. I'm losing my wife, Velma. She's had it. And the mobs got me by the gnarlies!"

Heads turned from every booth in the diner.

"Wow, dude. Breathe. Slow down. Let's keep our voices low. Remember, it's Gambler's *Anonymous*."

"Yeah, OK.

"Listen," Dan urged, leaning across the booth. "Our stories are so much alike. I need to learn from you. Your experience. How did you get away from the mob? The loan sharks? I'm into José for five month's salary. Or half of it!"

"Damn, dude. This is serious. I owed José and Pilar too. Finally paid them off two years ago. Ate rice and beans for months—took the T to work and back. Rented a one-room shit hole. A bed and a sink was all. Shared a shower with other guys. It was heaven though—I hunkered down. Sacrificed, man!"

"I may need to live in that shit hole too."

"All right, let's talk about gambling. We do call it a *compulsion* instead of an addiction, right? But it's the same damned thing. Ya gotta get your next hit. So what's your game?'

"Huh? Oh, craps. I love them dice. Always trying to get back to that first big win. Never seems to happen though."

"Yeah. This compulsion. It'll kill us. It's really a kind of slow death, is what it is. Ya know what they say, pecked to death by ducks. Like I said in the meeting, those damned cards were, are, my drug of choice. Some kinda high, I suppose—always searching like you to capture that feeling I got the first time I scored big—took the whole pot. You shoulda seen the looks on the faces of my poker buddies. I use buddies loosely, didn't know a one of them!

The waitress brought more coffee as Dan started to make his ask. He held off until she walked back behind the counter. "Anyway, I was wondering about this sponsor thing. What's that all about?"

"It's just an agreement between two guys to sort of watch over each other. The sponsor agrees to keep an eye out for the newbie. I leaned hard on my sponsor for the first year, called him a lot, at odd hours of the night when I'd get the urge. He'd talk me down, get my mind focused. Ya know, the one day at a time idea, or one minute at a time."

"So," Dan said with sheepdog eyes, "can you be my sponsor?"

"Maybe. That's a big decision for both of us. I already sponsor four guys. I'm about at my limit. Hey, that's funny—my limit, just like with dem cards! Maybe you should ask Mike instead." Then he paused and said, "Well, OK. But I'm not sure I can handle another Twelve-Step rookie—sponsorship. It's all about quality and TLC. My teat almost runneth dry, buddy."

CHAPTER 30

Tuesday June 11, 1968, 8:00 a.m.
Velma's World Caves In

"Oh God," Velma moaned to herself. "This office makes me feel so claustrophobic. The walls are closing in on me. And that damned bus ride felt like a nightmare. Every stop seemed like the end of the line for me—would José be stepping on board to torture me?"

As she sat at the typewriter, she hardly felt like typing at all. Worse, her hands shook uncontrollably. As Dr. R's latest dictation coursed through her nervous system and spilled out the other end of her IBM Selectric, she didn't really hear the content of his words—just typed what he said. Dr. R was good at dictation. Always dictated where Velma should insert the periods, commas, and quotation marks, and always, always spelled the big medical terms. She'd worked for other morons who skipped grammar class once too often. The office felt like a medieval cave, complete with chains on the walls to hang prisoners. Her morning enveloped her in abject shame.

"The bus ride in did one good thing—made me realize I have a choice!" Velma announced to no one. "I've gotta save Jeremy. I'll confess all to Dr. Rebovitz. Come what may, hell or high water. I still can't quite trust Dan. Don't know if his change of heart will stick—but *I'm* changing and right now this very day," she groaned as she double checked Dr. R's calendar. "He's in Juvenile Court, but should be back any minute." The wall clock clicked as every minute passed. Her nerves seared with the shame. A simple letter that should have taken her five or six minutes took twice that long. At 9:59 a.m., Dr. R strolled in and eyeballed Velma—she felt his look of contempt. "Good morning, Dr. R," she gulped out. "I need to speak with you when you have a minute. Your 10:00 a.m. appointment, Sgt. Fleming, called to say he'd need to cancel. Pulled a double shift."

"OK, come in. I've some concerns to share with you, too."

Velma grabbed a seat in front of Dr. R's desk, feeling like an errant grade schooler having her first visit to the principal's office. Velma never had gotten into trouble at school, had always toed the line and diligently studied. She should've gone on to college. She'd made good grades. But Mr. Dan caught her eye. Since she never dared to rebel, she cottoned to his air of contempt for authority.

"You go first, Velma." Dr. R said without emotion.

"Yes, well, there's so much to say and I'm in desperate..." Her composure collapsed as Velma burst into tears. *Why was it so hard to breathe?* She fell back in her chair and closed her eyes, too ashamed to face Dr. R's penetrating stare. He seemed heartless and all Velma could chalk it up to was her utter breach of his professional trust. She tried to speak but the words eluded her. The more she tried to say something, anything, the worse her sobbing and heaving became.

Dr. R stepped out from behind his desk and put a hand on her shoulder. He grabbed the tissue box and handed it to her. Even as angry as he was, he recognized her trauma. Yes, he would fire her today, this morning even, but he could offer her the solace of an ear for five minutes.

"Oh God! What've I become?" Velma began. "I feel so trapped. Like an animal that has to chew off its paw to escape the hunter's trap. But I lack the teeth to do the job. And where would I run to?"

"Slow down," Dr. R asked. "This is about the Hergenroeder family, isn't it? And that call you took from that screaming man?"

"His name is José. He's some sort of loan shark. He has a big goon named Pilar that's his enforcer. He and Pilar followed me home last Friday afternoon."

"You mean the time you supposedly needed to check at the garage for warranty service?" Dr. R inquired without a hint of sarcasm.

"Yes, I lied about that, too. They busted down our back door. Dan owes them $500 or, ah, more like $7,000 now. He has to fork over his paycheck for the next five months. My pea brain had the bright idea I could get little Jeremy to help us—make a prediction or two—help José somehow," Velma sobbed.

"Then you *did* breach patient confidentiality. You've lied to me several times and put the Hergenroeder family at great risk," Dr. R stated softly, which made it all the more damning.

"Yes, it's true. I don't care about me or Dan. I'd wanna kill myself if they harm little Jeremy. I was so selfish, so stupid. We, no I, have to save him and his parents from those monsters. I don't care about this job—it won't be worth living if they hurt that family."

Dr. R moved back around his big desk. He picked up the phone and asked the operator to get the police. While he waited, he said, "Velma, there's a detective of some notoriety I want you, us, to speak to. His name is..." The operator interrupted his train of thought. "I have the Police Department on the line for you sir. When I hang up you'll be on with the desk sergeant," the operator intoned.

"Thank you, ma'am," Dr. R said as she rang off.

"This is Sgt. Hudson. How may we be of service?"

"Hello. This is Azriel. Dr. Rebovitz, your friendly neighborhood psychiatrist...."

Before Dr. Rebovitz could finish, Sergeant Hudson interrupted, "How's it hangin', Doc. Always good to hear your voice! What's up?"

"I need to speak with Detective Rod McNamara. Is he in?"

"Yes, Dr. R, I believe he's in the squad room. They're having a special roll call, otherwise I'd interrupt. Can I give him your number?" Hudson asked.

"Please. Tell him it's urgent. Quite urgent...."

"Do I need to send a patrol car your way?" Hudson pressed.

"No. Well, I don't know yet. Sorry to be so vague. Just have Detective McNamara call me at 555–4527."

"Consider the message delivered sir," Hudson offered as he hung up.

Velma looked at Dr. Rebovitz, somewhat perplexed. "What's your plan?"

"Well we've got to warn the police. This is shaping up to be a kidnapping at the very least—of Jeremy and maybe his parents. If I were José and Company, I'd grab all three and use Jeremy's parents to persuade him to do his 'feeling people's heads' mind trick. How else to get him to do what you want?" Dr. R asked as he stared at the ceiling. "Velma, I've got to tell you..." Dr. R started to say as the phone rang. He picked it up. "Hello. Rebovitz Psychiatry, Dr. Rebovitz speaking."

"Dr. Rebovitz, I didn't know doctors answered their own phones. I'm Detective McNamara. Sgt. Hudson said you asked for me personally. A matter of some gravity, I take it?"

"Yes. I've read about your exploits and believe, accurately I hope, that you're a can-do guy. Correct?"

"Maybe. That's what my wife says, but not on the home front!" Rod Sr. said with a laugh. "What's up?"

"This is convoluted, but at heart it involves a loansharking operation, assault, and maybe a future kidnapping."

"You've got my undivided attention, Doctor. Tell me the who, what, where, when and most important, the why."

"OK," Dr. R said, as he placed the call on speaker phone so Velma could hear. "I'm about to breach a critical patient confidentiality. Can we keep this off the books or at least out of your notebook, except in the most generic terms?"

Rod thought for a minute. "All right, we'll start that way, but I gotta tell you I'm a visual detective—it's how I connect all the dots. I use my notepad to outline my cases. It's my Bible."

As she listened to the discussion, Velma felt the heat in the room rise 20 degrees. This was all her fault, the very definition of Hell. *Imagine facing St. Peter as he outlines all your life's sins and how each little one destroyed other people's lives and hope. A lattice of destruction.* She felt so stupid. With her face in her hands, she whispered under her breath, "Kill me now, God. I'm ready to take any punishment you care to mete out. But I warn you—dammit, nothing will surpass my grief if Jeremy dies or José hurts him." Suddenly she sat bolt upright, realizing that she'd not been listening. She caught Dr. R looking at her expectantly, the speakerphone on and no one talking.

"Detective," Dr. R broke the silence. "It seems Velma traveled to Chicago for a minute."

Rod said, "Yes, thanks. I thought we got disconnected. What's the story, Velma?"

"I'm sorry. I'm so crushed by what I've done. I've destroyed so many lives in such a short time."

Rod interjected, "I don't know about that. Dr. Rebovitz seems to think this might be a just-in-the-nick-of-time sort of situation. Let me get this straight: You advised this José character, the loan shark, that one of Dr. Rebovitz's young patients was a mind reader? Is that the gist of it?"

Toxic shame and crushing guilt cascaded all through Velma. She started sobbing again.

"Velma," Dr. R quietly intoned. "Please help us. Breathe a few deep breaths."

Rod said, "Stop. I'm coming to your offices now. Where are you located—save me the trouble of looking it up?"

Dr. R relayed the address and Rod bolted for his car.

The Fitchburg Police Department had great mechanics and Rod's car always started first time, every time. Best of all, in the muscle-car parlance of the times, it could and would haul ass. Rod grasped the magnetized bubblegum light and attached it to his car roof as he sped out of the police lot.

CHAPTER 31

Sunday June 9, 1968—7:00 a.m.
A Visit to Dr. R's House—Two Days Earlier

"I think this is it," Alex said, as she and Jeremy drove up the long driveway that fed into Dr. Rebovitz's modest mansion. A black Lab came running up to greet the car as Alex applied the brakes.

"Philada! You be a good girl now! Don't slobber on our guests. They're in their Sunday best!" Dr. R hollered from his front door.

Philada wagged her tail so hard her whole body shuddered. Jeremy hopped out and hugged her. Philada groaned her delight and whimpered for some lovin's from Alex, who happily obliged.

"Some guard dog, huh?" noted Dr. R in greeting. "She'd love a burglar to death—drown them in saliva maybe. But that's what I wanted. I do occasionally have patients come out here so they can drink in the bucolic setting—a change of scenery often is the best therapy. Welcome to our happy home. Right, Philada?"

As Philada wagged her delighted response, Alex looked around the well-manicured estate. Every tree trimmed expertly with the branches cut off flush, right next to the trunk so next year's bark could quickly heal the wound.

The gladiolas had begun to break out in all their glory, even as the hyacinths bade good-bye to spring, their radiant purple and pink hues a slowly ebbing memory.

"I see you're admiring my botanical contributions to the Fitchburg cityscape, Alex."

"Yes. You clearly have a green thumb! It's marvelous. And the dogwoods are in their full splendor," Alex said pointing.

"They dazzle me. I long ago vowed that if my parents and I ever escaped the Nazis, I'd surround myself with nature's bounty. It's the perfect contrapuntal to Paul Joséph Goebbels' Aryan designs."

"Wow. I'm not sure I'd have made that spiritual connection in a thousand years of meditation," Alex remarked. "I should be off so you and Jeremy can get to work. Thank you, by the way. I'll be back in one hour, 45 minutes, Jeremy. You leave Philada alone and join Dr. R inside."

"Thanks Alex, I'll take it from here. Jeremy, come on into my living room. Philada—you can join us. We don't want to hear you whining for attention at the window sill while we work!"

The three friends ushered themselves in through the front door. Jeremy looked in awe at the vaulted ceilings, the huge chandelier that pointed to an ample staircase, and art works large and small hanging in every nook and cranny. Most of it still lifes and flowers of every description.

"I see you're admiring my paintings, Jeremy. They are fine indeed. I've spent way too much money on them. But I believe in surrounding myself with beauty. I had a difficult childhood, which I understand you got a window into when you visited Mom."

Jeremy said, "Yes," as he daydreamed about Dr. R calling his mother 'Mom.' Older people didn't seem to do that, or maybe it was because they moved away from using "Mom" as part of growing up. He wasn't sure.

"Well, to whom do I have the pleasure of their company this fine morning, Azriel?" A woman in a bathrobe sang from the second floor.

Jeremy looked up to see a woman in curlers wearing a warm smile.

"Young man, please say hello to Mrs. Rebovitz. She's my boss!"

Jeremy laughed at the joke. "That's what my Dad says about my Mom, too. She's our boss, but not in a bossy way."

"Nice to meet you young man. Mr. Jeremy have you had your breakfast? I was just about to toast some bagels. Azriel?"

"No, I'm fine." Dr. R said.

"Me too," Jeremy followed.

"Let's retire to my study, Jeremy. The living room feels too vacuous and Mrs. R likes to abide there on Sunday mornings with her cherished *Boston Globe!*"

The two headed for the study, which featured a pool table and a sho' nuff Bally pinball machine, its lights beckoning to Jeremy. They sat facing each other and Philada couldn't decide whose company she preferred.

"Jeremy let's get to work. Your gift... I think is a fine quality and attribute, not one to be hidden or ignored. Does that make sense?"

"Yes, sir, I guess. But I thought I was supposed to filter it!"

"That's true. Have you ever heard the saying, 'Don't spread your pearls before swine'?"

"No," Jeremy said. "Why would pigs want pearls?"

"Ha, ha! Precisely! You're just so smart. No, what the saying means is that you, me, us—we shouldn't spend our gifts on people who will waste them. Don't tell everything you know, my mother warned me when I was your age. She knew I often heard her and my father sharing neighborhood gossip, which husbands were cheating on their wives, or which wives were cheating on their husbands. She didn't want me blurting out what I heard around the dinner table to folks we met at our synagogue, our Jewish Temple. Do you understand?"

"Yes, I think so. My Mom says the same thing. But she and my Dad spell out people's names or use initials when they don't want me knowing what they're saying or who they're talking about. Of course I can spell, though."

"Good man. You're starting to get it. The other thing I want you to think about is the spy game. Did you know our country spies on almost every other country in the world? We want to know what they're up to. So we send people from our country to theirs—to act like they belong there. Spain say, or Russia—the Soviet Union. The people we send speak Spanish or Russian—whatever language is spoken by the country we send them to. They go and just listen—all the time—and blend in. See what's going on and then call us back and report their findings. Do you understand? Ever heard of spying?"

Jeremy reflected for a few seconds, admiring the pool table. "Sure. It's like when my friend Jimmy brought over his new toy Commando Scope. We used it to see around corners without people knowing. We tried it around the neighborhood. Saw lots of moms doing chores or watching TV. It was boring!"

"Boy, young man, it's fun to watch your mind at work. Yes, that's exactly what I'm talking about. What would those moms have said to you if they caught you spying on them?"

"They'd a been angry. But they wouldn't have seen our scope or known what it was."

"Maybe. You see my point? Spying on people—seeing what they're doing—may frighten them. Or, they'd get angry. That's what I want you to avoid. See, you spy on people without even realizing it. Their thoughts, worries, future intentions just pop into your head without you even trying to spy on them. You can't help it! Right?"

"I guess. But I can focus," Jeremy offered.

"What do you mean, focus?"

"Like that spy scope. I can look at someone and feel their head."

"Yes, I guess you can. Again, you're teaching me about your gift. You've heard the Bible story of how David killed Goliath? All the other Israelite soldiers were too scared to take on Goliath—he was so huge, some say he was over nine feet tall or more. Anyway, Goliath was the champion of the Philistine army and challenged the Israelites to send a champion to defeat him. Day after day Goliath would appear ready for battle, but none of the Israelites dared take him on. One day David took the challenge and used his slingshot to hurl a stone at Goliath's head. He knocked him out and cut off his head. Really a brutal slaying. You see how tall I am, right?"

"Yes sir!" Jeremy exclaimed.

"Goliath was so big he may have suffered from a disease that made his pituitary gland go haywire. It caused him to grow much bigger than most people. One of the side effects of this disease is poor eyesight—he couldn't see very well from the sides, out of the corner of his eyes. We call it peripheral vision. David figured out Goliath's weakness and shot his stone from the side—from Goliath's blind spot."

"Boy I never heard that part of the story in Sunday school!" Jeremy said with glee.

"Yup, I'm big too, but I don't suffer from gigantism and my pituitary is fine. My blind spot is missing what some patients are really trying to tell me. What is your blind spot, Jeremy?"

"I don't understand. I'm not tall and I can see just fine."

"Good point. Let me ask the question this way. How do you decide when to T̲. E̲. L̲. L̲. people what's in their heads?" Dr. R asked, flashing quote signs with his fingers.

"I don't know. I just always told them. I didn't think they might not want to know."

"Excellent. Sounds like a blind spot to me. What do you think? I suggest it's not always that they themselves don't want to know. It's more that they don't want others to know or even you to know. Or, maybe they themselves aren't ready to know."

"OK," Jeremy said sheepishly.

"Please, don't misunderstand what I'm saying here. You have a gift to share. It's just that not everyone's ready to open it. Your dad's a minister, yes?"

"Yes!" Jeremy said emphatically.

"I want to tell you another Bible story—one of my favorite notions about Jesus. He had a gift or lots of gifts—at least that's what his followers believed. So he'd go from town to town and preach to people and tell them they should forgive their enemies and love their neighbors. But not everyone wanted to hear what he had to say. Particularly from a guy who liked to hang out with poor folks or people with diseases. Worse, he didn't have a job. No steady income, anyway. Every once in a while he'd run into a bunch of folks who really didn't like his message. You know what he'd call them?"

"No," Jeremy responded quizzically.

"Hard-hearted. So rather than spread his pearls of wisdom like 'Love your God with all your heart, your soul and your mind,' he'd go to the edge of their town and shake out the pebbles, sand and dirt from his sneakers and leave town! Just move on to the next hamlet. Made everyone happy! And the pigs could go back to their mud pies and rootin' around in their own filth. No wasted pearls!"

"Wow!" Jeremy said with a sparkle in his eye. "How do I know who has a hard heart?"

Dr. R laughed. "If I knew the answer to that question I could be President, Jeremy. And I'm a psychiatrist—if anyone should know that answer, it's me, by golly. But I do know one big clue: watch how people behave. See, a bully can *tell* you or me that he loves us and our neighbors. But when he starts picking on us or our neighbors, teasing all of us, what does that tell you?"

"That he's really not loving anyone." Jeremy paused for a moment and then said, "I've been working on my head, Dr. R."

"What does that mean, Jeremy?"

"I tried breathing real hard yesterday morning when I woke up. I was trying to see if I just breathed in and out and only thought about breathing, if that might help me."

"Did it? Help you?"

"Yes. I was able to turn off the feeling heads thing for a few minutes."

"Really? I think you should practice that technique more often. You know it's the whole point of meditation. Have you ever heard that word? Monks meditate— sometimes for hours on end. It's quite a discipline. They don't try to stop their thoughts. Instead they just let them fly by, sort of like ocean waves passing by your boat. Is that what you did?"

"I suppose. I just ignored other people's thoughts around the neighborhood. Sort of like that Superman story you told me."

"Once again, you surprise me. I'm proud of you. You know what that means?"

Jeremy looked into Dr. R's head and said, "Yes. Today's lesson is over, right? You're glad I learned to keep my mouth shut after I've felt someone's head."

"I couldn't have said it better myself, young man! Now let's go ask Mrs. R to toast us each a bagel! You too, Philada."

CHAPTER 32

Tuesday June 11, 1968; 12:29 p.m.
For Whom the Lunch Bell Tolls

It's almost time, Jeremy!" Jimmy said, pointing at the clock. "The bell's gonna ring in a minute and then we're free! Hurry up and finish eating your Ring Ding!"

Jeremy looked at the clock as he wolfed down his dessert. "Yup, I'm ready," he replied, still chewing. Jeremy thought back to Monday and the idea of getting two recess breaks. It almost made giving up his summer worth the time in school.

Jeremy gulped down his milk to the chimes of Edgerly's second recess bell. "Yeah!" the class shouted. Through the open windows, Jeremy heard similar muted cheers from the youngsters in grades 1 through 6. The kindergarten class quickly set aside their lunch boxes and threw out their milk cartons, all empty of course. Jeremy jumped up with his classmates and formed the two abreast lines that meandered toward the exit. Mrs. Murphy called for calm and pointed out, "Now children, it's a beautiful day. Get some air and remember your parents don't get recess!"

Pilar eased his black Caddy up to the curb on Highland Avenue, right behind the junior high building.

The front of the junior high faced the elementary school across a quadrangle right next to the recess yard. He shut off the engine but left the key in the ignition, the better to ensure a quick getaway. He and Ricardo had donned sports coats and ties in a feeble attempt to look professional. For the few minutes they'd be near the playground it didn't matter that they'd purchased out of style 1950s era coats from the local Goodwill. Briefcases finished the ensemble as they strode confidently toward the quad. They'd hatched their snatch and grab plan not 30 minutes earlier. "It's the only damn way," Pilar said, "Otherwise, we'll get into Jeremy's radar."

The hide and seek game was proceeding in earnest. Jeremy took his turn and rambled off the 10 alligator count as his classmates vanished into their hiding spots. He ignored the odd feeling of an ominous presence nearby. Squelching the tingling sensation of impending doom, he tried to focus on the game so as not to disappoint his peers. He saw Julie behind a bush and ran to home to declare her found.

Mrs. Murphy looked across the quad and wondered who the two clowns were dressed in tattered woolen sport coats, way too warm for such nice weather. *Ah, they're probably just vendors here to meet with college officials. Perhaps they had trouble finding a parking spot,* she assumed. Most student teaching assignments had concluded, meaning that all the senior education majors fell back to campus for final exams before graduation in 10 days. *They were lucky to find street parking,* Mrs. Murphy concluded.

Pilar nudged Ricardo as if to say "there's our man." Ricardo deftly vaulted back to the Caddy, turned it on, and backed it up toward the playground entrance. Pilar angled towards the hide and seek gamers and called out to Jeremy, who knew instantly Pilar aimed to grab him. Jeremy screamed, "Mrs. Murphy, hel...!" Covering Jeremy's mouth, Pilar hogtied Jeremy as he ran to the Caddy with his muffled prize. He couldn't help but think that the kid was a helluva lot stronger than he'd imagined for a five year old.

Seeing the kidnapping in progress, Mrs. Murphy stepped in front of the oncoming Pilar. He chuckled and easily bowled her over, her high heels' grip no match against Pilar's overwhelming force. She screamed "Kidnapping!" and "Help!" as Pilar jumped in the back seat, pushing Jeremy to the floorboards. Paula Lovejoy, who was serving as the other playground teacher, came running and helped Mrs. Murphy to her feet. Then Paula ran to the office to call the police. Meanwhile, Mrs. Murphy squinted in vain trying to make out the Caddy's license plate as the car peeled away in the swirling dust.

CHAPTER 33

Tuesday June 11, 1968; 12:47 p.m.
No Miranda Warning Needed

As they waited for Detective McNamara, Dr. R had Velma cancel his remaining afternoon appointments. Velma informed the patients that Dr. R had a patient emergency in Boston. Rod entered the office and introduced himself. Velma greeted him with, "Oh, thank God you're here." She took Rod into Dr. R's office and outlined in great detail Dan's gambling habit, his $500 loan from José via Dominic, their night from hell starting at Antonio's, the truck theft, and their attempts to ingratiate themselves with the Hergenroeders.

Amazed by Velma's searching moral inventory, Rod believed she sincerely sought to protect Jeremy, Alex and David. As promised, he took no notes.

"I usually don't disclose any data from my ongoing investigations but since you breached confidentiality, fair's fair, I'll share my inside Intel," Rod said. "As best I can tell this José character heads up a sophisticated smuggling operation. The syndicate's minions graduate from Fitchburg High's mechanics program and get jobs with local trucking firms. These kids, all Puerto Rican apparently, are snapped up as quickly as the high school mints them. The grads work for a base wage and why not? These grads not only drive—they repair the trucks also, tune the engines, etc. I've no idea yet what they smuggle. Clearly there is a budding connection with the shipping industry, else why bother with a penny-ante loan for $500 with Mr. Dan? That's chump change." Rod took a breath and eyeballed his two compatriots. "Does any of this ring true with you two?"

"Sure, but what Velma doesn't know is that Jeremy's gift is not a localized phenomenon. He can read people's thoughts across to California. Fortunately José, et al., remain unaware. But this child warned his parents about the impending RFK assassination five or six days before Sirhan Sirhan showed up at the Ambassador Hotel."

"Oh my God!" Velma exclaimed. "If José figures that out, Jeremy will never escape. He'd be too valuable. He could warn José that you're on to them, Det. McNamara!"

"All right we can go there, but let's not get ahead of ourselves. You say, Dr. Rebovitz, that you've been teaching Jeremy how to filter his pronouncements—if nothing else, so that he doesn't scare people too much?"

Dr. Rebovitz nodded, "Yes that's right. Sunday we held our first training session."

Velma interjected, "I didn't know about that visit and I certainly didn't have it on your calendar!"

Dr. Rebovitz shrugged. "Of course not, Velma. David and I both realized you were getting way too interested in Jeremy's case. We could only guess at this José character's involvement. That's why I destroyed, burned in fact, Jeremy's chart. Didn't want to leave a trail. David insisted that I do that, and I agreed. You and Dan were our main loose ends, I'm ashamed to say."

"Of course. How could you assume otherwise?" Velma said.

"Where is Jeremy now, this very minute?" Detective Rod queried.

"I suppose right now he's in his accelerated kindergarten class at Edgerly Elementary school. A nice public setting—should be safe, wouldn't you think?" Dr. R asked.

Rod shook his head, "I doubt it. These Rican Rangers, as they call themselves, seem pretty savvy. Let's call the school if you don't mind. But give me a second to think." Everyone paused for a breath. "OK, I got an idea. Just might work. Doc, let's use the pretext that you've heard about the accelerated class and you want to speak to the lead teacher, if she's available. Tell the principal you've had an appointment cancellation and you'd like to swing by—bring her lunch, offer her your insights from your juvenile specialty practice. Make sense?"

Dr. R scratched his head. "A bit. Not sure they'll buy it. Most folks don't take kindly to psychiatric visits—sort of spooks them. We can give it a whirl, though. Velma, please look up the number and call over there."

Velma found the number and called. "Hello, yes, this is Dr. Azriel Rebovitz's office calling. He'd be most appreciative if you could ring through to the teacher... What, excuse me, there's been a kidnapping... Hello?" Stunned, Velma said, "She hung up on me. I heard screaming—something about a child abduction. You don't suppose... Oh shit."

"Yes, I do suppose. Give me that phone. Hurry!" Rod demanded.

Rod called the department on the back line. "Hello, Sgt. Hudson? What's going on at Edgerly? Never mind how I found out! Child abduction... Name is Jeremy Hergenroeder. What else do you have? OK, black Caddy. Two kidnappers—Latino/Hispanic looking. Wearing wool suits and ties. You gotta be kidding me. Oh, these guys are clever by half. I'll be in my car, so radio me with any updates. Yes, we're looking for a ring leader named José Gutierrez. I know—no time to explain. Send a squad car to his last known address and assume he's armed and dangerous. He has at least two known associates who may be cousins or something. A Pilar and a Ricardo. I'm betting they're our kidnappers. Look up José's auto registration and get back with me ASAP."

Rod looked at Velma and Dr. R. "Let's hope Jeremy absorbed your filter lessons on Sunday. I'm off!" Rod hollered as he ran for the door.

CHAPTER 34

Tuesday June 11, 1968; 12:36 p.m.
Leaving Edgerly School Yard

"**H**ead for Route 2!" Pilar hollered from the back seat.

"I got it, I got it!" Ricardo shouted back as he rocketed down Highland Street. Without stopping he banked left onto Pearl Street. Several drivers honked and swerved out of Ricardo's way, one offering him a digital display of displeasure as the driver tried to exit the next cross street at Cedar. The Pearl Street hill fed them directly on to Route 2. Jeremy felt the heads of the angry drivers and knew one of them had already stopped at a small grocery store to call in a police complaint about an out-of-control Cadillac.

"Go the speed limit! We got the kid safe and sound. No need to draw attention to ourselves. Bad enough we're in this frickin Caddy!" Pilar pointed out.

"You shoulda seen the look on that teacher's face after you pushed her right on her ass. Like ya pile drived her inta da mat! The hell's she thinking? She looked like a spinning top that ran out of gas. Them high heels—no stability!" Ricardo said, enjoying the image.

"Yeah, I had no choice but to go right through her. She looked like a little girl. I coulda sneezed and she'd a blown outta da way. D'she get our license plate?" Pilar asked, worried.

Pilar had Jeremy squished to the floorboard next to the transmission hump. "Filter," he said quietly to himself. "Mrs. Murphy is panicking!" he mouthed a little too loudly.

"What's that you're saying, kid?" Pilar leaned down to ask.

"Nothing. Who are you anyway?" Jeremy asked. He focused on Mrs. Murphy and could feel her disappointment in not catching their plate number—too much dust flying around. She feared she'd never see Jeremy again, and that these attackers might return another day to grab more kids. All of a sudden he felt Pilar pulling him up on the seat by his pants' belt. Like a momma cat carrying one of her kittens by the scruff of its neck.

"Alright kid, no one's gonna get hurt. We need your advice, see. We got an important job coming up. We gotta know who's with us and who's against us. And you got the radar to tell us. Unnnerstan?"

Filter, filter. "No, I don't understand. Why'd you hurt Mrs. Murphy? I like her."

"I'm sorry, kid. She's OK. She'll recover—hell she practically bounced like one a dem pro wrestlers! So back to the main subject. Hey, Ricardo, up ahead, state fuzz!"

Pilar shoved Jeremy back to the floorboard. Jeremy saw a gun under the passenger's seat and some sort of knife. Both were lying next to some peanut shells and some crusty French fries. The gun looked as big as his head. *How big were the bullets,* he wondered? He listened to the confident thrum of the big Cadillac engine and heard it slow as they passed the Statie.

"Hadn't gotten out an APB on us yet, woo hoo!" Pilar guffawed. "We gotta get off this main drag, though. Let's lift a different car. Hey, head for that shopping center. Bet we can boost one of the employee's cars. They're always easy to spot—boss makes 'em park as far away as possible from the door. Can't have customers walking a country mile for their gifts and eau de toilette!"

Jeremy couldn't believe his ears. These guys knew about toilet water. *Wonder if they bought it for their girlfriends? Do they have girlfriends? What would their girls say about them stealing me?*

Ricardo swung into the Piggly Wiggly lot. Jeremy could see the pig icon on the big store sign smiling down at him. Smooth as you like, Ricardo slid out of the car holding some sort of flat metal shaft. A minute later Jeremy heard an engine rev up and felt Pilar grabbing him, saying, "You make even one peep and we'll hurt your mom."

Jeremy felt Pilar's head and knew he meant business. Pilar seemed a sad man—couldn't trust anyone, couldn't get a decent night's sleep. He'd been that way since he was Jeremy's age.

Pilar whispered, "Pretend you're sleeping kid—that way, I'm carrying my napping boy to his uncle's car. Close your eyes and go limp."

Jeremy complied and in seconds he felt the new floorboard. Another four door and another big engine. Nothing under the seats, clean as a whistle. He heard Ricardo tell Pilar he had bagged the gun and knife in a T-shirt and they were loaded for bear. Ricardo jammed the makeshift package back under the seat. They bolted out of the lot and Pilar dragged Jeremy up again on the seat.

"Listen kid, you do what we say, when we say it, and we'll get you back home to Pearl Hill Road and all your nice toys. Got it?"

"Yes, sir," Jeremy said.

"Oh, ain't we the polite PK? I thought all PKs was jerks. You puttin' on an act, Jeremy?"

"No sir, I'm just scared." Jeremy had quickly figured out what Pilar needed to hear. Hopefully this unique skill set would serve him well the next few minutes and hours, if he had them. He knew both his parents soon would be in danger along with Dr. R. But what could he do? Dr. R had taught him some filtering ideas— but he hadn't practiced much yet. Maybe he should travel across town, using his mind, and pay an uninvited visit to Dr. R's mom. He wished he could reach out to Granny Steele's cousin Grace, but she died long ago. No, he'd have to disobey Eva and soon. In the meantime, he might have to use his new breathing technique if Pilar and Ricardo tried to use his gift.

CHAPTER 35

Tuesday June 11, 1968
Two Hours before the Kidnapping
Gunplay Across Town

"**D**ang, it's hot out for a June day in Massachusetts!"
David hollered to Edward as he fired up the VW
and followed Edward out of the Rollstone parking lot.
"Look," David pointed, "The great sun disk God of
Egyptian fame haunts us with his glory."

With the temperature approaching 95, David and Ed
both opened their window vents to get a cross breeze. As
they passed Rollstone's front lawn, David admired the
robins and blue jays arguing over nesting rights in the two
big pin oak trees standing tall on the church front lawn.
*They'd stood the test of time for nearly a century. How
many of the birds' forebears had nested there? Following
Mr. Law & Order Ed sure is easy. The guy obeys the speed
limit, signals for every turn at least 100 feet beforehand,
and always come to a full halt at each stop sign.*

The two-car caravan paraded past Main Street up
toward Rindge Road, which fed all the way to
Ashburnham, Ed's hometown. The woods on either side of
the roadway seemed endless, a vast habitat away from
Fitchburg's industrial footprint. Ed drove a 1963 Lincoln

Continental, the kind with the back doors that open forward, which every backseat passenger appreciated on egress. Lincoln made the cars to ride plush and Ed insisted on buying one that the Ford factory built on a Wednesday, two days past the assembly line workers' collective weekend hangovers. He still changed his own oil and tuned it up himself, every 5,000 miles. Plugs, points, new rotor, new filters— this baby was gonna last.

As the pair approached Ashburnham, David wondered what the town's namesake, the Earl of Ashburnham, would have thought of a local minister getting target practice from a retired soldier.

Soon they found Ed's long serpentine driveway with the full bore security gate. Ed had installed a radio controlled servo that smoothly opened at the touch of some device David could see Ed push from his front visor. Ed's Doberman, Pinky, named after a favorite uncle of Ed's, waited patiently for his master to move through the gate. Pinky gave chase without barking, ignoring the noisy VW Beetle, whose maintenance schedule proved far more haphazard compared to Ed's Lincoln. David hadn't changed the oil since January, partly because his mechanic's reminder sticker had long ago lost purchase on the windshield, ending up with the rest of the detritus under his seat.

As they headed to the house, David admired the shooting range Ed had constructed, complete with archery targets and, to the left side, a berm that held four targets for longer range rifle work. There also was an odd looking bric-o-block building with a flat roof and a red front door. Ed hopped out of the Lincoln, petted Pinky and scratched his ears, which he had left intact despite the breeder's suggestion that they be lopped off. "If God intended Dobermans to have pointed ears, he'd have lopped them off himself," Ed warned the breeder. "Take off the dew claws, though, since I don't want my puppy handicapped and leave that tail be, I don't want it stubbed off either." Ed expected people to follow his orders without question and most folks took the hint.

Ed and Pinky headed for the building, which had its own impressive security system. Ed waved David over and started opening a locking apparatus. Pinky glared at David, but stuck near Ed. "Visit," Ed told Pinky. The dog demurred and went up to David to greet him. "This here's Pinky, David. He's hoping you'll pet him—and yes, he's already sized you up."

David liked dogs, always had. He recalled reading somewhere that early humans first domesticated wolves about 30,000 years ago. Cats came 20,000 years later, which explained why they still were semi-wild and could not easily be trained to heel, sit, roll over or guard a house. Pinky and David bonded for 90 seconds until Ed said, "C'mon into my shooting range."

As David walked through the doorway, Pinky stayed outside right by the door as if on sentry duty. Ed turned on the bank of overhead lights.

"Holy guacamole," David exclaimed. "This place is huge. It seems like it should be so much smaller from the outside. Say, is that a pile of coal at the far end? Oh, never mind. I get it. That's where all the bullets end up, right?"

Ed nodded and opened two of the huge gun safes. Both had nice backlighting.

"All right David, let's start here. I always lock up my guns, except the Colt that I keep by the bedside and the sniper kit I have in the trunk of my car. That kit is a whole 'nother story—I like to have my second M21 rifle with me since I also target shoot at the base. I got the two of them just a couple of months ago—they're prototypes. Here's one of them. Don't tell anyone, but they came with silencers," Ed said as he pointed to the second safe and pulled out a big rifle with a matte black scope sitting on top. "It's semi-automatic and takes a big cartridge or bullet. We call it a NATO cartridge, 7.62×51 mm. The rifle's got a muzzle velocity of 2,800 feet per second—that's how fast the bullet flies. I can shoot and hit a target up to 750 yards away. My killing days are over, however, so these two are just for practice."

"Now the one in the trunk is just part of the matched pair?" David asked.

"Oh yeah. I keep it in a portable carrier that locks. Sometimes I go to the range out at Devens. Nice to have that baby with me. Anywho, as I was saying, the movies and TV shows make gunplay look easy. But guns are like any tools you have in your shed. Treat them well, give them respect, and they'll serve you well. Think about it. Once guns showed up on the scene, those knights in shining armor were pretty useless. A bullet or two would knock a knight on his ass even if his armor deflected the shot. Once the knight fell to the ground, he became easy pickin's for his enemies."

Ed pulled out the pistol, holding it up for David to see. "Let's start with my favorite gun, the 1911 Colt 45. I've heard rumors that its inventor, a guy named John

Browning, designed the gun to stop an engine—you know if a car was running at you. Never put much stock in that theory though, and sure as hell wouldn't put it to the test by standing in front of a speeding car. The military calls this gun, 'Pistol, Caliber .45, Automatic, M1911A1 Colt.' No definite article. Sort of like that Christmas cantata my wife loves, 'Messiah,' and not '*The* Messiah.' You know the one where the choir belts out the Halleluiah Chorus and all?"

David nodded, still taking in all the artillery. Small arms, but more guns than he'd ever seen in one place. Unwittingly, David's jaw dropped as he took in the wide array of pistols and rifles.

Ed continued. "I've had to send both of these Colts, here, you hold this one, off to a machinist I know in Pennsylvania. He's an expert at retooling the slide so it's smooth as silk. I've also had him install Pachmayr grips—feels better in your hand. The machinist also Parkerized the gun's surface—it's an electrochemical conversion coating that protects against corrosion. Like Ziebarting your car. All this work cost me a pretty penny, but it was worth it. The guy has a waiting list of customers—so I didn't have these two puppies for almost a year, waiting for him to finish. You send him the guns with the list of what you want him to do—and the money up front. That's the thing with assembly-line manufacturing. Your goal is to reduce variation. Every gun should be the same, down to the micrometer. I've been to the Springfield Armory, the one founded by George Washington to make sure our armies had decent weaponry, and to the Colt factory in Hartford. I watched as these two Colts came down the assembly line. Yes, rank does have its privileges—especially when Colt's procurement team wants to curry favor with the military, their biggest customer by far, especially in war time.

"All right, snap to, David. Time to learn how to take the Colt apart. It's made in three main pieces—with about 54 parts altogether. This gun is what we call single action. It's semi-automatic, meaning you shoot one bullet at a time, but you don't have to pull back the hammer like those gunslingers of old had to do. Bullets are in a magazine." Ed pointed as he slid out the device. "The mag holds seven bullets." Ed popped one out of the top of the magazine. "Big, huh?"

David rolled the bullet between his fingers, stunned at the girth of the thing. He held it up to the light for a closer view.

"45 caliber," Ed noted. "The old military manual warned that when you shoot it at a big white pine tree the bullet will go into a depth of one inch or more. Of course, your distance from the tree would affect your depth too. They wrote that a one-inch depth meant a significant injury to your enemy. This gun's been copied by armies all over the world—because it's so damned reliable. Every time you shoot, its recoil operation—or the expanding combustion gases—creates enough force to cause the slide to move backward. There's a neat claw do-hickey, an extractor that pops out the spent casing."

David looked on, admiring the elegant mechanics of the thing.

"Once the slide stops, then its own inertia causes it to move forward, pushed by a big spring which brings up your next bullet—all ready to fire. It really means you can just keep shooting without worrying about cocking back the hammer. Unloaded, this gun weighs about three pounds. I like the double stack magazine because it holds 14 rounds. But I'm lending you my single stack—it's lighter and thus easier to conceal, which I think is important for you—since those clowns who are after Jeremy ain't never heard of a minister packing heat, right?"

"I suppose. This is all so...I don't know, surreal. Invigorating and frightening. At the same time."

"Good. I want you scared." Ed said as he disassembled the gun, cleaned and reassembled it. He then watched as David did the same, mixing up the order a bit, but finally getting the sequence down. He struggled a bit with his withered left hand, but managed to make decent progress.

"Now David, do it again but with your eyes closed! Pretend you're in the dark and it's a matter of life or death and your gun's jammed—now go!"

David closed his eyes and saw the gun assembled. He popped out the magazine, then played with the slide, got it off, along with the barrel and spring. Taking it apart was easier than he imagined. Clumsily, he spent the next 10 minutes trying to assemble the Colt. Easier said than done. He opened his eyes, but it didn't help since Ed had doused the overhead lights.

"Stop David." Ed said as he turned on the lights. "First time's a bitch. Let's do it with your eyes open a few more times so you get some muscle memory going in your favor."

As he practiced under Ed's watchful eye, David wondered about Jeremy. Meanwhile, across town, as Jeremy eyed the gun bag under the floorboard of car number two he felt his Dad's head and watched David attempt the disassembly and reassembly process.

Magazine? Jeremy wondered to himself. *What kind of magazine holds bullets? Not my Mom's Ladies Home Journal or Good Housekeeping. Could I get the magazine unhitched from Ricardo's gun?*

"Easy does it, Preacher. That's the ticket. Good—now you've got the hang of it. Time to shoot. Ready?"

David eyeballed Ed and nodded. "Is this the kind of training Sirhan Sirhan got before he killed RFK?" David asked under his breath.

"David, you mentioned going to the karate studio. Did the teacher talk about a stance?"

"Yes, yes he did. Mark had us put our right foot back and our left foot forward. Mark said our power started with the stance—moved up from our hips. Why?"

"Just like karate, good marksmanship starts with your stance. Assuming you're standing up, of course. Out in the jungle you may be crouched down or hiding behind a tree. Now here, it's just you and the target. OK, we'll have you take the same karate stance. Put your left foot forward."

David looked up and saw a target hanging from a guy wire about 15 yards away. It had a human outline on it— head and torso, no legs.

"Put these tactical ear muffs on. They look like fancy headphones, but they'll muffle the sound and protect your hearing. We'll have to speak up to hear each other. But the Colt is loud, like most guns. Sound sends a message, yes?"

"Yes!" David said, his voice muffled by the ear phones. He realized Mark had nailed it. "You hear gunfire and most folks take notice and run for cover. Or the uninitiated think it's just firecrackers."

"OK, put TV gunplay out of your head. All those images are wrong and dumb. I want to put you in what's called the classic Weaver stance. You gotta use your right hand, which I guess goes without saying. So put your right foot back. Left foot forward—just a bit. Watch—I'll try to push you," Ed said as he shoved David mid chest. David resisted and didn't budge, although he was a bit embarrassed at the seeming competition. *Lover, not a fighter,* he thought.

"Good. My point is that some guns have a kick to them, shotguns in particular. You want to live—then that means staying on your feet—in your stance with your eyes always on your target. Got it?"

"I think so," David nodded.

"Excellent. Now watch what I do...."

The pair practiced for the next 15 minutes with Ed helping David learn about the proper stance, how to sight in the target and actually hit the target.

Just then there came a knock on the red door. Mrs. Lily McPherson poked her head in, leading with her coiffed bouffant hairdo. "David, err, I mean Rev. Hergenroeder, there's a call from Linda at the church office. Sounds urgent. She said the police are trying to find you."

David and Ed brushed past Lily and bolted for the house with Pinky leading the way. Ed had the presence of mind to grab his Colt and two spare magazines. Little did he know he'd soon need his sniper rifle hiding in his trunk.

CHAPTER 36

Tuesday June 11, 1968—1:00 p.m.
A Good Day to Die

R icardo aimed the newly acquired Oldsmobile F-85
down Route 2. The damn thing had a standard shift,
on the column no less. Nor did it help that he was born a
southpaw. Thank God he'd learned on a stick when he
was a teenager. The good news, if it even mattered, was
that if the battery sputtered out, he could restart the car in
second gear by aiming it down an incline and popping the
clutch. He kept to the speed limit and then spied a
McDonald's restaurant outside Leominster. And a pay
phone!

"Pilar—I see a pay phone! Gotta get José on the line
and tell him we got the kid, have him meet us in Quincy
and get that stevedore union boss in for a meet and greet.
Get Jeremy to help us, right Jeremy?" Ricardo clucked as
he looked over the seat and eyeballed the PK.

"Yes sir," Jeremy said, deflated.

"Back on the floor kid, and stay down while we make
this call," Pilar growled.

Jeremy knelt back on the floor and spied the gun under
the seat. He had felt his Dad's head while David spent time

at Ed's gun range. Jeremy watched how David and Ed released the magazine. While Pilar kept watch for the cops or nosey passersby, anyone who would have glanced his way would have been struck by how odd he looked sitting by himself in the back seat. Jeremy took a breath and reached for the gun. He grabbed the release with his right hand and then held his left hand over his other hand's fingers. He deftly released the magazine as Pilar tried to hear Ricardo's conversation with José. To cool the car, Ricardo and Pilar had rolled down the windows. The open windows gave Jeremy plenty of ambient noise for cover. Jeremy jammed the magazine into the spring assembly that supported the ample front seat. The magazine found purchase between the spring curls and caught tight. Jeremy remembered that Ed said the gun weighed 3 pounds and was heavier with all the bullets.

Jeremy heard Ricardo shout, "I know, I know—we left the car at the Piggly Wiggly. Send one of the rangers to grab it before the employee figures out we stole his. The lot was busy with lots of moms buying their papas meat and potatoes."

José yelled back, "Christ—this is going to hell in a hand basket! Maybe we can get the car. I told ya ta just eyeball da kid during recess, remember?"

"Yeah and I told you his radar would've picked us up in a heartbeat. We saw him and grabbed him. That teacher got in my way…"

"Yeah, yeah, let's calm down already. I gotta think," José responded. "All right, this is what we do. I'll get Eduardo to grab your car. He'll have to hotwire it since you've got the stupid keys. He'd better scope out the lot for cops first. Do a drive-by. I'm sure there's an APB out on your asses now. Get another car and fast. Den meet me in Quincy at the yards. I'll take off right now. I'm getting Rick Sullivan on the line. See if we can square a deal—introduce Jeremy as my nephew, future Ranger."

Pilar and Jeremy both heard Ricardo mention Quincy. Jeremy clenched his teeth, jumped up on the seat and screamed at the top of his lungs, "This is a good day to die... This Is A Good Day To Die... THIS IS A GOOD DAY TO DIE!"

Jeremy continued screaming as Mr. and Mrs. Collin Anttonen exited the restaurant. Collin started complaining, "Honey, that Big Mac always feels like a bomb in my stomach...." His wife Lacey started to respond but then heard the screaming. She stared at the F-85 and the crazy kid threatening suicide at the top of his lungs. Collin stopped dead in his tracks, too, as he eyeballed Ricardo racing across the hot parking lot, his shoes popping the tar bubbles. Ricardo vaulted into the car while Pilar grabbed the boy around the face to shut him down. Ricardo fired up the engine and peeled rubber out of the parking lot, turning southeast back on to Route 2.

Collin noticed the pay phone receiver swinging from the momentum of Ricardo's haste to end the conversation. He swore he could hear some man screaming, "What the f...!"

"Something's bad wrong," said Collin. He had just retired from his solo CPA practice. The most excitement he had most days during his career was finding some extra deduction for one of his business clients. Now that was fun! Best of all the 1040 forms didn't talk back. He and Lacey had raised two girls and a boy, all of whom had flown the coop for Spokane, Washington after getting full rides to Gonzaga University. He'd never heard of Gonzaga until one of the kids' guidance counselor had suggested the school.

"Something's fishy," agreed Lacey. "Why was that man sitting in the back seat? It looked like he was hurting that boy."

"Best mind our own business, Lacey. We don't need to get involved at our age. I'm sure it's a family feud, don't ya' spose?" Collin offered, no confidence in his voice.

"Collin! If that were our grandchild Warren and another retired couple witnessed what we saw, what would you hope they'd do? I got the license plate. I'm calling the cops right now. You just go sit in the car until they arrive."

"You're right. I'm wrong. That kid's in trouble. Sure enough. I'd bet dollars to donuts those two clowns aren't related to the boy."

Lacey called the operator, who mistakenly routed her through to the Fitchburg Police instead of Leominster's finest.

"Hello, Fitchburg Police, Sergeant Finch Hudson speaking. Tell me your name and how we can help."

"I'm Lacey Anttonen and I'm standing here at the pay phone beside the McDonald's in Leominster."

"Ah, Ma'am, I need you to hang up and call the Leominster police."

"Look I don't know the number and I'm not running back into the restaurant for another dime. You listen here! We're just across the city line from Fitchburg. My husband and I just witnessed something awfully weird. Two guys manhandling a little boy. The kid seemed suicidal or something, the way he yelled at the top of his lungs."

"I'm sorry. Go ahead. I'll take down your information and then *I'll* reach the Leominster police. You say two men and a boy? And the kid was screaming. Could you hear what he was saying?"

"It's going to sound insane. He was shouting that he wanted to die or that it was a good day to die. He can't be more than five or six, but what a voice! I could've heard him three parking lots away. Look, they drove a four-door car, blue. License plate GRG-4HO. And the driver threw up a cloud of blue smoke burning rubber out of the parking lot. Quite impressive, actually."

"Lacey! Tell the cop it was an Olds F-85!" Collin yelped.

"What? Oh, my husband says it was an Oldsmobile. An F-85."

"It isn't stolen, at least from any reports we have. But I do have an APB out on a kidnapping that happened about 30 minutes ago—the kidnappers drove a Cadillac, though. Please describe the boy and those two men."

"The one man who was at the pay phone had snappy looking shoes on, a sport coat and he looked, I don't know, tanned, black hair. He didn't look European—I mean, he looked Cuban or something."

"You mean Latino, Hispanic maybe?"

"Yes, that's it! Hispanic—sort of a Fidel Castro without the beard or cigar. Big guy. Broad shoulders and, ah, no neck!"

"Which way'd they head on Route 2?"

"Left. I mean south, I don't know. I'm not good with directions. Are you sending a squad car to meet me?"

"No Ma'am. But the info you've given us helps a lot. Bless you."

CHAPTER 37

Tuesday June 11, 1968—12:55 p.m.
The Call to Ashburnham

"**H**ello?" David shouted into Ed's hallway phone. The McPherson's had housed their phone in a little cupboard all its own adjacent to a round piano style seat that pulled out from the wall. David noticed all the pictures hanging above the phone, including one with Ed and Gen. Douglas MacArthur in what looked like a M*A*S*H tent in Korea.

"David! Thank God I found you." Linda exclaimed. "Jeremy's been kidnapped. The police need to speak to you now! There's a Det. McNamara who's on the case. Seems pretty sharp. The desk sergeant can put you through—radio McNamara's car. Just call them—here's the number—2232."

For some reason, David had the presence of mind to grab the pen and pad sitting next to the phone and wrote down the number, just four digits. Fitchburg in the 1960s had a small enough exchange to accommodate abbreviated listings.

David heard two rings before the police answered. "Fitchburg Police Department, Sgt. Hudson speaking. What's the problem?"

David admired for a microsecond the sergeant's bottom-line approach. "Yes, please, this is David Hergenroeder. My son's been...."

Before David could spout out more, Sgt. Hudson barked, "Yes, David, I'm patching you through to Rod, I mean Det. McNamara, right now. He's leading our investigation. If you get cut off, call me right back at 2232. System is fuzzy sometimes."

David listened to static and then heard a click. "McNamara here. Is this David?"

"Yes! Where's my son Jeremy? Do you know?"

"We're not entirely sure, David, at least not yet. We know two guys nabbed him right off the Edgerly school yard during Jeremy's lunchtime recess. Assaulted his teacher, Helen Murphy. A brave one she is—they knocked her flat on her derrière, but she's OK. Gave us a description of the kidnappers and their Cadillac. I also just left Dr. Rebovitz's office and got some more background information. Tried to reach you at Rollstone. What else can you tell me?"

David took a deep breath and felt Ed's presence next to him. "I think that Dr. Rebovitz's secretary Velma and her husband Dan Brodie are part of some sort of conspiracy to abduct my son."

"I can assure you David, they are or were. I got the whole story from Velma herself. She 'fessed up to Dr. Rebovitz this morning and is feeling a death rattle at the thought that she and Dan put Jeremy in harm's way."

"I don't care about her emotional state, frankly. We've got to find my son before they hurt him or worse. It's some José character that's in with the bunch...."

"Yes, I have a lot of information about José and his trucking operations."

"Trucking? What could Jeremy do, I mean, why would a trucking company need him?" David asked as he instantly realized how a company might abuse Jeremy's gift, if they could get him to cooperate.

"That can't be our focus right now." Rod pointed out. "We just got an eyewitness report from a retired couple at the McDonalds in Leominster. Off of Route 2. They saw two Hispanic men trying to manhandle a small boy, who appeared suicidal. He was screaming about dying."

"Oh my God. No, he's not suicidal. We took a few karate lessons the last few days and our instructor Mark Gallagher taught us to scream, "Today is a good day to die" over and over. A way, I guess, to prepare for battle, deal with our fears and throw off our enemies all at once."

"Now by the eyewitness's account, a Lacey Anttonen and her husband, Jeremy had his kidnappers in fits. While one of them made a pay phone call, the other wrestled with Jeremy. Their windows were down thanks to the heat, so the Anttonen's and everyone else in a twelve-block radius coulda heard your kid. He scared them for sure and they burned rubber out of that lot. I'm guessing they'll boost another car any minute now. We found their Caddie at the Cleghorn Piggly Wiggly, up from the bike shop."

"How'd you manage to find their car?"

"We didn't. Some bag boy saw them steal his mom's Old's F-85. Where are you now?"

"I'm at a parishioner's house, Col. Ed McPherson's in Ashburnham."

"Where's your wife right now?"

"Alex... She's at home at 123 Pearl Hill Road."

"Good. Call her right now. Tell her to get to a neighbor's house this instant. Lock the house. I'm guessing these Gutierrez boys or whoever they are want some help handling Jeremy. Alex would be a logical choice, or God forbid, his teacher, Mrs. Murphy. The school's all locked down and we're notifying all the parents to come pick up their kids. You stay put. Give me Ed's number and I'll be in touch as soon as we have more information. I know it's gonna be tempting to get out and look for Jeremy. Please stay put. You don't have the dispatch tools we do. Please put Col. McPherson on the phone."

David handed the phone to Ed, his hand shaking from the trauma and fear gnawing at his innards.

"Hello, this is Col. McPherson. How can I help?"

"Colonel, I'm Detective Rod McPherson..."

Ed interrupted him. "Ah, I remember you. The savior to our elderly neighbors who almost got caught up in that roofing scam."

Rod rolled his eyes, embarrassed for a minute. "Look, I need your help calming David down. Please call and warn his wife, or at least be on the other line when he calls her—do you have a second phone?"

"Yes."

"Great. Call Alex now. Stay put please and we'll keep you posted. I'll leave instructions with Finch—our desk sergeant—to help you all stay in the loop. Got it? In fact, I think I'm going to deputize you if you don't mind. Are you still active military?"

"No, I'm mostly retired, but I help out from time to time at Ft. Devens with training new recruits for the all-volunteer Army.

"Fine. I need you to watch over David, make sure he doesn't do anything crazy. I've dealt with kidnap cases before and you never know how the parents are going to react. Got it?"

"Yes, I think I do. Understand I mean. I've seen all manner of men react oddly to intense stress."

"Of course you have. I shouldn't have couched it like that. So do you swear to uphold the law?"

"Yes, I swear. No worries," Ed said as they rang off.

"David, I'll get on the other phone—let's call Alex."

"OK. What'd he want with you?" David inquired, his voice changing pitch out of fear.

"He wanted us to stay put. Await further news."

"What did he make you swear for?"

"I don't know. For some reason he just deputized me. I think he thought I'd keep track of you if he had me join the police force. You know, duty calls and all that. Honestly, he said he'd had bad experiences with parents of kidnap victims in the past. They went crazy or something."

They called Alex.

CHAPTER 38

Tuesday June 11, 1968—2:05 p.m.
Route 2—Leominster, Massachusetts
Controlling a Five Year Old

"**A**ll right, kid!" Pilar screamed. "I'll shove a sock in your mouth if you scream that shit again. Got it?"

"Yes, sir. I got scared."

"Whatever. Back on the floor!"

Unbeknownst to the cops, Ricardo had doubled back on Route 2 after realizing that anyone who spotted Jeremy's crazy act at McDonald's would call the cops for sure. The threesome headed to Lunenburg, taking Route 13 North. As they wended their way into a quiet neighborhood full of Cape Cod style homes, Ricardo kept to the speed limit. They came to a high school nestled in the woods, but rejected it as too public for pirating another car. School buses sat in a neat line out front awaiting the closing bell.

Driving on, Ricardo found a strip mall with a Cumberland Farms convenience store next to a CVS pharmacy. He wound the F-85 around back, hoping to find a manager's car. Someone who wouldn't be leaving until closing time. Sure enough, he spotted a freshly waxed, spit-polished Ford Galaxie 500 LTD, with its windows down no less. He pulled up beside it, hopped in and within seconds hotwired it. He revved the engine and it thrummed like an Indy car. Pilar grabbed Jeremy and reached under the seat for their Colt 45. Jeremy wriggled in hopes of distracting Pilar's attention from the reduced weight of the magazine-less gun. "It worked!" Jeremy thought to himself. "Pilar seemed too worried about people seeing us."

"Make like a mummy, Jeremy, or else!"

Jeremy complied. As he pressed his face to the floor mat of the new car, he felt Ricardo's head and realized by screaming like Mark instructed, he had placed Dr. R in grave danger.

Ricardo started to put the gun under his belt and immediately knew the magazine was missing. "Smart move kid, smart move. Every other minute I'm underestimating you!"

"What the hell, Ricardo? Whaddya mean?"

"The minister's kid jammed our clip between the front seat springs! Hey, Jeremy, guess your mind trick don't always work that well, do it?" Ricardo guffawed. He reached under the seat and found the mag.

Pilar pressed Jeremy back down into the Galaxie's floor board. He just shook his head at the kid, thinking this all better be worth it.

"Pilar!" Ricardo motioned from the front seat. "Now that we've switched cars, the cops won't be looking for a Galaxie 500 for a few hours. At least until shift change. My guess is that the pharmacist owns this baby, nice as it is. I'm worried this kid ain't gonna help us unless we get some real leverage, ya unnerstan?"

Pilar agreed, "Yeah, fighting this kid ain't like taking candy from a baby. I never understood that line anyway.

Take candy from a baby, you still gotta deal with all the screaming and dirty looks. Whaddya thinking? Plus, you piss off the mom. Way I see it, we're already in the big time with kidnapping a kid. Gets us up to aggravated if we're gonna use his radar with those shipping guys like José wants. But we'll need help to force Jeremy to turn on his radar beam and make it useful."

Jeremy listened in horror as Pilar and Ricardo debated locking him in a nearby cellar until they could kidnap his mom or Dr. R. He finally realized they'd grab Dr. R, seeing as how it might be easier than a hysterical woman.

Pilar said, "His mom's gonna be too on edge and she'll never play along. We gotta grab the psychiatrist!"

Jeremy thought to himself. What can I do? I know Dr. R stands real tall and looks strong, but when I feel his head he doesn't like fighting. He's not like Mark or Col. McPherson. Jeremy listened to the thrum of the 500s big V-8 engine. Oddly, it calmed him down. He actually could see through Ricardo's thoughts as if he were in a movie theater watching the car headed to Dr. R's office. He'd never looked through someone's head that way. Did it mean he could feel people's eyes too?

Jeremy sensed Ricardo thinking Dr. R's office was maybe 20 minutes away. He thought, *I'll just have to get into Eva's head. Sneak into her memory of when those Nazis smashed her husband's shop. See all that broken glass. Hopefully, she'll understand.* Jeremy closed his eyes and traveled to Pinehurst. He found Eva in bed reading *Rumpole of the Bailey*, a story about some English lawyer.

Eva put down the book when she felt Jeremy rifling through her mind—searching around for Kristallnacht memories again. He focused on Dr. R as a boy and her fears for him never growing old, as the Nazis marauded down the street. Why would Jeremy disobey her so blatantly? Where was he now? Why now—when he'd been so scared of those images?

Then she knew. Somehow he faced grave danger. But her son? She madly pushed her bedside call button, but no one answered. The nurse tech had bathed her 30 minutes ago and dropped off her lunch, so they'd see her calling as a nuisance. She slowly got up from her prone position, her muscles stiff and long ago atrophied. But the adrenaline invigorated her. A chance to save her son! She eased off the bed into her slippers and pushed her smock down past her knees. If I can just get to the hall phone. Maybe if I scream for help? No, they'll just think I'm hysterical and up my meds to get me to pipe down. But how do I tell Azriel about my reverse mind reading? He'll just chalk it up to senility. Damn!"

She shuffled to the door, peeked out, and saw a lone tech headed away from her. Mr. Jesse Stevens, though, had an iron grip on the lone hall phone. Mostly deaf, he was screaming into the receiver at his son. "Yeah, it's hot in my room. Bring me some new shaving lotion and underrrrwearsss! Mine wore out and staff has lost several pair! I'm down to my last three!"

Eva realized a little white lie might work! She padded up to Mr. Stevens. "Jesse!" she yelled. "You're in luck. For some reason someone mistakenly sent me a gift package of new men's briefs. I'll give them to you if you let me make one quick phone call."

"What? Underpants? But I'm not done talking! I waited 30 minutes for the phone. You can wait your turn. My son will bring me the right size...."

Eva knew she had only limited time. She pushed down on the switch, hanging up Mr. Stevens' call. From somewhere in her depths she found Herculean strength enough to push his wheelchair 10 feet out of the way. Quick as lightning, she called Azriel's office.

"Hello, thank you for calling. This is Dr. Rebovitz's office. Velma speak...."

"Shut up Velma. This is an emergency. Get my son on the phone. NOW! This is Eva."

"Oh my, Ma'am. OK. Just a second."

"Hello, Ma. I'm in the middle of something. What do you need?"

"Good, now you listen. I'm not senile—not this minute anyway. Jeremy is in big trouble."

"Yes, I know. How in blazes do you know? Is it in the news? The kidnapping?"

"Oh for God sakes, he's been kidnapped? Listen, I know about his gift, OK? I had a friend during childhood who had it, too. Jeremy just entered my head..."

"What do you mean? I don't...."

"Shut up, please. I'm sorry to seem rude. But you're in trouble, too. I think Jeremy and the kidnappers are on their way to your office. Call the police now! If I'm wrong, you can put a pillow over my head and end it all next visit, dammit!"

"Wow, OK. A detective just left a while ago. I'll call him back right now."

Dr. R hung up as Velma watched. "She called about the kidnapping, didn't she?" Velma squealed. "How did she find out?"

"I don't know. She thinks, I guess, the kidnappers are on their way here. Now! I'm calling the cops." Azriel dialed.

"Fitchburg police, Sgt. Hudson here. How may we be of assistance?"

"Finch, err, Sgt. Hudson. It's Dr. Rebovitz."

"Hey Doc. How's it hanging?"

"Not good. I have information that Jeremy's kidnappers are making their way to my office for Lord knows what."

"No way. They were headed toward the Boston area, the last eyewitness report we had. Seemed reliable."

"Look, all the favors I've done for you all. Please indulge me. Send a squad car over to my office pronto."

"Sure thing, Doc. Didn't mean to short-shrift your worries. Least we can do. Lock up your office. I'm dispatching a cruiser to your location right now."

Hudson radioed for a patrol car and then called Rod, who in turn called the McPherson residence and got only Mrs. McPherson.

"Where are David and the Colonel, Ma'am?" Rod pressed.

"I'm sorry—they said I could man the phone while they headed into town. I can call them on Ed's CB."

"OK, I wanted to update you all as promised. The Massachusetts State Police just entered the case too. We have an APB out for a blue Old's F-85. Last we heard, it was headed toward the North Shore. But I just had a call

from Jeremy's psychiatrist. That's where I'm headed now."
Rod rang off.

Lily got on the CB and called Ed.

"Yes—what do you need Mom?" Ed chirped.

"That detective, Rod McNamara, just called. He said they think those kidnappers are on their way to Jeremy's doctor's office. You know that psychiatrist you like so much, Dr. Rebovitz?"

"Oh, shit. OK, we're right down the street. David and I will head there right now. Maybe we can cut them off at the pass."

Before Lily could protest, Ed rang off.

CHAPTER 39

Tuesday June 11, 1968—2:09 p.m.
Final Countdown

Ricardo pulled up the Galaxie 500 about two blocks away from Dr. R's office. As he scoped out the office, Pilar asked, "What's the plan?"

"I dunno. Gonna drive around and see if the guy has a back entrance. You know, a psychiatrist's gotta have a backdoor escape. Crazy patients might stalk them, who knows? It'd just be good business planning to have a back exit."

"How's about if we call the office—get Velma on the line? Warn her about how we hold Dan's life in the palms of our hands?"

"Nah—he might see her reaction. The good doctor's probably on to us. I say we ambush em! Storm their back door. I'll bust it down and let Mr. Colt 45 do the talking. We gotta high-tail it outta here anyway. And fast."

Ricardo drove around the rear of the office and saw only one car lot. He quietly parked and started to get out when he thought he heard a siren far off. Then he heard the front left tire explode and a funny metallic clanging sound. As he stood up, he looked down at the tire, but his brain couldn't register the odd timing of the blowout or the misshapen rim. "Must've hit some glass or a nail," he complained. "Bad timing. Damn. May have to borrow doc's car." Next he heard Pilar yell, "Something wrong? I felt a jolt!"

"Yeah, tire blew out. Hell, looks like half the wheel got destroyed with it."

Col. McPherson aimed his sniper rifle for Ricardo's head. He and David had climbed to the top of an adjacent two-story building that sat right behind Dr. R's office. By mere minutes, they had beaten Ricardo and Pilar *and* the patrol car to the office location.

Ed asked, "David, what you do see in the backseat? I can't see Jeremy."

Looking through Ed's combat binoculars, David scanned the car and could only make out Pilar's head, sans neck. "I see a guy hunched down in the backseat."

"Well, we've got two choices," Ed said, as Ricardo looked at the blown-out tire. "One, we wait for the cops and watch the OK Corral play out with your son in the middle. Two, I take these guys out—back-seat guy first, and...oh shit, front-seat guy has a Colt 45 in his hand!"

Before David could speak, Ed fired and blew off Ricardo's left hand. Ricardo's pistol skipped across the pavement. Then as Pilar looked up at Ricardo in shock, Ed fired again grazing Ricardo's left thigh. Ricardo collapsed immediately. Pilar jumped out of the backseat in a panic, leaving Jeremy on the floorboard. As confusion reigned, Pilar looked around for the gun. He saw Ricardo's Colt 45 and ran for it. Ed wasted no time shooting Pilar in the right femur. Pilar collapsed, his face scraping the gravel just like Dan had done next to Antonio's dumpster in Boston's Combat Zone.

David rushed down the fire escape and made a bee-line for the car, praying Jeremy was alive. A patrol car pulled in with its lights blazing and the siren turned off. Rod's car followed immediately, just as David reached into the car to grab Jeremy. He found him lying quietly on the floorboard. They hugged as David bawled uncontrollably.

"Lemme guess, Jeremy," David sobbed. "You felt Col. McPherson's head didn't you?"

"Yes, Dad. I also took the magazine thing out of Ricardo's gun. But he figured it out. I wanted to make him like the Abominable Snowman after Hermie removed his teeth!" Jeremy offered, remembering how the family enjoyed watching the Rudolph holiday special.

Ray and Rod ran up to the car, turned and saw Col. McPherson descending the fire escape, jamming his sniper rifle into its carrying case. The other two patrol officers eyeballed Ed as they tended to the wounded Pilar and Ricardo, and called for an ambulance.

"Glad everyone's OK. I thought I asked you to stay put, David!" Rod shouted. "And Col. McPherson! I deputized you to stay put as well! I thought we agreed you all would wait for our dispatch and I'd keep you in the loop. What're you doing here?"

David responded, "Yeah, well, the Colonel is not real good at taking orders from civilians. *He* thought we could lend a hand. Who am I to deny one of my parishioners a chance to save my son? I'm amazed we got up to the top of that building in time to do any good."

"Detective," Ed offered, "I'm turning myself in. I disobeyed your direct order. That's a breakdown in the chain of command. All we did, I did, that is, at first was blow out their front tire. Then I saw the Colt 45 in Mr. Front Seat's hands and I sensed trouble. I took him out of the picture to save Jeremy. When Mr. Back Seat sat up and got out to make a play for the gun, I took him out, too. They should live. Sorry about the blood and guts on the pavement. Figured it was worth it, though."

A crowd started gathering across the street, gawking at the scene. More patrol cars arrived as Dr. R and Velma exited the back door. Rod looked at the crowd and then turned to Rev. Hergenroeder. "David—and I guess I'll explain to you, Velma and Azriel—we picked up José or rather the state patrol did as he made his way toward Quincy apparently to that big shipyard. They arrested him for kidnapping, loan sharking and extortion. That's just for starters."

"Wow," David said, otherwise speechless.

"What I don't get," Rod said, "is how everyone knew these guys planned to come back this way?"

"A woman's intuition, Detective," Azriel offered.

"You mean Velma?" Rod asked.

"No, my senile mother, Detective. Turns out she adores David and Jeremy. They are the best of friends."

Rod just shook his head—glad the day had ended safely for Jeremy and the Hergenroeders, not to mention Dr. R. He figured he'd get to the bottom of the trucking conspiracy in the next few days. There'd be plenty of time to interrogate José, and the two kidnappers, who soon would be locked under tight security at Fitchburg's Burbank Hospital. Time to put in a call to that bad ass D.A., Christopher Johnson. He'd jump all over a case like this—and he didn't have much of a neck, either.

EPILOGUE

Tuesday June 11, 1968—5:30 p.m.
Fitchburg Sentinel—Late Special Edition

Police Thwart Juvenile's Kidnapping

By Kristen Brigham

L ate this afternoon, Fitchburg police arrested two men outside a local psychiatrist's office following a gun battle. The two, Pilar and Ricardo Gutierrez, allegedly had kidnapped a five-year-old boy whose name is being withheld by police.

Detective Rod McNamara, who led the hunt for the boy and his abductors, said the arrests flowed from a wider investigation into an extortion ring. The Gutierrez men kidnapped the child hours earlier during the lunch recess at Edgerly Elementary School.

Edgerly is the main teaching facility for students on the campus of Fitchburg State Teacher's College. Neither the police nor the Gutierrez men fired their weapons. Eyewitnesses, however, saw two men descending from the roof of a nearby building and one was seen stuffing a rifle into a duffle bag of some sort.

Details are still sketchy, but one anonymous police department source theorized that the boy's father, a local minister, may have been the real target. The source went on to say that the kidnappers likely thought they could pump the minister for church funds as their ransom.

The Gutierrez men are cousins of a third man, José Gutierrez, whom the Massachusetts State Police arrested earlier today on Route 2. State Patrol spokesperson Lawrence Kirkland said the latter Gutierrez was under investigation for extortion, loan sharking, and conspiracy to transport stolen goods across state lines using local trucking firms.

When this reporter asked if the kidnapping charge had anything to do with the Edgerly student, Kirkland refused to provide further details, citing safety concerns for the family.

As this breaking story unfolds, The Sentinel will publish further details in tomorrow's edition.

The End

ACKNOWLEDGEMENTS

W ithout my wife Wendy Overlock, whose constant refrain the last 25 years has been, "When are *we* going to get your novel written?" this book would not have been possible. Wendy has edited almost everything I've ever written—at least that mattered. She put me through graduate school and is the true minister in our family, even though she didn't get the M-Div. degree I did. She paid for the tuition—so I could focus on my studies.

This book is semi-autobiographical, so a lot of the references to Massachusetts generally and Fitchburg specifically come from my memories of growing up there. My Nanna really did take me on that tiger hunt when I was five and my grandfather Jake Overlock really did carve a long rifle for me. The residents of Fitchburg often bragged that their fair city was the second hilliest in the United States, and there really used to be a Piggly Wiggly grocery store in town. My father served as pastor of Rollstone Congregational Church and kids (me included) really did dial 888 on the hall phone to get it to ring.

Time for additional gratitude. I have to thank my parents, The Rev. Dr. Donald Everson Overlock and Sally (Potter) Overlock. My Dad read a first draft of this book shortly before he died—finding two or three key mistakes.

Mom warned him not to tell me, fearing that doing so might discourage me. His criticisms and comments had the opposite effect—like all good editors.

Tom Bird and his publishing concern deserve my utmost praise. Tom's classes and "write your novel in a weekend" retreat taught me to shut off the left side of my brain—that hypercritical editor that paralyzed my writing for the last quarter century. How many times had I sat down to write a suspense novel, only to get bogged down in the research or outlining?

There was no outline for this book—just a few ideas that birthed everything you have read here. That may seem counterintuitive, but it was part of my problem with prior novel writing attempts. If you've always wanted to write a novel, then look no further than Tom Bird's web sites: www.tombird.com or www.writeyourbestsellerinaweekend.com.

My sister Kristen Overlock and her partner Anna Forkan introduced me to an individual who shall remain nameless who has Jeremy's gift. After meeting that person and experiencing his brain scan of me, he advised me that I had a strong feminine side and offered me some predictions about what my life might look like in the next few years. I've met two or three other people during my life who had varying degrees of this "feeling heads" capacity. The first such soothsayer I met on the community train track in the foothills outside of Montego Bay, Jamaica. To our utter astonishment, he used his gift both on me and two *Sea Semester* classmates. Our ship, the 120-foot staysail schooner *RV Westward*, had just docked in the Bay three days before Christmas in 1980. Our captain had given us several hours of shore leave to explore the local environs.

One such gentleman happened upon us and offered to take us up into the foothills to meet and greet his family and friends. It was a glorious day and he introduced us to the soothsayer. Like my sister's seer friend, I often wondered about both of those gentlemen's "growing up years." I tried to imagine what it would have been like growing up with such a gift. How could it be abused? How would such an individual and his or her family protect the secret? Thus, this story.

My friend and colleague Nancy McCullough, RN, a clinical trials nurse at Nashville General Hospital where we both work, graciously offered to serve as my first editor. As we discussed her first redline she blurted out that as soon as she started reading the third chapter she realized *the chase was on*. So she gave me the title, for which I am both grateful and reminded of the power two minds together can harness.

Finally, I owe a debt of gratitude to Dr. Ron West who counselled me in the art of gun play. Ron worked with me for several years at Nashville General Hospital, where he was the Pharmacy Director. It was only later in our friendship that I learned of his expertise with fire arms. I realize that the sniper rifle Col. McPherson used at the end of the book may have been too much firepower for the job at hand, so forgive me for that literary license.

All the errors in this book are mine and mine alone. In that regard, I sinned boldly.

Made in the USA
Columbia, SC
10 August 2017